I0685529

Mudd's Luck

T.S. O'Neil

I write about good guys who are a little bad

Dedication

To my dear friend, the real Ken Kelley, who generously agreed to let me use his name as a moniker for the antagonist in this book. More importantly, he agreed not to sue me for doing so. The real Ken Kelley is a true friend, a great guy and the epitome of a man's man. The only character trait that Ken shares with the villain in MUDD'S LUCK is a taste for an occasional Guinness.

CONTENTS

ISBN-13:978-0692413005 (TSONEIL)

ISBN-10:0692413006

Disclaimer

This is a work of fiction. Names, characters, businesses, places, events and incidents are either the products of the author's imagination or used in a fictitious manner. Any resemblance to actual persons, living or dead, or actual events is purely coincidental.

Mudd's Luck

Chapter One – Briny Deep

Kelley spied his quarry below him at sixty feet—give or take a foot or two—stalking a large Black Grouper on the other side of a circular outcropping of coral. Kelley was behind and above him -- he was sure that he remained unobserved. Diving with a mask handicapped one's peripheral sight and divers tended to focus on what was directly in front of them—effectively rendering everything else invisible.

Kelley would wait for the man to fire and then begin to retrieve the catch before making his move. It was a nice fish—in the range of forty pounds—in his opinion, close to the limit he would want to take with a spear. He figured even with a good hit, the guy would have a fight on his hands. If it was Kelley, he would hit it with a spear, draw it close and then jam an ice pick in its eye.

In any case, the guy would be distracted. The clamp he had specially designed would snap on the valve and not allow it to be opened without a special wrench. He was told to make it look like an accident—so he had studied the man's habits and decided that scuba diving was the correct way to make that happen.

Kelley wore a Draeger Mark 25 rebreather instead of a regular scuba tank—the closed circuit computer-controlled device continuously scrubbed carbon dioxide from the attached oxygen tank, allowing the diver to stay under water a long time—up to several hours. Since it was a closed system, no air bubbles escaped to give away his position. The apparatus was actually a computer-controlled mechanical system that had a depth limitation of about seventy feet. This should not be a problem, given his quarry's current depth.

Kelley heard the whoosh of a spear being released from the man's pneumatic spear gun and watched as it struck the fish immediately behind the gill—a good shot, but not a kill shot. The grouper shuddered from the impact of the spear and swam downward while the man speedily reeled it in—no doubt closing the distance so he could dispatch it with a blow or a blade.

Kelley descended slowly—closing the distance while the man struggled against the still fighting grouper. He reached for the Pillar valve on the top of the man's scuba tank and turned it counterclockwise shutting off the air supply. Next, he slid the clamp on the knob and snapped the other end over the top of the regulator locking it into place. Now, no matter what his victim did, he would not be able to take the device off and turn on his air.

This will be interesting to watch, thought Kelley. The man tried to breathe and came up short. He panicked and dropped the spear gun—the fish saw it as an opportunity to escape and darted toward deeper water, towing the spear and gun along with it. The man reached behind him, felt the valve and knew immediately that something was very wrong.

The man started an emergency ascent to the surface, allowing the air in his lungs to escape, lest its expansion rupture his lungs. Kelley couldn't let him reach the surface. He swam to the man, enveloped both of his legs in a hug and swam downward—his fins powerfully generating waves of propellant force pushing them deeper. The man kicked in the opposite direction with all his might, and Kelley was surprised at his strength. But, that would serve his purpose—it would burn up the precious oxygen and sooner or later, the bodily reflex would cause him to gulp in the sea water and it would be over.

The man then did something that Kelley hadn't anticipated—he grabbed Kelley's mask, twisted it and ripped it from his face. It was an experienced move—an attack, not something one does in a panic. Kelley's eyes flooded with sea water and he let go of his prey. The man, freed from the anchor-like weight, began swimming upward towards the surface.

Had the man held on to the mask, he would have easily escaped as Kelley was functionally blind without it. He felt something hit his flipper and instinctively closed his feet to trap the descending object. Kelley retrieved it, placed it back on his face and cleared the mask by blowing air into it.

Kelley looked up towards the surface and saw that the man was a good fifteen feet above him. His situation called for rash action—he fully inflated his buoyancy compensator with compressed air. The immediate increase in buoyancy caused him to rocket upward—until his head bumped against the underside of the man's flippers. He purged the compensator to arrest his assent and then ripped the man's flippers off his feet—handicapping his swimming ability.

Kelley expected the man to continue to flail upward towards salvation, but instead, he bent at the middle and brought his right hand down in a striking motion towards Kelley's head. Kelley caught the glint of something long and shiny in the man's hand. He let go of the man's legs, just as the descending arc of the strike missed his head and instead hit his shoulder.

He grimaced in pain and looked down at his right shoulder to find a black rubber handle protruding from it. Blood began to seep from the wound. Kelley looked at the man and was surprised to see his dead, unseeing eyes stare back—his target had used his last gasp of life to try and take Kelley with him.

He swam to the body, towed it to a nearby coral outcropping, and guided it atop its surface. Kelley retrieved a wrench from a pocket in his wetsuit and used it to remove the skirt he had placed over the valve earlier. He turned the air back on and then swam off to retrieve the dead man's flippers—which luckily had landed nearby. Once the flippers were back on the man's feet, Kelley inflated the corpse's buoyancy compensator with one short burst and watched as the body began to slowly rise to the surface.

Kelley would see to his own wound once he got back to his boat. They hadn't bothered to mention that Kelley would be killing someone with training in martial combat—that omission irritated him.

Chapter Two – Dinner Party

The late afternoon sun cast long shadows on the two figures reclining on the stern fly bridge of the *Good as Gold*. Michael was sprawled lazily on a teak chaise lounge, while his fiancée Sofia reclined in tandem—her lush shoulder-length black hair spread like a lustrous fan across his bare chest.

He drank an ice cold Corona encased in an insulated neoprene jacket while she sipped dry white wine from a flute. She turned and regarded him through a set of blue topaz color lenses attached to the Costa sunglasses he had bought her in Cozumel. Aaron Lewis' *Endless Summer,* wafted out of the Bose outdoor speakers attached to the upper corner of the bulkhead.

"Michael, are you serious?" said Sofia in slightly accented English. She was Colombian born and bred, but had studied medicine in London and had grown up totally bilingual—the benefit of being from a wealthy family. Her father was a successful emerald dealer in Bogota and her uncle was a long-term senator in the Colombian Senate.

"Sure, Honey, why wouldn't I be? I want you to meet my mom."

She turned her lithe body around to face him—brushing her breasts against his bare chest. "Oh. Michael," said Sofia, "you've made so happy!" She gripped both armrests and propelled herself upward to kiss him.

Ramos had introduced her to Michael after they had reconnected following the mission that someone had eventually named Starfish Prime. Michael's intention in seeking out Ramos was to personally thank him for helping to salvage a mission badly gone awry.

He found Ramos at his family's house in the green forested hills overlooking Bogota. Michael intended on only staying for dinner, but he met Sofia and stayed for a year. She was Ramos' first cousin and Michael didn't know if it was a surreptitious arrangement or blind providence—he didn't care which. He fell in love the moment she spoke to him. She had a little girl's lilt to her voice and when she spoke, her lips pouted as if she was considering something.

They kissed and Michael felt his manhood twitch. *Shit, she still excited him like it was their first time.* She reached down and gently fondled him as if she had read his mind.

"No time for that, I'm afraid, the guests will be here in a few minutes," he said while consulting his watch.

"Okay, but don't get too drunk, as I have plans for you," she cautioned.

Michael looked at her and smiled, "Honey, there is no way to keep a good man down." He grabbed his beer and emptied it in a long swig.

There would be a lot of drinking tonight. Michael and Char had met Nicky Flynn about two years ago, when they wandered into the bar that Nicky frequented on Ambergris Caye in Belize.

Flynn was a charter boat captain, but the boat's overworked engines required an overhaul which was being done in Tampa. Flynn had fiscal discipline that made a drunken sailor look cheap. He needed to earn money to pay for the costly repairs so he organized junkets to Belize for bone fishing and scuba diving.

Michael and his father, Char, had met Flynn in San Pedro, the main town on the island after wandering into a garishly painted, beachside bar called Hurricane Sally's. Flynn stood in the back of the bar, busily engaged in schooling the tourists on an ancient snooker table. The gringo tourists, more used to the larger pockets on pool tables, had trouble adjusting to the more narrow holes used in snooker. It took finesse to sink a shot and therein lay Flynn's expertise.

Char had learned to play snooker in Vietnam and still played occasionally, but was way out of practice. After initially being fleeced for two hundred dollars by Flynn, Char retired for the evening to plot revenge.

Flynn had a charter the next day, and Char spent the time practicing on the table and recapturing some of his prior expertise. Upon Flynn's return, Char was ready—after luring him in with a few thrown matches, Flynn became incautious and began downing Belikin beers on an empty stomach. Char waited for the beers to affect his play and then pounced. Before it was all over, Char had won his money back and looted Flynn of his profit from the junket.

Rather than leave the man penniless, Char allowed him to

work off his debt by being their fishing guide for the next three days. During that time, Flynn took them fly fishing to some of the least known fishing grounds on the coast. The bonefish ran from about three to five pounds and after a short lesson on how to properly cast a fly rod and set the light hook, both he and Michael were able to catch more than a dozen. Flynn cooked them up on the beach as he did for his other clients, and they became friends.

Flynn was now guiding a spearfishing charter with his repaired boat and they had stopped at the Dry Tortugas to allow his guests to tour the Fort Jefferson Historical Site. It wasn't blind luck that they had met. It was a normal stop on his itinerary, and Char had used his satellite phone to call Flynn and arrange a dinner. The Dry Tortugas seemed the most logical place to meet as the *Good as Gold* was headed to Key West and Flynn's boat, the *Blue Marlin*, would eventually be returning to Tampa.

Flynn had sent a launch over with fish for the afternoon meal—a large yellow mouth grouper that he had speared that morning and three rock lobsters he had spotted hiding beneath a coral ledge while retrieving the fish. Char was busy filleting and breading the grouper, and he was planning to put the lobsters into a bisque, since there was no other equitable way to share them among the six diners.

Flynn, as the captain of a fishing charter, sometimes grew sick of perennially eating seafood. Char and Michael also wanted a break after being at sea for weeks. Therefore, Char added three recently defrosted Colombian beef filets that he would barbeque on the back deck.

As for liquid refreshments, Char had several bottles of chilled Argentinean Pinot Grigio, as well as some light red blends from Sonoma County—although he figured most of the guys would be drinking ice cold Coronas that were in abundant supply since replenishing in Cozumel.

Johnnie and Earl served the meal and then sat down to join the rest of the party. The two had been with the *Good as Gold*, since Char hired them over a year ago in Port of Spain. They planned on jumping ship in Key West, but Char figured they might change their mind as he was an easy boss who paid them well, and he treated them more like buddies than employees.

Nicky Flynn arrived at three o'clock, looking like an ad for Tommy Bahama. He was as tan and wind worn as a well-used saddlebag, and the benefit of an active outdoor life had left him with a runner's physique.

The creature comforts on Flynn's sixty five foot boat were sparse—divers normally slept four to a cabin, and paid handsomely for the privilege as it was all about the spearfishing. Therefore, Flynn welcomed a chance to relax in the luxurious splendor of Char's eighty foot Hatteras.

Cocktails were served and everyone stuck to either beer or wine, it being still too early in the day to break out anything harder. Michael introduced Sofia to Flynn, who was visibly impressed with the tall raven haired beauty—even more so after learning she was a doctor. Once they were seated at the long teak dining table, Flynn continued flirting with Sofia, who seemed more amused than charmed by the older man's attention.

Johnnie did his waiter imitation—scurrying around the long table, topping off wine glasses and delivering the bisque to be followed by medallions of beef topped with crab meat or fresh grouper filet. Char had purchased the beef in a shop owned by a local rancher in Bogota. Earl, the other mate, had caught the crab fresh that morning on a shallow portion of an outlying reef before they arrived at Fort Jefferson.

"I spent a little bit of time in London—can't say I liked it—too dreary and full of Englishmen, said Flynn with a sly smile. "A beer costs twice what it does here—although they do pour an Imperial pint. So tell me, Sofia, why would you want to waste time there?"

Sofia smiled—somewhat surprised the man would be so forward. "I wanted to undergo instruction in English as I thought it would help me to get truly fluent, and I had dreams of practicing there, but it didn't work out that way."

If Flynn sensed any reluctance to talk further he ignored it. "And why not?"

"Mister Flynn is certainly the curious type," said Sofia to the rest of the party.

"He just doesn't get a lot of female attention on that floating sausage fest, so he feels he needs to make up for it when he gets the chance," said Char.

"Well then, Mister Flynn, you deserve a complete explanation, but only if you tell me about the history of this huge brick fort named after your president. Sofia pointed out the salon's large port window towards a gigantic red brick structure that sat a short distance away across the aquamarine-colored bay.

"You mean Fort Jefferson," said Flynn.

"Yes, of course," replied Sofia. "Michael promised to give me a tour tomorrow," she said, squeezing his hand, "so I'd like to be well versed in its history."

"Fair enough, Sofia," said Flynn smiling brightly, "I will tell you all I know about the fort—after twenty three years of leading groups of spear fishermen here, I hope we have enough time to cover it all."

She smiled, sipped her wine and regarded Flynn, "Well, Mister Flynn, I left Colombia because I became a target for kidnapping by the FARC, and my father felt it was best that I go to school overseas. However, when I became certified as a physician, he asked me to return and serve my country. I worked as a rural physician for the Colombian Red Cross and later as a medical coordinator for the international branch of that organization, based in Bogota. This was probably not his intention—but we all must choose our own path and I believe everything happens for a reason. Had I not returned, I would not have met the love of my life."

Michael reached over and squeezed her hand. She smiled warmly at him and then leaned over and gave him a short peck on the lips.

Flynn nodded. "Please call me Nicky."

She nodded. "Fine, Nicky and now you know all. As Michael would say, if I tell you anything more I will have to kill you." The table erupted in laughter. *Oh, to be thirty years younger*, thought Flynn.

"And now, tell me all you know about the fort," said Sofia.

Flynn nodded and began a short discourse about the history of the islands and the rise of the fort. "Following the War of 1812, a group of forts from Maine to Texas was planned to provide defense of the fledging American republic. Fort Jefferson was built to protect the southern coast. The citadel is a hexagon shaped building constructed of over sixteen million handmade bricks. The wall consists of an outer wall generally 8 feet thick, and an inner wall, with flooring stretching nearly twenty feet between the two. The design called for a three-tiered fort, mounting over 400 heavy guns. The walls met at corner bastions, which are large projections designed to allow defensive fire along the faces of the walls they joined. The heavy guns were mounted inside the walls in a string of open casemates, facing outward toward the sea through large openings. Basically, Fort Jefferson was designed to be a massive gun platform, invulnerable to assault, and able to destroy any enemy ships stupid enough to approach within range of its massive guns, but it was never used as a fort as it was already obsolete before it was completed. So, they put it into use as a prison. And now, you know all I know," said Flynn, raising his wine glass in a toast.

"No, there is more," protested Sofia, "Michael told me the doctor who treated the assassin of your president was imprisoned there."

"Ah yes, Doctor Samuel Mudd was the fort's most famous inmate. He was imprisoned here for aiding and conspiring with John Wilkes Booth in the assassination of President Abraham Lincoln." said Flynn as he signaled Johnnie for a refill of his wine glass.

"Did he die here?" asked Sofia.

"No," said Flynn, "He assisted in the treatment of the other prisoners and guards during a yellow fever epidemic and was eventually granted clemency."

"Yes," nodded Sofia with a slight smile, "A doctor is always obligated to treat the sick regardless of circumstance. So, you could say that being a doctor both got him into and out of two very difficult situations."

The fresh grouper filets proved to be the highlight of the meal. Char had breaded them and fried them in light virgin olive oil until they were golden brown. They had turned out to be light and flaky underneath a crunchy cornmeal crust. Dessert was a Key lime pie that Earl had whipped up, substituting Mexican limes for the smaller fruit indigenous to the Keys.

After this, they retired to the arm chairs and couches in the main salon and Char offered cigars from the humidor and brandy from the bar. Only Sofia demurred, as she found the practice unhealthy, but had not yet pushed the case with Michael.

Flynn's satellite phone rang and he retreated onto the back deck to answer it. Loud animated talk punctuated by profanity filtered in through the half opened slider and he soon appeared back in the salon.

"Got to go, we've got an emergency—one of our divers hasn't returned. He was due back about a half hour ago."

"Anything we can do to help?" asked Michael.

"Sure, you can help search. I'm getting the coordinates of where they dropped him—we'll start looking for him there, both on the surface and beneath it. The current is running east. I'll give you directions to where I want you to search once I have a better idea where we'll be," said Flynn.

Flynn knew that this was the kind of thing that could destroy a business like his that operated during the best of times on a very tight profit margin. Add a lawsuit for wrongful death and it was all over.

A skiff soon approached from the *Blue Marlin*. Michael signaled for the mooring line, but Flynn jumped on board once the boat got within a couple of feet. The pilot turned the rudder, throttled up the engine, and sped back towards Flynn's boat.

Char came back to the stern and watched his friend depart. "Hope they find him alive," said Char.

"You and me both," said Michael.

Chapter Three - Floater

By the time Flynn got back to the *Blue Marlin*, he was already in full risk management mode and didn't want any witnesses, should the diver turn up dead due to shark bite or propeller blade. The sun was lower in the sky and he knew that they had better find the guy or the body before dark. There is no twilight in the Caribbean—it's as if someone pulls a dark curtain across the sun.

Flynn took the skiff out himself. A strong offshore wind had kicked up and generated white tipped swells. All the drop sites were well known to the crew and were always around a coral reef or other landscape feature as that's where the fish tend to congregate. A crew member in a skiff would drop divers off at different sites and record where they were dropped on an acetate covered map with a grease pencil.

The missing diver's name was Harold Dennison of Enterprise,

Alabama. Flynn remembered him from the welcome aboard mixer, mainly because his head was as bald as Mister Clean. He was also somewhat of a 'Joe Diver,' sporting different diving or spearfishing logos on everything from his T-shirt to the bag he used for stowing his dive gear. Most times guys like that were over-compensating, but Dennison looked and talked like an experienced spear fisherman—offhandedly mentioning far-flung places he had dove and fish he had speared. What little else was known about him was being gathered by his first mate.

The spot they had dropped him at was known as a grouper hole, but it was reported to have been fished out, so most of the other divers went elsewhere that afternoon. Flynn circled around the submerged coral atoll that served as the center of the site and began slowly circling outward. He continued doing so until he was about a half mile from his starting point. It was then that he saw what he thought was a tank bobbing at the surface.

He cut the motor, grabbed a boat hook, and scrambled to the bow. The boat drifted forward and he let go of the hook as the boat passed close enough so that Flynn reached out and grabbed the tank stem with his hand. The man's bald head was wrinkled from immersion. He attempted to pull the body into the boat, but found it to be impossible with all the dive gear.

Flynn removed the buoyancy compensator from around the man's torso and pulled it into the boat. The body started to slip beneath the waves, and Flynn panicked before plunging both arms into the water and catching the zipper leash on the back of the man's wetsuit. He secured the leash to a boat cleat, reached into the water, undid the man's weight belt and pulled it onboard.

Thus lightened, the body floated higher in the water, and Flynn figured he could get it over gunwale. He knelt down, reached under the corpse's armpits and pulled, but he barely raised the body from the water. After a few futile attempts, he untied the anchor from its line, wrapped the anchor line around the man's torso and winched it onboard. Once back at his boat, he would use a lifting harness and a hydraulic davit to lift the body onboard. Flynn covered the corpse with a tarpaulin, started the outboard and motored back to the *Blue Marlin*.

***

Kelley knew something was badly amiss when he removed the ice pick from his shoulder. Frothy pink bubbles flowed out of the wound as he watched in the small mirror over the sink in the head. He tossed the pick into the basin, walked into the galley and rifled around in a cupboard until he found a roll of plastic wrap. Unrolling it, he ripped off a sheet, folded it into a palm sized piece, and slapped it on the wound. He located a roll of duct tape, tore off several long pieces, and painstakingly placed them about the perimeter of the plastic wrap. Thus secured, it felt better until he felt pressure building within his chest.

This had happened once before after a British SAS troop had shot him in the chest during a failed ambush. Normally, they would have left him to bleed out, but the American media was on hand embedded with the troops. He should have known better—they were so sure of the outcome; they brought their own publicity with them to record it. A sniper's bullet found his lung and others in his cell were similarly targeted as the patrol moved on down Falls Road unmolested.

Kelley had felt as if an anvil was strapped to his chest. He found out later a precise counter ambush had been emplaced well before they had set in to defend the barricades of this most famous of the 'no-go areas' in West Belfast. He lay there in a pool of frothy blood trying to breathe while he watched a tall blond haired woman reporter in a British army helmet and oversized flak jacket vomit onto the bluish gray cobblestone street at the sight of the carnage. The medics arrived shortly afterwards and got to work on him.

"Lucky for you that American reporter is here, Taig," said the medic, using a derogatory term for an Irish Catholic, "Or you'd be deader than Michael Collins." The medic roughly slapped his face to stave off the rapidly approaching state of shock. "Look here, Mick, I'm trying to help you. You've got a tension pneumothorax—basically a collapsed lung that has leaked lots of air between your chest wall and the lung, building up pressure and pushing the lungs over to the other side of your chest." The medic used his palm as a stage and his fingers to pantomime the scene.

"If the pressure increases too much, you will develop dangerously low blood pressure resulting in you slipping into shock, passing out and probably dying. Rather than let you die and become another bloody Catholic martyr, I'm going to suck the air out of your chest cavity so that we can put you in a nice cell we have prepared for you in H Block at the Maze," said the medic.

Kelley looked up at the man with a pleading expression and whispered something. The medic couldn't hear him, so he lowered his ear to within a few inches of the wounded man's mouth.

"PUTT-TO!" Kelley loudly spat a gob of bloody phlegm into the medic's ear. "Go fuck your mum, you bloody wanker!" said Kelley.

It turned out the Limey bastard was right—Kelley did pass out.

Chapter Four - House Call

Earl was manning the bridge, making preparations to move the *Good as Gold* wherever it would be needed to support the search efforts, when the bridge's satellite phone buzzed. Earl turned to the stairway to the galley and shouted, "Skipper, you've got a call on the sat phone. It's Flynn." Char bounded up the stairs and grabbed the receiver.

"He's not breathing, but my guys are giving him CPR. The certification agencies say we have to continue until a doctor pronounces him dead. The fort only has a couple of park rangers that are EMTs, and they are telling me the same thing. If I don't do this right, I'll be liable. Can Sofia come by and make the call?" asked Flynn.

"I'm sure she will," said Char. In the short year that he had gotten to know the doctor, he had found Sofia to have a default disposition of kindness towards all and nearly limitless patience—

except when dealing with corruption, criminality, or intentional stupidity.

Johnnie had used the yacht's electric davit to place the skiff in the water. He stood at the center console with the engine at idle as Sofia, Michael, and Char filed out of the main salon and hopped onboard. Johnnie turned toward Char to await the nod—he had been around his boss long enough to know that Char expected him to facilitate making shit happen. Char untied the single line and nodded. Johnnie pushed the throttle lever full forward and steered the small launch towards Flynn's boat, which now sat tied up to the long composite pier at the fort.

The victim lay on a backboard atop the dining table in the small main salon. Char was bothered by the mob of bystanders crowding the people trying to render aid.

The three men and one woman giving the man CPR worked in shifts of two, one giving chest compressions while the other worked the manual bag resuscitator to feed air to the victim. They were closely crowded by most of the crew and clientele, some shouting words of encouragement, while others fought for better vantage points. This chaos angered Michael and he started to say something…

"Gentlemen, please, I am a doctor, and I require your immediate exit of this area so I can examine this patient," said Sofia. "If you are not administering CPR or standing by to do so, out you go."

She said it loud enough for everyone to hear, but she had not raised her voice much above a normal tone. However, there was a firmness to her words that left no doubt that she was in charge, and the lookie-loos best exit the salon. The crowd of divers and crew filed out while Sofia bent over the victim.

"Please continue," she instructed the first responders. Sofia felt along the line of the chin for an extended period of time and then removed a penlight from the pocket of her shorts, switched it on and opened the man's eyelids—shining the beam into both eyes several times.

She opened a small black kitbag and withdrew a set of shears. She handed them to Michael and directed him to cut through the wetsuit on both legs. As soon as he was finished cutting the neoprene from one leg, she examined it by roughly pressing her hands along their length, looking for the stiffness of rigor and the pooling of fluids. Flynn stood close by her side.

"At what time did you find him?" she asked.

"Four fifteen or so," said Flynn.

"When did you start CPR?"

"When we got him on board. About ten to fifteen minutes after that."

Sofia gave me a skeptical look. "And why not sooner?"

"I was alone and had trouble getting him in the boat," said Flynn, suddenly sounding defensive.

"That was a mistake, but he was probably dead already," said Sofia. "There is rigor in the jaw and legs." She addressed the two rangers applying CPR, "You may stop. Thank you for trying to save this man." She looked at the medics who had spent the last half hour trying to breathe life into a lifeless body and wanted to do something to bring closure to their efforts and perhaps make them feel that it wasn't futile. Sofia smiled slightly while making eye contact with each medic. "Please join me in a short prayer for the departed."

She offered her hand to Char and to the woman ranger, who in turn took Michael's. The others followed and they formed an oval around the dead man.

"Lord God, your own Son was delivered into the hands of the wicked, yet he prayed for his persecutors and overcame hatred with the blood of the Cross. Relieve the sufferings of the innocent victims of war; grant them peace of mind, healing of body, and a renewed faith in your protection and care. Grant this through Christ our Lord."

"Amen," they all said in unison.

"Please forgive the prayer, we used it for the victims of war and it's the only one I know by heart in English. A British surgeon who served in a clinic in Rwanda during their civil war taught it to me. Sadly, it may well be appropriate," said Sofia.

"What do you mean?" asked Michael.

Sofia didn't answer but signaled for Michael to follow her. She approached Flynn, who was forlornly staring at the body, and she spoke to him quietly, "Please take me to the man's scuba equipment."

They all filed out of the cabin. Flynn, cognizant of the fact that there would be an inquest— at the very least, had checked the tank for air, then stashed it in his cabin and locked the door. Flynn unlocked the sliding door to the cabin, pointed to the tank and stood by the open doorway. Sofia walked to the gear, turned to look at the pressure gauge and then showed it to Michael.

"He had plenty of air left—how does a man with a little less than half a tank drown?" asked Michael.

"The logical assumption was that he had a stroke or a heart attack and drowned. But if that's the case, the heart attack occurred after he started drowning as I could feel the fluid in his bloodstream. We can't be sure without an autopsy, but it would seem that someone wanted to make the man's death look like a drowning caused by a cardiac arrest," said Sofia.

"That's absurd," said Flynn. "There was no one in sight when I found him. I would have seen another diver or a boat."

"Perhaps so, but aside from air bubbles floating to the surface, scuba divers can be hard to see," said Sofia.

Disconcerting thoughts flooded into Michael's head—Flynn had discovered the body and that made him a suspect. "So, what now?" asked Michael.

"The rangers told me that they've notified the Coast Guard and they will send a Cutter to evacuate the body. I believe I'll have to go along," said Flynn. "I would imagine they would need a statement, Sofia."

"They will have it," said Sofia softly.

"It could be a while, as she is coming in from patrol in the mid gulf, according to the rangers. You'll be more comfortable on that floating Taj Mahal of yours than on this meat locker."

Sofia didn't immediately understand, but Michael nodded. "I'll have Earl monitor the radar for the cutter. When we see it, we'll come right over."

Johnnie had sat in the bow of the skiff with his shirt off, apparently napping in the gentle heat of the late afternoon sun. Char jumped onboard and startled the dozing mate, who leapt to his feet and wiped the sleep from his eyes.

"Sorry, I didn't know how long you were going to be, and I was up late last night playing spades with Earl."

23

"That's fine, Johnnie, just get us back to the boat. It's been an emotional afternoon for everyone," said Char.

Michael enveloped Sofia in his arms as if to ward off bad thoughts. Sofia had seen more than her share of violence and suffering in her homeland and had told him of her desire to lead a more tranquil life—*una vida tranquila*. It was a life that Michael had promised to deliver—*a dubious promise, if not an outright lie,* he thought regretfully.

Johnnie motored towards the *Good as Gold*. Earl, ever the cautious pilot, had anchored far out in the harbor to avoid any possibility of scraping bottom. To get there, they had to pass by a Mainship Pilot 30 II, a vessel with the similar appearance to a down-east lobster boat. They were constructed to be highly buoyant, if not virtually unsinkable. It was definitely a craft more suited to frigid northern waters than the Keys. They were built to be spartan, but not completely devoid of creature comforts. It was the boat of choice for small lobstering operations in Northern New England and Eastern Canada.

"She's not anchored and there's no one at the helm," shouted Johnnie.

"She's drifting—let's take a look," said Char. Michael grabbed a boat hook and moved into the bow.

"Stay here, Honey," Michael made it sound like more of a request than an order—Sofia did not respond well to them.

"Be careful, dear," cautioned Sofia.

Johnnie maneuvered the bow of the skiff toward the open stern compartment and Michael hooked the boat hook around a handrail and tied off the skiff. He and Char leapt aboard and approached the cabin door.

Char knocked loudly for a few seconds and then shouted "Ahoy, Char Blackfox from the yacht *Good as Gold*, are you alright?"

There was no reply, and Char looked at Michael as if to ask 'what now?'

"Well, we didn't come onboard to be stymied by a door," said Char. He flung open the door and peered inside.

Chapter Five – Boarding Party

Kelley was close to death—the long ice pick had entered the rib cage from just below the shoulder blade and punctured his lung. He had solved the immediate problem of the injured lung sucking in air from the outside, but it continued to exhale air into his chest cavity.

He had motored towards the fort, figuring that they would be able to help him, but had grown weak. He had made a fateful decision to shut down the engine and drift as he wanted to avoid the possibility of colliding with something under power, should he pass out. He grew cold in the open cockpit and crawled into the cabin—hoping to reach his bunk, but settling for the floor.

Kelley wheezed horribly and grew dizzy from the lack of oxygen. The pain in his chest increased to a point where he wasn't sure what would kill him first—the lack of air or the fact that the deflated lung could stop his heart from pumping by pressing on it.

He passed out on the cabin floor and waited to die—figuring he reaped what he had sown these many years.

Michael and Char saw him collapsed on the floor of the small cabin and knew something was amiss. Michael bent down and looked into the man's face and noticed distended veins on his neck. *A junkies dream,* thought Michael. He felt for a pulse and detected a faint one.

"Better get Sofia," said Michael.

Char exited the small cabin and returned a moment later with Sofia carrying her small doctor's kit. She wasted little time— immediately bending down to examine the man, while removing a stethoscope from the bag.

"Guys, take off his shirt," she ordered.

Michael unbuttoned the man's shirt, while Char pulled it off his body, revealing the field expedient plastic wrap bandage on his back.

"I know what that is," said Char.

"Sucking chest wound," said Michael.

"Ten points for you both." She pointed to the mess table. "Michael, clear off the table and find something to clean it. I've got to needle the chest, but I don't know if the needle will be long enough. Either way, if we don't do something soon, he's a goner."

Michael retrieved a sponge and some dish soap and gave the table a quick, but thorough scrubbing.

"Okay, let's get him on the table," said Sofia. Char bent down and placed his arms under the man's torso and lifted him onto the table.

Shit, the old man is still a strong bastard, thought Michael.

Sofia withdrew a three inch long hollow needle known as an Angiocath, a catheter, a marking pen, and a dark bottle from her kit bag. She skillfully probed the man's chest until she located the top of the third rib. Once she found it, she used the pen to mark the spot and swabbed the iodine-based antiseptic over a large area on his chest. She then sunk the needle up to its hilt and bent her head to listen. Satisfied that she heard an audible hiss, she removed the needle and attached a catheter.

"That will allow the pressure in the chest to decrease and in theory, the lung should re-inflate, but he'll need assistance. Send Johnnie back to Flynn's boat for the resuscitator. He's going to need us to help him breath for a while."

Michael knew what that meant—they would work in shifts feeding the guy air until he could easily breathe on his own. It was going to be a long night.

Chapter Six – Dreams of Eire

For just shy of three hours they took turns working the bag—helping the man breathe. At a few minutes after ten, he suddenly regained consciousness and roughly pushed the respirator away. He began breathing on his own, but soon fell once more into unconsciousness. This was not surprising in light of the fact that Sofia had shot him up on morphine to combat the pain.

"The worst of it is probably over, she announced. I'll stay. I want to make sure he doesn't thrash around and rip out the catheter."

"Nothing doing," said Char. "You and Michael go get some rest—I'll babysit tonight."

"I agree, said Michael. He placed both hands softly on her shoulders. "You've had quite a day. Let's get some rest."

She shook her head in agreement. "It started out to be a beautiful day and now all this. She looked up at Char. "Don't move him. If he's better tomorrow, we can put him in a bunk."

After they left, Char used some spare rope to securely tie the guy to the dining table. It was about five feet long and his lower legs hung over the side, but even with the restraints, the man seemed comfortable enough.

Char planned on transferring the guy to the *Good as Gold* when he seems able and then on to the nearest hospital—probably in Key West and leaving him, but it would be left to Sofia to determine when this would happen.

The boat was almost completely devoid of creature comforts—the kitchen was little more than a top loading refrigerator, a two burner gas stove, a sink, and a few cabinets, while the sleeping arrangements consisted of a fold down double bed and two small berths in the bow that could be curtained off for privacy. It did boast a good size marine head with a shower stall—which seemed extravagant in light of the boat's other spartan features.

About an hour into his shift, Earl arrived with a small red cooler containing a grouper sandwich and a six pack of Coronas. Char checked on his patient from time to time to make sure he was still able to breathe on his own, but otherwise stationed himself on the stern watching the stars and smoking a Cohiba. In the morning, he would have his yacht brought closer, but he didn't want to risk moving it through the shallow water at night.

Kelley dreamed of his childhood in a drug-induced slumber. He was back in his boyhood home on Glen Road on the Upper Falls area of West Belfast. His mum and dad, both long dead, had been resurrected in the dream. Mum had made him a traditional breakfast of sausage, eggs, brown beans and blood pudding, while his dad read the paper sipping his morning tea. Kelley tried to read the headline, but could not quite make it out. The photo showed a Provo sniper stationed on a rooftop aiming an American-made

M16 at something. Kelley looked closer and he recognized the sniper—it was his older self! The scene dissolved and he found himself back in Maze Prison, where they had sent him for staging the failed ambush. As if being shot wasn't punishment enough, he had to endure six years in the Maze.

Kelley went in an idealist youth believing in a free and united Ireland and got out as a cynical criminal interested in using his associations to foster his lawless career. While in prison, Kelley had met an associate of Michael McKevitt, former Quartermaster General (QMG) of the Provos. McKevitt left the Provos to start the Real IRA, a more militant group, engaged in bombings and direct combat with the Brits. McKevitt armed the Real IRA with arms stolen from a weapons store he had set up while QMG of the Provos.

To earn favor while in prison, Kelley and another prisoner executed a Loyalist Volunteer Force leader. The other prisoner, already doing life for another murder, copped to the charge and let Kelley escape scot-free. In the dream, he relived the murder of the Loyalist, remembering the bullet he put in the man's forehead. But this time the reanimated corpse actually talked to him, telling Kelley he would wait for him in Hell. That was when he began thrashing, but eventually quieted down enough as he entered another dream state.

Char checked on the man and listened to him breathe. His breathing was regular and seemed normal—it was indeed a vast improvement over when they found him—wheezing and turning blue due to lack of oxygen. He took the man's temperature with an electronic thermometer that Sofia had given him. A fever would indicate the start of an infection—although she had also given him antibiotics to guard against just such an eventuality.

His nurse's duty over for the time being, Char returned to the stern and was soon dozing on the back deck. The expansive night sky was blanketed with stars made more lustrous by the absence of competing artificial light. He was nursed to sleep by the gentle warm breeze and awoke with the false dawn. He checked on the patient again, considered having a beer, but vetoed that idea in favor of lukewarm coffee in the thermos that Earl had brought.

The *Good as Gold* arrived with the true sunrise and anchored fifty feet away to avoid the shallow water where the trawler sat at anchor. Sofia and Michael returned in the skiff. She boarded, hugged Char and kissed him on both cheeks.

"Well, good morning beautiful. You certainly look well-rested," said Char.

"I am in fact. Michael almost carried me to bed."

He gave Char a look, "and then I left her alone after that," said Michael.

Char was about to make a comment, when Sofia abruptly changed the subject. "How's he doing?" she asked.

"A bit of thrashing around, so I tied him down. Other than that, it looks like he had a good night's rest," said Char.

"Good, I'll go check on him and see if he's awake. Michael and I will stay with him. Johnnie has got your breakfast waiting for you. Go get some rest," said Sofia.

Michael looked at Char. "You heard her—doctor's orders."

She disappeared into the cabin and busied herself examining the patient. He was still asleep and that was good—she had to remove the tube and stitch the wound shut, and it would be better if he was unconscious for that. She expeditiously completed her tasks, and he began to stir as she finished closing the wound with a few small stitches. His eyes fluttered open, and he looked at her. He tried to move, but Char had effectively hogtied the man.

"Water," he said.

Sofia had anticipated that and had brought a plastic glass with a lid and integrated straw—the sort of cup they sell you on a cruise boat. She held it to his lips and he sucked the cool water until it was empty.

"More?" she asked.

"No, I'm okay for now," he said hoarsely. "Who are you?"

"Doctor Sofia Ramos of the International Red Cross. And you are?"

"Ken Q. Kelley, late of Sneem, County Kerry, Ireland. I take it you are responsible for saving my life?"

"Yes, my fiancé Michael and his father, Char also helped you. Now that you're out of immediate danger, we should take you into Key West for follow-up. I did the best I could with what medical supplies I have, but there is a danger of infection that they will be better able to treat."

"Why am I tied up?" he asked.

Michael opened the door to the cabin and looked down at the man. "Sorry, my dad said you were thrashing around, so he had to tie you down to stop you from pulling the catheter out."

"Can you sit up for me?" asked Sofia. "Michael come help us."

Michael descended the half dozen steps into the cabin, expeditiously untied the man and helped him to sit up.

Sofia touched the back of the dinette bench seat. "Perhaps you would be more comfortable sitting here."

Michael assisted him to his feet and helped him to sit down on the bench. "Who the hell are you?" Kelley asked.

"Mister Ken Q. Kelley, this is my fiancé, Michael Blackfox, "said Sofia.

"Grand to meet you, but I could eat the lamb o' Jayjus through the rungs of a chair."

"Excuse me?" said Michael.

"I'm hungry," replied Kelley.

Sofia smiled warmly. "I thought you might be, so we've brought you breakfast—hardboiled eggs, toast and ham. There is also coffee. Michael, get the cooler."

"What's the Q stand for?" asked Michael.

"Quincy, like your President Adams," replied Kelley. "Sorry, lad, but she said something about food?"

Michael opened the cabin door, picked up the igloo from the deck and brought it to the dinette table. He opened it and withdrew several Tupperware containers, popped off their lids, and placed them before Kelley.

Kelley tentatively withdrew an egg, examined it for a moment before pushing it into his mouth whole and ravenously chewing it. He followed with a piece of toast and then another egg. Michael withdrew a quart of orange juice, opened it, and handed it to the man. Kelley drank deeply and wiped his mouth on the back of his hand. He withdrew a ham slice, rolled it and alternated eating it with another egg. Once all the food was gone, he finished the last of the juice and regarded his audience. "That was bloody good."

"Glad you enjoyed it. Now, we'd like to take you into Key West for a more thorough exam," said Sofia.

"No, I can't agree to that."

"And why not, Mister Kelley? You need to be placed on an antibiotic and anti-fungal regime or the outcome could be grave. Pneumonia, wound infection, or relapse of the tension pneumothorax are just a few of the possibilities," said Sofia.

Kelley looked at Michael and then to Sofia. "I had a bit of a dust up in Key West a few days ago and I'd just as soon give the place a wide berth."

"Is that how you got the wound that caused the collapsed lung?" asked Michael.

"I borrowed money from a guy to restore this boat and he claims I never paid him. He brought a couple tough gougers with him to take the boat and one of them stabbed me. I got out of there, treated myself and felt the pressure building in my chest so I headed towards Fort Jefferson where I knew they could give me first aid, but I passed out on the way, "said Kelley.

"Funny the way things happen, there was another incident at the fort, seems a diver had a heart attack and drowned just yesterday," said Michael.

"Well, then brace yourself boyo," said Kelley, "Because you know what they say—everything bad happens in threes."

Chapter Seven – Rule of Three

Michael had sought Char out immediately upon his return from Kelley's boat. He found him on the bridge, running diagnostics on the starboard engine. Char lightly tapped the blue screen display. "It's running hot—probably the water pump—I think it's on the way out. How's the patient doing?"

"Eating like a horse, but still pretty weak. Claims he got stabbed over a loan on the boat."

"I don't like the sound of that," said Char. "Who gets stabbed over a loan?"

"Yeah, well, not our problem. Let's get him well enough to pilot his boat and then the guy can go wherever he wants," said Michael.

"As far as I'm concerned, load him up on antibiotics, give him some food and send him on his way. I'm done saving the world," replied Char.

"It's Sofia—she feels responsible for the man."

"Let me tell you something about women…" said Char.

"Save it Dad—your longest relationship since Mom left is a two-for-one lap dance you had in Bogota."

"Maybe so, but it was a hell of a dance. Just remember, Sofia has a big heart and she's a crusader—she thinks she can save the world—one wounded man at a time," said Char.

"There's something about that guy rubs me the wrong way," replied Michael.

"Something? How about everything? The guy has a bullet wound in his chest. It's scarred over, but a small caliber bullet did it—it looks like a five point five six round."

"Military or ex?" asked Michael.

"Maybe, but it could be something else. In either case, talk Sofia into cutting him loose. Call your mom—tell her you're engaged and in route to Key West. You know how she is about throwing parties."

"Sure. An engagement party is an easy out. Hell, I'll even invite the guy," said Michael.

"Let's give him another day to recuperate. That way, Sofia will feel she did her duty," said Char.

"That will work—I still have to take her on a tour of the fort. I thought we'd take the paddle boards over."

Chapter Eight - Ann Sullivan Blackfox

Until recently, Michael's mother had managed an art gallery in Crawford Notch, New Hampshire. An avid hiker with a passion for the outdoors, she fell in love with the simple, rugged charm of the White Mountains and moved there from her childhood home in Nashua, shortly after graduating from art school. Ann Sullivan Blackfox could have been used as inspiration for the state's motto—*Live free or Die* as she was the epitome of a free spirit, with a strong entrepreneurial streak.

She had met her husband, Char, during a Spring Break trip to Daytona Beach in the late eighties. They fell in love over the course of the week long trip and a month later she moved back down to marry him. They had a simple yet touching sunset ceremony on Ormond Beach, presided over by a Seminole Shaman who also happened to be an ordained minister. Michael was born about ten months later.

Their life together lasted a scant four years, as Ann quickly grew tired of Char's life on the run—from what, she didn't know.

She retreated back up north with her young son in tow and settled into an old farm house. She converted one of the empty rooms into a studio and returned to painting the White Mountains, but there were plenty of other artists doing that.

Money was tight and she was one step away from returning to live with her mother when inspiration struck. She had started a portrait of her husband in traditional Seminole Long Shirt and red leggings, but never completely finished it.

Crawford Notch hosted an art fair once a year and Ann begged a friend to share an exhibition space. A few of Ann's paintings garnered offers, but the portrait of the Seminole Warrior sold outright for the listed price of $600—it was obvious she had stumbled onto something.

She began doing paintings of local indigenous people, such as the Penacook, Winnipesaukee, and Ossipee, before the arrival of the White Man. No one else was doing this at the time and she quickly gained some renown as a local artist.

Char was a pretty good absentee father—he pulled his trailer up north to escape the repressive Florida summers and took the boy camping in the White Mountains. In the fall, he returned and Char even took the boy hunting—Michael shot his first deer when he was twelve years old.

Ann didn't mind the boy being a hunter—although she associated with an artsy crowd, she was firmly grounded in the need to provide for her family. Her paternal grandfather had fled the Great Famine in Ireland and told her stories about having to eat kelp and wild plants to fill their bellies. It was a lesson well learned and nothing filled the larder as well as a three hundred pound white tail deer.

Eventually Ann saved enough to escape the cold mountain

winters. She choose Key West as she knew it to be an artist's enclave and she had found an old general store that could be converted into a small gallery. She planned to permanently change her focus to painting early nineteenth century Seminoles, while also showcasing local artists.

Michael hadn't seen his mother since before he deployed to Iraq, but knew from their infrequent telephone calls that she was moving to the Keys. Flynn ran his boat out of nearby Stock Island and spent most of his free time birddogging eligible female tourists on Duval Street. Michael told Flynn about his mother and Flynn mentioned seeing a local news story showcasing an entrepreneurial artist with the unique last name of Blackfox. The news story showcased her efforts at building a new edition to Key West's art and business scene.

Ann had divorced Char, but kept his last name because it gave her a certain level of gravitas within a community that valued ties to progressive causes—including indigenous people. Michael used the satellite phone on the bridge to call information and get the number for the Blackfox Gallery. He let it ring ten or so times and just as he was about to give up, she picked up.

"Hi Mom," said Michael cheerfully. She had the uncanny ability to transform him into a guilt ridden eight year old every time he failed to keep in regular touch with her.

"Who is this? It sounds just like a son I once had, but I think he must have been swallowed by the ocean as I haven't heard from him in nearly a year."

"It's been more like three months, Mom."

"Of course, Michael. I'm overjoyed to learn that you and your miscreant father are still alive," said Ann Blackfox. "How nice of you to let me know. Where the hell are you?"

"We stopped at Fort Jefferson on the way to Key West."

"Did they finally catch up with your father and lock him up?" she asked.

"Come on Mom, they haven't used it for a prison in over a hundred years."

"More is the pity. It's the kind of place I imagined he would end up in one day."

It was his Mom's way, and ironically she wasn't that far off the mark. She was a usually joyful woman who loved her son, but had the dry sarcastic wit of her Irish ancestors and was unhappy she heard from her only child on a sporadic basis—if at all. He managed to send her emails or call her on her birthday and Mother's Day, but she hadn't heard his voice in a long time. He needed to redirect the conversation before it became mired down in a discussion of his father's many failings.

"Mom, I'm getting married. I thought you would want to meet her."

Michael could detect a subtle change on the other end—as if his mother's mood was undergoing an actual metamorphosis.

"Is it the same woman you met in Bogota—the doctor?" asked his mother.

"The self-same," replied Michael.

"Well, don't let this one get away."

"That's the idea Mom. I need you to do me a favor, however. Can you host a small engagement party this weekend? It doesn't have to be anything special."

"It's your lucky day, Michael. I have a couple cases of wine and assorted appetizers left over from the gallery opening yesterday. People don't eat like they used to—everyone is either a vegan, on a low carb diet, or doing some other silly shit."

"That should work, Sofia's a bit involved treating a boater that had a problem breathing," said Michael, deciding the less said about Kelley, the better.

He ended the call and felt relieved. He wouldn't have to lie to Sofia to get her to disengage from treating Kelley. The last few times over there, he noticed the man's demeanor had softened. He wasn't as suave as someone like Flynn, who worked the ladies with a practiced panache that was always on, but Kelley was definitely turning up the charm as he recovered. He wasn't worried about some 55-year old putting the moves on his fiancée, it was more like Kelley had something else in mind—Michael just wasn't certain what that was.

"We're on for tomorrow at seven," said Michael.

"Good. Key West is about two hours from here. That will give you enough time to show Sofia the fort and say good bye to the patient," said Char.

"Yeah, I think we're going to take the paddle boards over tomorrow morning," replied Michael.

Char shook his head. "I wish you would do something with those things. You and Sofia used them once on Roatan and they've been taking up space on the fly bridge ever since."

"I think I'll go give Sofia the good news and see if she wants to repay me in kind. She hasn't been too affectionate lately. I guess she's in doctoring mode," said Michael.

"Maybe she's practicing for after you're married," said Char with a grin.

Michael didn't laugh, but a sly smile spread across his face. "Oh, before I forget, Mom sends her love."

Chapter Nine – Sister M

Ken Q. Kelley became addicted to morphine after he was shot during the troubles—Ireland's revolt against British home rule. Kelley's idealism faded as his addiction to morphine increased. It took every ounce of self-discipline he had and then some, to wean him off the drug the first time and now he remembered why—it was an outstanding high that washed over him like a warm bath.

They made sure he was well fed and at first, she had kept him well-juiced with morphine. But yesterday—the morning of the third day since they found him near death, she had substantially decreased the dosage. The young blond hair kid who looked like a surfer, had come over with the evening meal —shepherd's pie and a thermos full of coffee.

Kelley always seemed to be sitting on the dinette's wooden bench seat, facing the door as if waiting for something. "Where's Sofia?" he asked.

"She's got the night off. You've got me tonight. I brought you a shepherd's pie—Earl thought you might like it. He's a pretty fair cook." Johnnie removed an earthenware crock from a small cooler, placed it before Kelley and removed the lid.

Kelley examined the mashed potato topping with a spoon for a moment, sunk it deep within the stew and shoveled a heaping spoonful into his mouth. He chewed slowly before swallowing—as if considering a comment.

"Maybe so, but he doesn't know fuck-all about Irish cuisine," said Kelley.

"I thought that was an oxymoron—you know, like sober Irishman," said Johnnie.

Kelley's face flashed red with anger. Then he forced a smile. "Funny bloke, you are. Acting the maggot with me?"

"Yeah, don't sweat it old timer, I was just fucking with you."

"Right, well bugger off and let me eat," said Kelley.

"Fine by me, you're not my idea of a good time either. Sofia says she'll come by tomorrow and give you a final once over, and if everything checks out, we're heading in to Key West."

"No shot for pain?" said Kelley.

"No, but she did give me some pills," said Johnnie withdrawing a small brown bottle from the pocket of his board shorts. "She said take two every four hours for pain."

Johnnie placed the bottle on the table in front of the man.

"What are they?"

"Aspirin, 325 milligrams per tablet," said Johnnie.

"Aspirin—fuck me to Hell," said Kelley.

"There are a hundred tabs, you might be able to catch a buzz if you take enough," said Johnnie.

Kelley just glared at him.

"Sorry man—it was just a joke."

Kelley pointed a knife he was using to butter a piece of bread at Johnnie.

"Didn't you say you were buggering off?"

"Yeah, I was just leaving. Have a good night."

Kelley said nothing in response, but Johnnie didn't care—the old Mick gave him the creeps. He exited onto the stern cockpit, jumped in the skiff and motored the short distance back to the *Good as Gold.* He thought he should have a word with Michael.

Kelley cursed. "Fuck me to tears!" He pitched the shepherd's pie against the bulkhead, breaking the bowl and scattering the contents around the cabin—*it was shit anyway.* He had again become accustomed to getting high and was looking forward to another evening in the embrace of sister morphine. It was going to be a long night.

***

It had been almost four days since they had made love. Sofia had been totally consumed with saving Kelley and everything else was forgotten. Johnnie hadn't said anything about Kelley's demeanor, otherwise she would have insisted on a house call. She had run out of morphine and regardless of his complaints, the wound was healing nicely and a simple analgesic could manage any residual pain. Still she felt guilty for not going herself to tell him of the change.

The lovemaking had at first been as powerful as it was quick. Sofia felt like she was riding a tsunami of Michael's lust. The second time was slow and romantic. He employed the patience and skill of a concert pianist in tickling the appropriate keys to make her sing. Had there have been an audience, they would have applauded in unison on their feet.

Then they slept. Michael was up before her. He let her sleep in, pulled on a pair of board shorts and a sleeveless t-shirt and slipped into the passageway. He climbed up to the main deck and into the galley for a cup of coffee. The Keurig was already on. He selected a K-Cup—Green Mountain Roaster's Double Black Diamond, placed it in the machine and dispensed his coffee. He retreated to the long teak dining table, took a seat and began reading a week-old *International Herald* he purchased in Cozumel. Ten minutes later, Johnnie came up from his cabin to begin preparing breakfast.

"Morning, Michael. I went looking for you last night, but you had already, ah.......gone to bed."

"Yeah, I was tired," he said with a slight grin.

"Listen," said Johnnie, "that fucking guy, Kelley, is a head case. I mean, I thought he was going to stab me because I brought him aspirin instead of morphine. I would be careful around him."

"No worries, Johnnie. Sofia checks him out in a few hours, then we cut him loose. He can go wherever he wants as far as I'm concerned."

"Well, if I had to render an opinion, I'd say he's gonna go score some heroin somewhere."

"Not my problem. After Sofia is satisfied she provided better than average care, he can go chase the dragon of china white with a black tar heroin chaser for all I care, "said Michael.

Johnnie shook his head slowly, maybe not agreeing so much as acknowledging that the diminutive, but wiry Irishman didn't worry Captain Michael Blackfox, whose last assignment was commanding a Marine Corps Special Operations team in combat.

"How do you want your eggs, Mike?"

"Hardboiled," he replied.

Yeah, just like you, thought Johnnie. It occurred to him that the difference between people and what they accomplish or don't comes down to fear and the level that they are willing to tolerate to get what they want. The more fear they can stand, the greater potential for accomplishment. It was the same for a high stakes poker game or combat, except for in the former, usually no one dies.

"Coming right up, Boss," said Johnnie as he retreated into the galley.

Sofia appeared a half hour later dressed in a lightweight wet suit, carrying a waterproof backpack that Michael usually took with them when scuba diving. She approached Michael and gave him a deep kiss.

"Morning, my love."

"Morning. No breakfast?" asked Michael.

"I had a granola bar, that should last me until lunch," said Sofia. She was notorious for going without food for extended periods of time and then feasting when there was opportunity to do so. It was a trait she developed when working different emergencies with the Red Cross. Once during a mudslide in southwestern Colombia, she had gone two days without eating—

subsisting on a locally made electrolyte drink until the triage she ran slowed down enough to allow her to eat a quick meal of beef and rice.

Char came down from the fly bridge and went straight for the coffee maker, mumbling a few salutations on the way. He grabbed his favorite coffee mug—one with a Navy diver's helmet badge embossed on the face, filled it and sipped deeply. He walked over to the table and stood at one end. "I had Earl drop the boards in the water. You can board from the stern when you're ready."

Sofia clapped her hands in excitement and ran to the stern, with no plan other than that.

Michael started to follow her, but Char grabbed his arm, "Johnnie told me about our patient's mood last night, so I don't have to tell you to watch your ass over there. More importantly, watch your fiancée's ass."

Michael laughed. "It's okay, Dad—nothing's going happen on my watch."

"You want, I'll go over and give the guy a final exam and you two can just paddle over to the fort," said Char.

"No, it's important to Sofia—otherwise it'll look like I'm controlling her."

***

Kelley hadn't slept much during the evening. He had swallowed at least half the bottle of aspirin, but it did little to stifle the throbbing in the side of his chest. But, the real pain was the physiological withdrawal from the morphine.

Michael knocked and waited a few seconds before descending into the small cabin. Sofia followed closely behind him. Kelley sat in the booth and stared at them.

"Morning Mister Kelley, how are you feeling?" asked Sofia.

"As if you gave a care—you left me to suffer through the night with nothing other than some aspirin."

Michael looked around the cabin and recognized shards of the earthenware and small piles of meat and potatoes scattered about the cabin. "Didn't like the dinner?" he asked.

"It tasted like a pile o' shite," said Kelley.

"Beats starving," said Michael.

"Michael, please! This is not helping," said Sofia. She turned to Kelley, "Ken, please take off your shirt, I'd like to examine the stitches—if you're experiencing discomfort, it could be a sign of infection."

Kelley was wearing the same lightweight, button-down shirt he had worn since Sofia treated him. It had dried salt rings around both armpits and a blood stain on the back, where he had been stabbed.

Michael assisted him off with the shirt and held it, unsure of what he should do with the soiled garment. "Got another shirt, dude?"

"In the drawer under the bunk behind me," said Kelley with a jut of his chin. Sofia busied herself examining the original wound as well as the incision she made to deflate his pneumothorax.

Michael walked past the man, found the drawer and opened it. He searched through the drawer for a clean shirt, found something similar to the one Kelley had been wearing under a small pile of hand towels and pulled it from the drawer. Something rolled off it and fell to the deck when Michael pulled out the shirt. It clattered to the wood floor, bounced off Michael's neoprene bootie encased foot and then rolled under the bunk.

Hearing the noise, Kelley attempted to turn toward Michael, but Sofia objected, "Please, Mister Kelley, hold still while I check your stitches."

Michael returned with the shirt. "How about I bring some soap and water, so you can wash up?" asked Michael.

"I'm fine," protested Kelley.

"Oh, no Mister Kelley, I beg to differ," said Sofia with a wrinkled nose, "You stink. I suggest you let Michael help you get cleaned up."

Michael didn't wait for further argument. He returned to the drawer and pretended to search for a towel while he reached under the bunk and retrieved the object—a nine inch long ice pick, before retreating into the head. He placed the towel containing the ice pick onto the shelf over the wash basin and exited to the galley. He searched the cabinets until he found a large bowl and returned to the head to fill it with water.

Once back in the head, Michael examined the blade. The tip and about one half of the blade were coated with what appeared to be dried blood. It had a molded six inch black rubber grip topped with a waterproof lanyard. He examined the grip and noticed the initials H and D burnt into the handle—probably with a soldering iron.

Michael was sure that the initials were the same as that of the diver who had died on Flynn's boat three days ago. If that was the case, he would notify the rangers at the fort and they might take Kelley into custody. He briefly debated whether to take the ice pick or leave it, but decided that the rangers would require some evidence substantiating the tale he would tell.

Michael placed the ice pick into his rubber booties, with the point sticking into the heel. He pulled the wet suit's leg over the handle, but it created a large and noticeable bulge on the back of his ankle—it would have to do.

He grabbed the soap, filled the bowl with water from the basin and returned to give Kelley his bath.

Sofia was just finishing up her cursory exam when Michael returned. "Well, Mister Kelley, it looks like you will live."

"Yeah, thanks to you, I will. Don't think I'm not grateful, it's just that this bit of business has put me out of sorts."

"I understand," said Sofia.

"So do I," said Michael. He placed the bowl, towel, and soap on the dinette table. "There's your bath—you can help yourself. The tide is going out and we have to get a move on."

Sofia looked surprised, but said nothing. Kelley smiled at Sofia, "Might I ask you one last favor? Give me something stronger than aspirin for the pain?"

Sofia nodded, opened her waterproof backpack and pulled out several physician's sample packs. "I forgot I had these. Here are twelve morphine pills. The correct dose is one pill every four hours—after that, you're on your own."

Kelley smiled, took the packets and embraced Sofia, who although taken by surprise, hugged him back.

"You'll be leaving then?" asked Kelley.

"Yeah, we're going to check out the fort and then head to Key

West."

"I'm going to meet my new mother," said Sofia as she hugged Michael.

There was little more to say and Michael badly wanted to leave. Sofia looked at him and sensed his discomfort. "Okay, Ken, we will leave you to your bath. Farewell," said Sofia. Michael led her up the short stairway and out the cabin door.

Once outside, she turned to him with a look of concern on her face, "Michael is something wrong?" He held his finger to his lip and she nodded in understanding. He slipped over the gunwale and onto his paddle board. She walked further back towards the stern and did the same. They cast off their lines, picked up their paddle and put the Irishman behind them as quickly as their mode of transport allowed. Michael felt relieved to be moving away, but strangely disquieted as if there was someone watching him depart.

Chapter Ten - Kiley Reilly

Kelley remembered he had tossed the pick in the drawer and knew that the guy, Michael, had seen it, but so what? He went to the drawer pulled it open and searched through the clothing. *Nothing,* thought Kelley. *The bastard had actually taken it and was in route to the last law enforcement outpost in Florida.*

Kelley climbed out of the cabin and watched them paddle away through the helm's windshield. Seeing them on paddle boards brought back memories of long ago—when he had just arrived in the states after he was released from the Maze. He had done his job and kept his mouth shut and for that he was sent on an arms buying mission. McKevitt, Commander of the Real IRA, liked him but wanted him out of the picture as the murder he committed had generated lots of calls for retribution from the loyalists.

It was a good gig—nobody looking over his shoulder, but better still was that no one was counting their change. He was told to purchase two hundred fifty handguns and half that number of assault rifles. He used straw purchasers—which necessitated meeting guys willing to take a chance for a bit of profit. He chose Florida based on its sunny climate, as it was winter when he was released. He set up a base of operation in a motel on Treasure Island, within walking distance to the beach and began frequenting dive bars looking for lads who were a bit down on their luck. He'd buy em drinks, a bit of food, whatever, until they trusted him and then he made the offer—buy me a forty-five automatic or nine millimeter and pocket a cool hundred. He made a lot of friends quickly.

The most upscale of the places frequented was a steakhouse called the Billabong Grill in downtown St. Petersburg. It was meant to play off the love of the Australian mystique brought to the states by Mel Gibson in *Mad Max* and Paul Hogan's character, Crocodile Dundee. The restaurant did pretty well when it first opened in the late '80s—until Outback Steakhouse arrived on the scene. After that, it survived through a mix of long happy hours, cheap food, and most importantly—the all-female staff of servers wearing Australian flag bikinis and bush hats.

Kiley Reilly was a tall twenty-two year old blond haired bartender with a voluptuous figure and a mercenary desire to get ahead. She worked the regulars like a seasoned professional—they drank all night long and at the end of the evening were presented with a check for eleven or twelve dollars. The jolly drunkards thought they had won the lottery and tipped Kiley most of the money they would have used paying the actual bill. Even on a slow night, she managed to squeeze a couple hundred dollars of reallocated profit from the joint.

Kiley had always wanted to go to visit her grandfather's birthplace, but after meeting a true son of Eire, she reasoned that sleeping with an Irishman was the next best thing. They were married in the Sunken Gardens, two months later and set themselves up in a beachfront apartment on St. Pete Beach.

Kelley's job necessitated traveling about the state, making friends in bars, pitching the offer and then, hopefully, taking delivery of the firearm. Now that he was married, he drove a harder bargain—instead of offering a C-note, he dropped the commission to fifty dollars, and was forced to see even more desperate clientele.

Kiley's luck took a turn for the worse. A disgruntled customer who hadn't received the benefit of her creative bar tab accounting, complained to the boss. He began monitoring the number of drinks he served and reconciling them to the bar tab. She was eventually let go.

In retrospect, Kelley should have known that a young, horny wife, who was suddenly terminated and therefore lacking in self-esteem is like a satchel charge that's all primed and ready to go. It just needs someone to push the detonator. That role fell to a thirty-two year old Australian surf instructor, who also rented paddle boards from a small stand on Sunset Beach. It wasn't important to know how they met—she gave off so much raw sexuality it was likely that he just followed the aroma. There was the usual juvenile attempt at subterfuge after he noticed the abrupt change in her routine and her equally sudden disinterest in sex—at least with him.

One of his clientele, who was also a former customer of Kiley's from her days at the Billabong, spotted them frolicking in the surf and then paddling off together at sunset. After paddling out a good distance, she climbed on to his board and appeared to straddle him for a spirited cowgirl-style lovemaking.

Kelley's straw man buyer dangled the information in front of him in the hope of garnering a tip for his trouble. When Kelley took the bait and offered a C-note, the man offered to take him to the very spot in the hope of witnessing his young wife perform an encore. They witnessed nothing that night, but Kelley believed the man and followed him to his small apartment on the island to take delivery of a .38 snub nose revolver he had bought and commiserate over a bottle of Jameson's whiskey.

Kelley took delivery of the revolver and twenty boxes of copper jacketed hollow points. They had finished half the bottle when it became clear what must be done. He claimed to have never seen such ammunition as it was prohibited in Ireland. He took one round out of the box to examine it and surreptitiously placed it into the pocket of his jacket where the newly purchased pistol already resided. He then excused himself to take a leak.

Upon returning, Kelley grabbed the pillow, shoved it into the man's face and pinned him to the couch. He pushed the short barrel deeply into the pillow and pulled the trigger just once. It was louder than he thought it would be and the smoke from the burned cordite didn't dissipate—causing him to fear that the smoke detector would go off. He pulled the pillow away and looked into the unseeing eyes of his victim—he wasn't even sure of the man's name—Ken something or other. He reached into the man's rear pocket, retrieved his wallet and flipped it open. He removed the man's license and stared at the picture. There was a passing resemblance.

"Well, at least you're Irish," he said as he slipped the wallet into his back pocket.

He closed the man's eyes, gave the pistol a thorough wipe down, placed it near his right hand, took the ruined pillow and departed. He threw the pillow in a dumpster behind the apartment building and thought that'd be the end of it, but he was in Pinellas County and that made all the difference in the world.

Kelley waited until the following day when he was scheduled

to travel to Miami and spend the night. That meant that his cheating wife might take advantage of his absence to repeat her sunset paddle board sojourn.

There was a high-rise hotel that had been vacant for years and was scheduled for renovation, but construction had not yet started. The upper floors provided a panoramic view of much of the coastline of Pinellas County. Kelley walked by the faded pink high rise concrete monstrosity that had once been the Sea Shell Hotel. It had been encircled by construction fencing from which no trespassing signs hung at regular intervals. The fencing extended onto the beach and therein lay the way in.

He walked around the beach front side of the hotel and found that whoever had placed the fencing was not particularly concerned with insuring that there was no clearance between the bottom of the fence and the sand. In various places, the sand had piled up in a small dune and there was an opening of at least a foot between the two. He found what appeared to be the largest opening, pushed his backpack through, and low crawled after it. He walked with practiced nonchalance to the fire escape he had spotted earlier, lowered the base ladder and climbed up to the first landing.

At first, he thought it might all be for nothing. He had met the Australian earlier in the day while his wife was sleeping off a suspicious hangover. He was a big bronze bastard, with a perfect set of white teeth and a cockiness made more salty by the accent he accentuated to advertise his uniqueness. Kelley hated him the second he met him. He inquired about surfing lessons and the guy almost laughed at him.

"A little long in the tooth for that, aren't you mate?" and that was when Kelley was just forty three.

"Just looking for something to do on vacation," he replied.

"Well, there's always the pub—you missed high tide. But come back tomorrow if you want to give it a go. I open at nine," said the Aussie.

But not tomorrow, thought Kelley.

The hotel was art deco style—its exterior was supposed to resemble the curved lines of a ship. Kelley climbed to the top of the wall, slid over the parapet and surveyed the roof. A couple of old metal folding chairs sat off to the side of a bulkhead—no doubt an improvised smoke break area. He grabbed one of the chairs and carried it to the edge of the roof. Sitting down, he was concealed behind the building's beach facing wall, but if he stood, he could observe the Aussie's beach stand.

One of his prized straw purchases had been of a Heckler and Koch 93 SG1. What made it special was the fact that it was a sniper grade variant of the popular assault rifle. It boasted improved telescopic sights, a bipod, and some tuning of the trigger mechanism. Most importantly, it broke down to a very compact size that could fit into a briefcase or knapsack. He opened his old canvas haversack and removed a high impact plastic case containing the rifle.

Kelley watched the Aussie through the rifle's telescopic sight and it appeared that the guy was nervously awaiting someone. He waited an hour and even in winter, the sun was intense.

He hadn't brought anything other than the weapon and he cursed his lack of preparedness. He contented himself with tobacco—chain smoking because he was nervous—murder of a loyalist was one thing, but killing his wife was another. Still, she had cheated on him and loyalty meant a lot to a bloke who had gone to prison rather than give up his bosses in the Real IRA.

She literally danced into the crosshairs of his scope. Kiley jumped into the Aussie's arms and straddled his waist with her long legs. Any hope that the Aussie hadn't fucked his wife faded with that casually obscene display.

A few minutes later, they grabbed two paddle boards leaning against the side of the shack and slowly paddled out to watch the sunset. He couldn't afford to wait until then as there wouldn't be sufficient light to make a shot. He couldn't decide who to shoot first, and that was when it occurred to him that he would take them both with one shot. He watched them misalign themselves half a dozen times as they paddled out to some unknown spot in the gulf. Finally, The Aussie slowed his paddling and Kiley inched closer behind him until they were perfectly aligned. Kelley fired once.

The memory faded. Kelley watched Sofia—his savior, and her fiancé paddle towards Fort Jefferson and made a decision. He climbed behind the helm of his small craft, started the diesel engine and used the windlass to retrieve the anchor line. He turned to the bow of the yacht, waved to the tall older guy on the bridge and then throttled up his boat.

Chapter Eleven – PBK

Char waved to the departing boat. "Well, I guess that's that." He hopped out of the white leather captain's chair and handed the M4 carbine to Johnnie.

"Watch the radar—make sure this guy is headed out of here and put this back in the weapon's locker. I'm gonna have Earl make me a Spanish omelet." Char had forgone breakfast to provide over-watch to his son and Sofia. They were now out of sight and no doubt arriving at the long wooden dock outside the Sally port at the fort.

"Good call, boss, that's one of his specialties," said Johnnie.

***

Kelley throttled up the boat's modest diesel engine and turned east toward Key West then turned north to pick up the Dry Tortuga's ship channel. He followed the channel north around the coral reefs that encircled the island. Anyone observing him from the yacht would think he was headed to Key West. He passed the western side of the immense brick structure, throttled down the engine to about one quarter and made a slow turn around the northeast side of the island—looking for a landing sight. His boat's shallow draft and the high tide allowed the boat to pass over the reef with a couple of feet to spare.

A moat encircled the entire structure. He kept up a slow circumnavigation of the small island and spotted a short beach about one hundred yards to his southeast. The beach was adjacent to some old pilings that looked to be the ruins of an ancient dock. It would do for his purposes.

Kelley brought the engine speed down to an idle and let the boat drift until it ground on the soft sand. He had landed by the ruins of the North Coaling Dock. Kelley opened the storage locker beneath the bench seat cushion and removed the waterproof box containing the same HK assault weapon he had used nearly a decade earlier to kill his wife and her lover. He had acquired a suppressor for it—which would obscure the sound of the rifle shot.

The ferry from Key West had not yet arrived—which was both bad and good. There was no chance to get lost in the crowd, but there was also less chance of getting spotted when he prepared his firing position. He popped two morphine pills earlier and so felt no pain—Kelley wanted to be numb for what he had to do, but not so anestanized he'd have trouble doing it.

Kelley straddled the gunwale and hopped down into the shallow blue water and then pulled the black plastic case off the boat and waded to shore. He shuffled down the beach line towards the Sally port that served as the entrance to the fort—sweating profusely in the early morning sunshine. The sally port was at least a quarter mile away.

Once at the entrance, signs directed him inside the office

where guests bought tickets—but Kelley had other ideas. It was early and the post was not manned, so he jogged left until he found a steep circular stairway inside one of the bastions. He climbed the stairs as quickly as his wounded, drug-addled state would allow, and ascended to a landing where a sign directed him to the cell of Doctor Samuel Mudd.

Kelley found a gun casement overlooking their direction of travel and quickly set up a hasty firing position. Workers were repairing one of the casement walls and several bags of cement were left at their worksite. He tried to pull the heavy bag towards the opening and groaned from the effort. He dragged another bag over and placed it so that the two bags formed the shape of a V. Kelley opened the case, retrieved the HK, fitted the suppressor to it, opened the bipod legs, inserted a loaded magazine, and took up a good firing position. He searched Bird Key Harbor and at first didn't see the two paddle-boarders. He scanned one hundred eighty degrees of his position and spotted them off to the right, less than a hundred yards away—heading towards the main dock.

The guy, Michael, was in the lead and Sofia followed a short distance behind him navigating the water between the ruins of the South Coaling Dock and the main ferry pier. If he shifted his position by forty-five degrees he should be able to take them both out with one shot.

Kelley was certain that Michael intended to report him to the rangers. He was pretty sure they weren't the law enforcement kind of rangers, but they could call in the Coast Guard. Any in-depth scrutiny of Kelley's background would uncover enough skeletons to fill a large walk-in closet. Any subsequent search of his boat would turn up at least a dozen firearms he had never bothered to ship to his mates in Belfast. *Killing these two here and now was definitely easier than allowing them to report him and having to kill everyone at the fort*, Kelley reasoned.

He shifted his position and brought the crosshairs of the scope onto center mass of his target. Sofia followed closely behind Michael, perhaps trying to beat him to the dock. Kelley watched them for a while and had almost given up his impulsive desire to recreate in some form the murder of his wife and her lover. He wasn't sure why he wanted to do so—other than the need to duplicate the feeling of omniscience that his first double murder had given him.

***

Michael saw something shiny reflect from the second floor of the fort and became uneasy. He remembered feeling the same way in the Venezuelan jungle about a year and a half ago and the experience had taught him to trust that feeling. He stopped paddling forward and stared at the spot in the wall where the reflection had originated. He heard the rumbling of an outboard in the distance that sounded like the hundred horsepower Mercury they had on the launch.

Michael looked to his right and saw the Boston Whaler approaching at full throttle across the top of the reef to the south of the fort.

What the fuck is Dad up to, he thought.

Then he heard it—the short staccato crack of an M4 carbine on burst mode—pop, pop, pop. Michael turned to the spot on the wall, saw a bright flash that looked like a suppressed muzzle burst. He felt something hard hit his left side and knock him from the board. He fell into the shallow water and sucked in a lungful of seawater.

Michael sank to the bottom, touched his shoulder, and felt pain. He pulled his hand away and saw blood flowing from a thumb size hole on the left side of his shoulder. He heard another splash and remembered Sofia. Michael surfaced and tried to locate her—he was in seven feet of water about twenty feet from the ferry dock.

The launch was still at full throttle and closing rapidly and Michael was suddenly worried that it would run him over or hit him with the propeller. Someone cut the motor, but the shooter continued firing at the casement. Michael rotated his head and then treaded water in a circle until he found her—floating face down about ten feet away from him on the far side of her paddleboard.

"Sofia!" he yelled frantically, but there was no response. He swam to the board and towed it with him, planning to use it to transport her to the dock. Several rangers appeared on the shore running frantically back and forth unsure whether the mad man in the boat was attacking the fort or had shot the people on the boards.

Michael swam to Sofia, turned her over and stared into her lifeless eyes. A small bullet hole in the center of her chest was at least evidence that she had not suffered much. He cried out and awkwardly pushed her body onto the board. He was frantic, but he started to realize that he could do nothing to save her—she was already gone. He felt tears of anguish and helplessness fill his eyes. He pushed the board towards shore. Two of the rangers waded in to help, while one on shore pointed a shotgun at the launch.

"Drop the weapon," yelled the ranger aiming the shotgun. With a practiced motion, he jacked a round into the chamber of the twelve gauge to punctuate the order. It made an audible "che-chunk" as the round was propelled from the magazine into the chamber. The ranger looked barely old enough to vote, but the cold steady stare and the way he handled the scattergun told Char not to trifle with the guy. He slowly placed the M4 carbine on the deck and his hands in the air.

Something to the far right caught Char's attention. Incredulously, he watched as a black case was thrown from the casement, followed a few seconds later by a man plunging two stories into the moat.

Char looked to the left and said something to Johnnie, who stood at the helm. The launch was perhaps twenty feet from the dock but slowly drifting past it.

"Bring that boat to the dock," the ranger ordered.

"Bet he's got a round of double ought loaded," said Char.

"Could be a rifled slug," countered Johnnie.

"Feeling lucky?" asked Char.

"Not particularly," replied Johnnie.

"When I drop to the deck, hit the throttle, pull the wheel to the right and drop below the gunwale."

"Oh man. I've got to find another job," said Johnnie.

"Is that a yes or a no?" asked Char.

"Yes," he replied.

Char fell behind the thick gunwale of the Boston Whaler as Johnnie pushed the throttle forward to full. The engine roared to life and rooster tailed a frothy wave of seawater into the air. It surged past the dock and turned abruptly away from shore. The shotgun toting park ranger ran forward and fired, two of the pellets impacted the stern gunwale and the rest fell outside the boat. The ranger jacked another round into the chamber and pointed it at the boat, this time compensating for distance by aiming high, when the weapon was slapped out of his hands with such force that it knocked him off his feet. Michael pointed the shotgun at the prostrate ranger, "Enough!" He expertly ejected the four shells left in the magazine and tossed the empty shotgun on the man's chest.

"I've already lost my fiancée—I'm not gonna let you kill my father." He started to walk away while his right leg gave out. He landed on his knee while his left leg completely collapsed. He passed out, and the rangers ran to the prostrate body.

Chapter Twelve – Pursuit

Kelley was so focused on lining up his victims he hadn't seen the Boston Whaler approach and so was surprised when rounds started hitting the cement bags he was using to support his weapon. The cement inside had hardened in the damp air and the rounds hitting the bag propelled a white cloud of dust and rock fragments into Kelley's face. He got off one round before abandoning the shooting position in a coughing, wheezing retreat.

He grabbed the waterproof case and decided that returning through the main entrance was not an option. Kelley ran east through the main corridor between the gun casements towards his boat. It never occurred to him that there would not be another exit until he reached the base of the stairs and found it only emptied into the enormous internal courtyard.

He climbed the stairs back to the second level, rested at the top for a few minutes to catch his breath and turned northeast down the hexagon shaped building—wanting to get as close to his boat as possible before abandoning cover. He ran to one of the open casements that were once portals for cannons to fire and saw his boat bobbing in the relative calm of the small bay perhaps one hundred yards away. About twenty five feet below was a moat containing choppy green sea water—he hoped it would be deep enough to break his fall.

Kelley quickly broke down the HK into its component pieces and repacked it in the waterproof case. Once that was done, he carefully tossed it through the opening and watched as it splashed into the water and bobbed to the surface. He couldn't tell how deep the moat was, but there was no other viable option. He jumped and tried to flutter his arms in a vain attempt to slow his decent.

He hit the water and it momentarily knocked the wind out of him. He touched bottom and estimated the moat to be less than ten feet deep. Something long, dark and slithering swam up through his legs and past him—escaping with a powerful stroke of its long reptilian tail—he had apparently landed on top of a slumbering crocodile! He took solace in the fact that the beast had been startled and had made a direct route to escape—rather than a feint to strike him.

Kelley surfaced and looked for the case. It floated a short distance from the moat's outward edge. He swam to it, grabbed the handle and wrestled himself ashore. He looked back in the direction of the Sally Port and saw the ranger fire at the Boston Whaler that inundated him with suppressive fire—*it had to be that big bastard called Char*, thought Kelley. The boat turned sharply and headed his way. He ran towards the beach where he had moored his boat. If they could pass over the reef without grounding, they would beat him to his boat and no doubt put a bullet or two in his head.

He turned towards the Whaler to check its position and watched as Char brought the weapon up to his shoulder and fired. A round zipped over his left shoulder—close enough that he thought he felt the air disturbed as it passed.

Another round hit the water a few feet ahead of him—it would seem Char was trying to walk his rounds on target. He dove into the water and swam the twenty five feet to his boat, pushing the rifle case ahead of him while bullets zipped around him. *He waited for one that he felt was inevitable, given his less than stellar treatment of his fellow man. He felt the devil himself would be standing behind the trigger—as anxious as he was to have ole Ken Q. Kelley by his side,* thought Kelley.

He pushed himself as far as he thought he could go and then surfaced and gulped in air. Incoming rounds still hit the water, but they were far less accurate now and Kelley saw why—the Boston Whaler was stranded by the sand bar that ran between the fort and the Key. Despite the pain and exhausted state, Kelley laughed. He reached the stern platform of his boat, placed the waterproof box atop it and laboriously dragged himself out of the water.

I made a right bags of that, he thought as he stripped off his wet clothing. He walked naked to the wheel, retracted the anchor and started the engine—intending to put more distance between him and the survivors of his latest carnage. He pushed the throttle to half and piloted the boat through the sea channel towards the open ocean. He looked back in the direction of the fort and didn't see the whaler. *Nothing is ever that easy,* he thought. If Kelley were in their place, he would follow the ferry boat route around the island and intersect his route to foil his escape.

Kelley placed a bungee cord around the wheel to keep it in place, and disappeared below. He found the dwindling supply of morphine the doctor he had just killed had given him and swallowed two more tablets. He then searched through the clothing drawer, retrieved a pair of board shorts and a wife-beater t-shirt and slipped them on.

Once back topside, he opened the waterproof case and reassembled the assault weapon. Char had a M4 carbine and its short barrel limited the range to about four hundred yards, while Kelley could put rounds on target out to seven hundred or more. He would have to make that differential work in his favor. *Aye, I'd love to put a thirty caliber round through that asshole's hat rack,* thought Kelley. Johnnie swung the whaler around and throttled up past Fort Jefferson's dock. The ranger on shore watched them speed by, retrieved his radio and spoke into it—apparently, they were being tracked. Char came back and sat on the bench seat behind the console—the butt plate of the M4 rested on his knee.

"What about Michael?" asked Johnnie.

"He's fine. I'm not sure about Sofia, but we aren't in any position to help her and the rangers are." Johnnie nodded slowly as if understanding, but not agreeing with Char's summary of recent events.

Char knew that look. It was a combination of, 'you've got to be shitting me,' with a dose of 'is this going to get me killed?' thrown in. After spending about two weeks with him traveling up the Orinoco, Char became accustomed to Johnnie regarding him thusly.

"We try to tie up at the dock and we'll end up in a firefight for sure," added Char.

"Whatever you say, Boss," said Johnnie. He stared straight ahead and mentally started putting a résumé together. He supposed he could rephrase 'adept at dealing with a crazy person' into 'excellent people skills.'

The launch traveled around the perimeter of the small island that housed the gigantic fort—its tall brick facade starting to crumble in different places. It was a beautifully mild September morning—the sea was calm and there were scattered clouds in the sky. Normally, Char would have at least noted it, but his mind was lost in a swimming confluence of strong negative emotions. He had loved Sofia like a daughter he never had and she was such a positive influence on Michael that it was almost like he had been changed into another, more thoughtful and thankful person. To have it all wiped away by this madman—especially since she saved his miserable life, struck Char as a particularly heinous act. Kelley must be made to pay.

"There he is!" said Johnnie. He pointed to a boat a short distance ahead of them that appeared to be moving at full speed—which Char estimated to be around twenty-five knots. The throttle on their boat was already pegged, but the lighter frame meant that they were traveling at least ten nautical miles faster.

The problem was their dwindling fuel supply—they had a twenty-four gallon gas tank and the gauge was at one quarter. However this ended, they would probably have to call the *Good as Gold* and have Earl pick them up.

"Get me closer," ordered Char.

Johnnie brought the Boston Whaler close enough so he could just make out a figure in the open pilot house steering the boat. Char moved into the bow, laid down in the prone position on the bench seat that ran along gunwale and aimed the M4 at the retreating boat. He would wait until he had the guy's melon in sight and then he intended to split it with a stream of lead. He aimed over the guy's head—figuring that he could perhaps lob a bullet into his body, as they were still outside effective range of the short barreled carbine. He fired a three round burst, looked for a sign of an impact and saw none. He aimed higher and fired a long burst. This time he was sure he saw two rounds hit the stern—just above the swim platform.

Johnnie heard a whopping siren over the engine noise and looked to his stern. A small Coast Guard response boat mounting a bow machine gun was riding their bow wake and closing fast. Johnnie throttled down the boat and raised his hands above his head.

"What the hell are you doing Johnnie?" asked Char.

"Trying to stay alive," replied Johnnie. He definitely would be looking for a job as soon as the Coast Guard released him. Char stood up tentatively and looked at the approaching patrol boat, sighed deeply and cleared the weapon and opened the upper receiver. He popped the firing pin of the bolt, tapped it against the side of the receiver, removed a tiny part from the lower receiver and dropped it overboard.

Chapter Thirteen - USCGC MOHAWK (WMEC-913)

"Suppose you tell me again, smart guy," said the Lieutenant Junior Grade (JG) Gandy. He was the commander of the law enforcement detachment that had interdicted Char's launch and interfered with his effort to deliver some expedited justice. He was a tall thin guy with the hard edge of a former NCO—he was too old to be the product of the Academy wearing the rank of a junior officer.

"The part where I tell you to go fuck a sea snake or the part where I tell you I want my lawyer?" said Char.

He and Johnnie were sitting in an interrogation room immediately outside the brig on the Cutter Mohawk—handcuffed to a metal pipe that had been welded to the bulkhead. His M4 carbine had been taken from him and signed into the arms room.

"Right now, we have you for a bunch of charges including a

federal firearms violation for firing and possessing a class three automatic weapon."

"Suggest you fire the weapon. I was just pulling the trigger fast, but I'm not saying anything more until I speak with my son."

"He's in sick bay. He was hit in the shoulder—his companion was not so lucky—she took a round in the chest. Her body is in the morgue."

"Is he under arrest?"

"It's not currently against the law to be shot, so no."

"And you don't have arrest authority over civilians, isn't that correct?" added Johnnie.

"That depends," replied Gandy.

"You searched the boat and didn't find any drugs, right?" asked Johnnie.

"Roger, that."

"We're both U.S. citizens as evidenced by the identification, we've provided you," said Johnnie. Char sat contently, allowing his pilot to plead their case.

"So, aside from the possibility that we're pirates, you've got no reason in the world to hold us," said Johnnie.

"Well, there is the matter of firing a weapon in a national park," countered Gandy.

"My employer was merely defending his son and fiancé against attack by a madman. The truth of that is in evidence in your morgue and sick bay."

Gandy looked at Johnnie, "Are you a former guardsman?"

"Nope, I was a Petty Officer in the Navy—Special Boat Squadron, we cross trained with you guys in maritime interdiction."

"So, that's how you knew about our mission parameters," said Gandy.

"It is indeed," replied Johnnie.

"Okay, it appears that that may well be the case, but I'm going to refer the case to a U.S. Magistrate and they may want to file charges. Also, we're running a background on you all. If there are no wants or warrants, you'll be released when we get to Key West. I've called ahead to have the Medical Examiner meet us at the dock. It's standard procedures in wrongful death cases. You guys hang loose down here. I'll have a Food Service Mate get you a meal."

They sent up four ham and cheese sandwiches and a couple cans of cola. Neither he nor Johnnie had eaten since morning and it was now closing in on two o'clock. Gandy returned after the meal. "We should be arriving in Key West by three or so. We'll tie up at Trumbo Point and you're free to go," he said to Johnnie. There is a deputy marshal who wants to speak with you, Blackfox," said Gandy.

Char looked at Johnnie and then shrugged. *Oh, sure* thought Johnnie, *why wouldn't there be?*

"Does he have a name?" asked Char.

"Carl Davis."

A shiver ran up Char's spine but his outward appearance remained unchanged. If Gandy was looking for a reaction, he didn't get one.

"Oh, yeah and you were right, according to our armorer, the M4 carbine is missing a sear that would make it automatic, so the weapon will be returned to you, once the deputy marshal is done talking with you."

"Can I see my son?"

"Sure." Gandy unlocked the handcuffs and led Char and Johnnie to a small, but well equipped sick bay. There was a treatment room with an examination table with a high intensity medical light mounted over it and several cabinets for storing drugs and medical supplies. An adjoining room served as a convalescent area where Michael was currently resting. A hospital corpsman was filling out some paperwork. Gandy pointed to the man. "This is Petty Officer First Class Beauregard. He treated your son."

"How is he, Doc?" asked Char.

"Physically, he's fine. As they say in combat—if you have to get shot, it's the kind of shot you want to get. The bullet was a large caliber—probably 7.62. It creased the top of his left shoulder, penetrated the trapezius muscle and exited without doing much damage. I cleaned out the wound, stitched it up, and pumped him full of antibiotics." He started to say something else, but Char cut him off.

"That's great news, Doc. Can I see him?"

"Let the man finish," cautioned Gandy.

"Thank you, sir. As I started to say, physically he's in good shape, but emotionally, he's a wreck. I knocked him out, but you can see him. I wanted to talk to someone about the deceased and your son wasn't up to it."

"Shoot, I'm your man," said Char.

"I need all the deceased particulars I'm afraid. I have to submit a report of a marine fatality. It's a web form. Let's step over to my workstation and get her done so we can release the body once we land," said Beauregard.

"Sofia," said Char.

"Sorry, Mister Blackfox. Let's get this done, so we can release Sofia when we land," said the corpsman.

Char tried to talk, but his eyes filled with tears and he choked on the words. Beauregard had seen a lot of tragedy in the four plus years he had been working afloat. Someone was always special to someone else and the worst was the unexpected death of a loved one. In this case, it was a beautiful woman who looked like she was all of twenty five years old.

"Let's take a couple of minutes. Want some coffee? I was going to brew a fresh pot," said Beauregard.

Char nodded. "I need a smoke."

"Nasty habit," said Beauregard. He opened the drawer of his desk and pulled out a pack of Marlboro Lights. Let's go topside."

They went out to the fantail, rear of the hanger deck to the stern where the Cutter's Short Range Prosecutor pursuit boat sat. Next to it, sat Char's Boston Whaler.

The smoking area was designated by three butt cans—small buckets painted red set on wooden stands and filled with sand. Beauregard offered Char a smoke and withdrew one for himself. He pulled out a battered Zippo embossed with the Coast Guard's seal, lit Char's cigarette and then his own. The Corpsman inhaled deeply and exhaled into the wind. The smoke quickly dissipated in the airstream created by the ship's forward momentum.

"I haven't had a cigarette in four days," said Beauregard.

"Close to the same number of decades for me," said Char. "I think my last smoke was the one a corpsman gave me after I was wounded outside Da Nang in '72."

"So, we are continuing a tradition?" said Beauregard. He immediately regretted the comment and searched for something to say to change the subject. "Would you happen to know why Michael would be carrying an ice pick in his bootie?"

Char was inhaling and coughed when he inadvertently inhaled smoke up his nose. "No, he had no reason to be. Do you still have it?"

"Yeah, technically I should have turned it over to Lieutenant Gandy, but I didn't want to overcomplicate the situation." He reached down into the cargo pocket on his uniform, retrieved the tool and handed it to Char. He held it in both hands to examine it and felt rather than saw the initials carved into the handle.

"They're the initials H.D. Seems to me to be the same initials of the drowning victim we evacuated from the spearfishing boat four days ago."

"I wouldn't know," said Char.

"According to the report, Doctor Sofia Ramos rendered medical assistance. You and your son are also listed as witnesses," said Beauregard.

Char became annoyed. Suddenly, the corpsman had morphed into the grand inquisitor. "So, there's no law against that."

"No, there's not. I'm just curious to know whether she suspected that the cause of death was not unintentional drowning."

"Take unintentional out of the sentence and you have the true cause of death," said Char. He flicked his cigarette butt into the butt can as if to add an exclamation point to the sentence. "Now, let's say we finish that report, so I can be on my way."

Chapter Fourteen – Carl Davis

Deputy Marshal Davis waited on the Coast Guard pier at Trumbo Point in the hot sunshine of the mid-afternoon, perspiring heavily into the supposedly lightweight, quasi-military apparel. It was the kind of clothing agents who normally wear suits slipped into if they were going into the field.

Davis had been pushing papers since Char had left him handcuffed bare ass to a bed in a townhouse outside of Santo Domingo about eighteen months ago. Since then, Carl had been placed on administrative leave, suspended, reduced in grade and then reinstated, to the asset forfeiture department located in Miami. He had dreamed of the day that Char would turn up as he had a well-worn forfeiture order for his yacht, *The Good as Gold,* as it was once the property of a Tampa-based Mafia capo and was also used in the commission of multiple felonies.

Char had taken it from the capo and Carl had been in the midst of seizing the yacht when he was lured into drunken tryst with two

Dominican prostitutes. They had slipped him a mickey as they say in the old detective flicks that Carl had recently become fond of—sobriety frees up a lot of time formerly dedicated to drinking. Most drunks experience significant weight loss after gaining sobriety as all those empty calories literally dry up—but Davis just replaced them with soft drinks.

Char had been pardoned for actions he wasn't privy to, but the seizure order for *The Good as Gold* was still in force and Davis was going to take it right out from underneath that smug prick.

He watched the 270-foot cutter slowly steam into port, approach the pier, and execute a short series of berthing maneuvers before tying up. The gangplank was secured into place and Davis stormed aboard, his Deputy Marshal five pointed star-shaped badge in hand. The officer of the deck approached.

"Carl Davis, U.S. Marshals Service."

"Yes, Deputy Marshal, they are waiting for you in the officer's mess."

A Guardsman escorted him to a small dining room. Davis looked through the circular window in the door and saw Char seated behind the polished oak table. He pushed open the door and approached Char.

"Hello, asshole," said Davis.

Char looked at the man, but said nothing. Gandy returned with a cup of coffee and placed it in front of Char.

"Agent Davis, I'm the ship's Tactical Law Enforcement Officer, Lieutenant Gandy." The two men did not shake hands. "Per your request, I have asked Mister Blackfox to remain aboard so you could conduct an interview. My understanding is that the point of the interview is to ascertain the location of an asset for which you have a seizure order, is that correct?"

Davis nodded, somewhat taken aback by the overly officious nature of the Coast Guard Officer. Davis approached and placed two meaty perspiration covered hands on the mess table.

"Where's the *Good as Gold*, Blackfox?"

"Wish I knew, Carl. One of the guys I hired in Port of Spain stranded me on Cozumel a couple of weeks ago and I'm just working my way home."

"Bullshit!"

"No, really. I meant to write you about it as I knew you had that order, but I didn't know where you ended up," said Char.

Davis reached across the table and slapped Char across the face. Char saw the strike coming and had pushed back his chair, rendering Davis' strike impotent.

Gandy grabbed the deputy's arm "Deputy Davis, control yourself or I'll have you removed from this ship." said Gandy.

Davis shook his head and pulled his arm away. "Whose side are you on, squid?" He realized immediately he had made a mistake, but Davis was the type of guy who didn't apologize for anything.

Gandy stood up and walked to the door. "The interview is over."

"Well, I ain't leaving until this prick tells me where he's hiding the boat," said Davis.

"That's fine. Help yourself to the coffee. Mister Blackfox, you may go. The armor is waiting with your weapon at the gangplank. Good day and Godspeed to you and your son."

Char nodded. He turned toward Carl, "Good luck finding your white whale, Ahab."

Chapter Fifteen – Ahab

Char walked out into the passageway, feeling a bit guilty about having misjudged Gandy. He felt a sense of relief wash over him as he walked out into the waning daylight of the later afternoon sun. He looked toward the stern and saw their launch being lowered into the water from a hydraulic davit—apparently Johnnie had arranged to get it offloaded while he was otherwise engaged. Char found the gangplank and walked across it and onto the wide concrete pier. A half-dozen other cutters and buoy tenders were tied up along its length.

Johnnie walked over to him visibly relieved that Char was not being led off by the deputy in handcuffs, as he had imagined.

"Hey boss, you okay?"

"Been better Johnnie."

"Yeah, it's been a rough couple of days. The ambulance was here a while ago. They took Michael to Key West Medical. The hospital technician told me to ask you to wait for the medical examiner, so you can sign the release for. . ." Johnnie hesitated, "Sofia," he said finally.

"Where's Earl?" asked Char.

"He's offshore a few miles, waiting for the smoke to clear. I told him to hold there until you decided what you wanted to do."

"Good, take the launch out to the *Gold*. You both head for Madeira Beach. Find a marina and lay low until you hear from me," said Char.

"Anything else you need to tell me, boss?" asked Johnnie.

"Yeah, there is a seizure order for the *Good as Gold*. If they find it, they will take it, so you need to be invisible."

"Okay, we'll have to fuel up somewhere, but we'll figure that out. What are you going to do?" asked Johnnie.

"You ask a lot of questions, kid."

"It's because I care, boss," said Johnnie with a slight grin.

"Well, Johnnie, since you asked, I'm going to visit my ex-wife and tell her that her only son is in the hospital and his fiancé is dead. Once that is done, I'm going to find a bar somewhere and have more than a couple stiff drinks."

The M.E. arrived a short time later, and Sofia was brought out to him. The watch officer must have alerted Petty Officer Beauregard to his arrival. Four guardsmen carried the stretcher off the boat and down the gangplank. Char felt his lip quiver and his eyes tear up. He bit his lower lip as hard as he could to keep from crying. Just yesterday, a vibrant and beautiful woman had been alive and in love with his son. The kid had finally been dealt the four aces he deserved—only to have the jackpot ripped from his hands.

It was over in a flurry of signatures and an exchange of contact information. State law mandated that the body be autopsied and that true next of kin be notified—which meant that Char had to call Ramos, let him know that his cousin was dead and ask him or some other family member to come and claim the body. Perhaps he should move having a couple stiff drinks higher on the agenda.

Char still had Ramos' number from the time they spent together traveling from Cartagena to Bartolomé de Las Casas—figuring that having the number for the rich son of a Colombian senator might come in handy someday. He didn't figure that it would come to this. He called and there was no answer, so he left a message.

Char walked off the base and stopped in the first pub he found. The Marlin Bar, or something like that. It had the same ambiance and decor as the Old Popeye movie with Robin Williams and Shelley Duvall. Char didn't care if it looked like the set of the Texas Chainsaw Massacre—as long as it sold whiskey.

A bartender who looked like he could have starred in either movie took his order—a double shot of Jack Daniels and a beer chaser. The bartender delivered the shots in old style fluted glasses that held about one and a quarter ounces of whiskey. He was in luck—they didn't charge for the chaser and it was one per shot. He downed the shot and followed with a long swallow of beer. He turned his attention to the second shot and repeated the process. The whiskey warmed his stomach, tamped down his feelings and dulled his senses. It was the perfect way to spend the rest of the afternoon, but he knew that wouldn't be possible. As if to punctuate that thought, his cell phone vibrated and Char looked at the screen. One word was displayed in the window—Ramos.

Chapter Sixteen - Blackfox Galleries

The bartender delivered a second double after he got off the phone with Ramos—it was happy hour and Char relished the kind of relief that the alcohol had delivered thus far. It was then that it occurred to him that he had somewhere to be—his ex-wife's art gallery on…. He had forgotten the address in all the commotion! He had a smartphone, but the thought of trying to look up the address on the little browser after drinking caused him to seek more antiquated alternatives.

"Hey, Nate," Char had read the man's name tag when he had delivered the first round—it paid to be friends with the man delivering the booze. The bartender stood several feet away cleaning up the food and drink residue from another customer's afternoon binge.

"Whatdya need?" he said without looking up.

"Heard of the Blackfox Galleries?"

"What if I had? You don't exactly look like an art aficionado," said Nate.

"Why so cautious? It's not like I'm gonna rob the place—just looking up an old friend."

Nate stopped cleaning up and regarded Char. "And who might that be?"

"Ann Blackfox—she's my ex-wife."

"That would explain the heavy drinking," said Nate, not unkindly. "You're in luck—the place is about two blocks away on Fogarty, near the corner of 4th Street."

"You sound like you know her," said Char.

"Yeah, I guess you could say we're friends. She used to stop in here when she was refurbishing that old store. She did most of the work herself. I helped out when I could—hauling crap away in my pickup, moving furniture and some lighting work—I was a licensed electrician in another life. She did a wonderful job—I don't think a professional could have done it any better."

Char liked the guy. If Ann befriended him, he was probably okay, although she had befriended Char once. He finished the last shot, shook Nate's hand and headed to the door.

"Go straight across the street one block, take a right on Fogarty and head toward town—you can't miss it," said Nate.

Char crossed the street and semi-staggered down the sidewalk. He hadn't eaten anything since lunch on board the cutter, and the whiskey had crept up on him. His head buzzed with undulating waves of numbness, but it was that detachment he craved as it swept the ugly reality from his thoughts.

Char saw the silhouette of the hanging sign from three houses away—it was a wooden sculpture of a leaping black fox over gold lettering that spelled out gallery. He opened the old style glass front door which rang a brass bell and walked in to the stylishly spartan interior. In the center of the room was a large banner that someone had painstakingly scribed 'Congratulations Sofia & Michael.' A well-stocked bar had been set up on an old mahogany sideboard and several chafing dishes sat atop a long portable table next to cheese and relish trays.

Ann walked through the swinging door from the kitchen with a bottle of Dom Perignon champagne in hand. She looked at Char and smiled. "You know what they say—it's not a celebration without Dom."

They embraced and she kissed him on both cheeks.

"You've been drinking." It wasn't a question. He nodded.

"Something's wrong." Another non-question—like a mechanic who could tell just by sound that a lifter tick is due to dirty oil deposits, Ann had the intuitive ability to sense the same imprecision with people.

"Is Michael okay?" she asked.

Char nodded affirmatively. "He's okay, not great, but he'll be all right."

Char walked to the bar, found a bottle of Belvedere Vodka and poured several fingers into a glass with a couple of cubes of ice.

"You might want to sit down," said Char.

"Char, please stop being melodramatic and tell me what's going on."

"It's his fiancée, Sofia; she was shot in the chest by a madman at Fort Jefferson. She's dead."

He handed her the glass and she started to take a drink, then stopped herself. "Where's Michael?"

"He's in the hospital. He was wounded, but it's not life threatening. I think he's in shock because of Sofia's death."

She went to an antique roll top desk in the corner of the room and retrieved her cell phone.

"Key West Medical?" she asked. He nodded.

She called information and got connected. Spoke to the reception desk, waited an interminable time on hold, repeated Michael's name several times, spoke to someone for a few minutes and then hung up.

"He's been sedated. They suggested that we come by in the morning after nine. I'll take that drink now."

"I've got a plane to meet sometime tomorrow, and I'll need to rent a car."

"Take me to the hospital, come up and see Michael and you can take my car."

"I need a big vehicle—a Suburban or Escalade," said Char.

"There's a Hertz out by the airport. I can drop you after we visit with Michael. Who are you meeting?"

"Sofia's family," said Char. "They're flying in to escort her back to Bogota."

"What type of people are these Charles?" asked Ann. She was the only one who called him by his full first name.

"Very rich, powerful and connected people, my dear."

She upended the glass—swallowing the two ounces in one gulp. "Now please tell me how it is that our son and his fiancée came to be shot."

He went to the bar poured himself a glass of Jack Daniels and retrieved the bottle of vodka to refill her glass. "It's a long story and we're bound to get thirsty."

Chapter Seventeen – Star of Tampa

Ann and Char had spent most of the evening discussing the events that had led to Sofia's death and Michael's injury. They were famished, so they made dinner of the hors d'oeuvres. Char was grateful for anything to soak up the inebriants, and Ann had taken great care in preparing some especially delicious appetizers for her gallery opening. They munched on mini beef skewers with chimichurri sauce, coconut shrimp, and fresh fish ceviche that Ann had served with a spicy mango sauce. The discussion took an unexpected turn after they had finished eating.

"So, how did my near itinerant ex-husband come to be in possession of an eighty foot yacht?"

"Long story," said Char.

"We have all night, Charles."

"Fair enough," he said, unsure how he should begin. "Have you heard of the *Star of Tampa*?"

"Vaguely. Isn't it that gambling ship that sunk in a hurricane in the gulf a long time ago?"

"That's it. It was a casino boat that hosted a one-armed bandit with a million dollar payoff."

"Okay, ancient history, what does that have to do with you having a four million dollar yacht?" asked Ann.

Char took a drink of whiskey—warming to the tale he had told just a few times before. "Maritime authorities figured out that the ship was hit by a rogue wave that sank it sometime during its maiden voyage on Halloween night in 1974. All aboard were lost and no trace of the one million dollar jackpot has ever been recovered. What they didn't figure out is that the ship was robbed of its gold, and the passengers were robbed of their personal possessions before the wave sank the boat."

"How would you know that?" asked Ann—afraid to hear the answer.

Char swallowed the rest of the whiskey and poured himself another one—figuring that she might show him the door after he confessed.

"Because me and a bunch of other guys robbed it." She looked at him with wide-eyed incredulousness as if she was hoping he would tell her it was all a big joke—it wasn't.

"And all those people died?" she said finally.

"They would have died anyway—the robbery had nothing to

do with it," replied Char. He waited for a reaction and didn't get one. She stared straight ahead.

"You can't know that," she said quietly. "That's just what you tell yourself to ease your conscience."

"No, that's what the weather service said. It was the leading edge of a hurricane that went undetected as it was outside the umbrella of our then nascent ability to detect severe weather," said Char. "Had the wave missed, they still would have faced a hurricane." The line had been used many times, but it did not come off as scripted. He really believed what he said.

Ann seemed satisfied for the moment with the explanation—at least for the time being. "Why did you do it?" she asked.

"The owner of the ship, an Aussie tycoon by the name of Simon Block, stole my girlfriend—the women I intended to marry." *There were other reasons, but that was one he hoped she'd understand.*

Ann nodded, "Vodka," she said. He grabbed the bottle and poured her a short one. *Well, she's not kicking me to the curb, yet,* he thought.

She took a medicinal sip and then tipped the glass towards him "Go on,"

"The same wave that hit the *Star* impacted our boat as we were about to land at Fort Desoto—the state park by St. Pete."

"I know it," said Ann.

"Our boat was wrecked while docking at the park. It seems that guy who bankrolled the job, a Mafia capo by the name of Sally Boots, planned to kill us and take it for himself. They killed my friend, Tommy, but his brother, Jimmy, managed to hide the gold and other loot in the park. The problem was he was caught crossing the causeway into St. Pete, and he was an escaped bank robber. He ended up being convicted for the robbery and escape before anyone could find out where the gold was hidden."

"Such nice friends you have," said Ann.

"Had—he's long dead," said Char.

She nodded. "Not surprising."

"Fast forward thirty years and Jimmy suddenly finds himself freed from prison, and we recover the gold. The same guys who double-crossed us in '74 were still around—looking for the gold."

"And they killed Jimmy? "Ann asked.

"Yeah, they killed him and then some," said Char as if reliving the event a little in his head.

"Hasn't gold gone up a lot over the years?"

"Yes, but not as much as you might think. The fly in the ointment, however, was the fact that a lot of the stolen gold was fake. Still, we managed to reap about a million from the deal."

"Why was it fake?" she asked.

"Block was leveraged to the hilt and couldn't quite put a million in gold together in such a short period of time."

"And the yacht?"

"We stole a boat to recover the gold. Sally Boots shot up that boat, so we took his," said Char.

"It's as simple as all that?" asked Ann.

"No, it's getting late, and I need to know whether you're going to throw me out or not so there's still time to get a hotel room."

She couldn't help it, but Ann was enthralled by the tale that Char was spinning. To her, it was ancient history and his actions—while criminal and despicable, happened a long time ago. He had always been an exciting guy, who lived on the edge—truth be told that was part of the reason she had been attracted to him. She now knew why he was always looking over his shoulder.

"I have a couple more questions for you, Charles, and I suggest you tell the truth," said Ann. "First, was Michael involved with any of this?"

Char thought about lying, but he realized Ann knew him too well—even though they had been estranged for years. She could always read him—if not like a book, then like the funny pages.

"Yeah, he helped recover the gold and probably saved us all from being killed," said Char. "Next question."

"There is no one looking for you—nobody who talks with a Brooklyn accent and likes his pasta fagioli after a hard day of breaking knee caps?"

"Nope, not a one. I heard Sally Boots got capped by a cop the night we got away."

"Don't get cocky—you may still get kicked to the curb yet. Are you a fugitive from justice?" she said, sounding strangely officious.

"No, funny story, but both Michael and I were pardoned for any and all peccadillos that had to do with that particular event."

"And how did that come to be?" asked Ann.

"How much time do you have?"

Ann retrieved the bottle of vodka, poured herself a splash and then added a few ice cubes. "Why Charles we have until tomorrow morning, but if you talk fast, we might even get a little sleep tonight."

Chapter Eighteen – Ken Q. Kelley

The sun was just starting to retreat behind the mangroves protecting the inlet when he pulled into an old marina on Geiger Key. The place was built when the largest pleasure boats were in the 30-foot range and had never been expanded to include larger vessels so business was limited.

Kelley was hungry and in need of a fix—he swallowed the last of the pills Sofia had given him after seeing the Coast Guard pursuit boat nab the Boston Whaler. It was good for Kelley that they had as Char had gotten close to putting a bullet in him.

He pulled into a vacant slip, hopped out, and tied off the boat. The time-worn boards of the dock were rotted in places and repaired with new pressure treated planking in others—giving it a patchwork appearance. The marina had a bar and restaurant housed in a tropical thatch-roofed bohio that served a pretty mean conch ceviche—at least they had years ago. *If times were different, I could see myself settling down at one end of the bar and drinking a few Coronas and perhaps a shot or two before digging into a grilled sea bass or some fish and chips,* thought Kelley.

He found the office and paid for an overnight dockage fee and asked them to call him a taxi for a trip into town—he wanted to get a drink and score some smack before the night was over. He had a bill that was past due and badly needed to be paid.

The taxi cab was driven by a dreadlocked Jamaican who reeked of marijuana. He had all the windows of the mini-van opened, but it still reeked with the sickly sweet aroma.

"Where can I take you, mon?"

"I need to get a drink," said Kelley.

"Ah mon, lots of places to do that in Key West—you got to be more specific."

"I also would like to score some smack."

The driver laughed a great throaty chuckle. "That's not exactly what I meant, but at least I know what kind of bar you be looking for."

He drove down the overseas highway into Key West and turned down A1A and then a few side streets until he pulled up in front of a line of at least a dozen American-made motorcycles aligned with near military precision. The once glass store front had been replaced with thick plywood and the door looked to be covered with aluminum diamond plating. The sign over the transom announced the name of the place.

"The Drunken Hag," said Kelley, "charming."

"Hey man, you want to score some Harry, you got to go to the right place," said the driver.

Kelley tossed the guy a twenty on a nineteen dollar and ten cent fare, got out and examined the outside of the club as if deciding whether to enter or not. The driver wanted to protest, but his marijuana-induced lethargy disinclined him from doing so.

Kelley felt the reassuring weight of the Chief's Special .38 caliber revolver in the cargo pocket of his shorts and decided what the hell. The dark interior smelled of cigarette smoke, stale beer, and leather. A bar ran down the right side of the interior, and ten or so booths took up the left side. In the middle sat an equal number of small circular black tables. A dancer lazily swung from a brass pole on a stage in the back of the room.

He climbed atop a black vinyl barstool and waited. A woman behind the bar wore nothing but a sleeveless leather vest and jean shorts cut down so much that they amounted to little more than a G-string. She had full-sleeve tattoos on both arms and a heart and rose atop one of her breasts. Kelley didn't know whether he should be titillated or frightened.

"Whatdaya need?" she asked.

"Jameson, straight up."

"We got Bushmills— you want that?"

"I don't drink Protestant dishwater," said Kelley.

The bartender looked at Kelley and then off to the right side of the bar. "Nothing is still an option," she said.

Kelley regarded her for a moment, trying to decide whether to backpedal a few steps or pistol whip the bitch when he felt a large hand on his shoulder. He turned to confront a black bearded bear of a man blocking out the only overhead light in the center of the bar.

"Hey, easy there Paddy,"

"The names not Paddy, chum. It's Kelley."

"Fair enough Kelley. Sherri, get Kelley a Jack Daniels and put it on my tab. Hell, get me one too. Any objection to drinking Tennessee Whiskey?"

"None here. You the owner?" asked Kelley.

"No, just the bouncer," he said while offering Kelley a catcher's mitt-sized hand. "My name's Sean, actually of Irish decent, but don't know much more than that."

"So, you heard my accent, and you wanted to buy me a drink?" asked Kelley.

"I'm a mellow guy—I like to sort out issues before they become problems."

The shots arrived, Sean grabbed his and clicked Kelley's glass. "What is it you Micks say when you toast?"

"Sláinte?" said Kelley.

"Yeah, that's it, Sláinte," he said before drinking down the shot.

Kelley ordered a reciprocal round. They ordered beers after that—the Guinness that while not tasting the same as in Ireland, did quench Kelley's thirst.

Five shots and two beers into it, Kelley felt sufficient kinship with his new friend to inquire about his need. "Sean, how would I go about scoring some drugs around here?" said Kelley after a sip of his beer.

"That's a tough one braugh, see I was told by the boss to kick anyone selling drugs to the curb. And I've been doing just that."

"So, there's no drugs to be had here?" asked Kelley.

"I didn't say that—I got coke, speed, and grass. Anything else I outsource to another dealer. What do you need?"

"Heroin or morphine, "said Kelley.

"Yeah, that will be Les, everyone calls him Lester the Molester. He likes to get underage girls hooked on heroin and then slip it to them. He's got half a dozen young girls slinging ass down on Duval Street—I don't like being around the guy, but hey the customer is always right—know what I mean?"

"Sounds delightful," said Kelley sarcastically.

"Want me to give him a call?" Kelley nodded affirmatively.

"Okay, here's how it will work. Lester will drive by here. He's got an old Chevelle SS—it'd be a classic car if he treated it right. He'll wait thirty seconds; you get in, go off do your deal and be gone. Don't come back here holding—got it?" Kelley nodded.

Looking embarrassed, Sean self-consciously opened a flip phone. "It's a throwaway." He punched in a code, spoke a few words into the receiver, listened for a moment and ended the call. "He'll be here in ten—we have time for another shot."

They drank another round, Kelley paid the bill, finished his beer and waited. The throaty rumble of lightly muffled dual exhausts announced Lester's arrival. Kelley bounced out the entrance, griped the door handle of the sedan and slid into the ancient bucket seat.

"Sean sent you?" the driver asked.

"Yeah, you Lester?"

"It's just Les—you got it. I don't know what they told you, but the fucking name is Les!" Kelley paused to regard the man. He had a weasel-like face with a long pointy nose, dark beady eyes and buck teeth badly in need of alignment. He also sported a receding hairline made more obvious by the fact that his remaining hair was tied into a grey-tinged ponytail. He gunned the engine and accelerated down the side street at an imprudent speed.

"Sure, Les. No problem."

"So, how much do you need?" asked Les.

"How much for a couple of grams?"

"$600," said Les.

"Bloody hell, $600? That's a bit much, don't you think? I mean, it's like bleeding $80 a gram in Miami," said Kelley.

"Yeah, well this ain't Miami, my limey friend—I can sell you coke for a $100 a gram, but you want smack—it's going to cost you."

Les pulled the car off to the side of the road and parked. He reached down beneath the seat and withdrew a Ziploc bag about a third full of small balloons. "So, we going to do a deal or not?" asked Les.

"I'm Irish, actually," said Kelley.

"Irish, English—same fucking difference," said Les.

"So, Sean tells me that you offer the services of young ladies for pleasure," said Kelley.

"Yeah, sure you want that, we do a deal, I'll take you down to Duval Street, and you can take your pick."

Kelley squinted and lowered his voice to a conspiratorial whisper, "how young?"

Les smiled—warming to the subject, "I've got an eleven year old, but she's special. I keep her for myself, but I got three or four thirteen year olds I can hook you up with for a C-note." He withdraw a cigarette from a packet above the visor and lit it with a match.

"You mind rolling down the window?" asked Kelley.

"What's the matter my limey friend, a little smoke bother you?" said Les mockingly, as he lowered the glass.

"No, not really, Lester. I just don't want to get blood on the window." Les started to do something—Kelley was never sure in retrospect whether he was searching for a weapon or reaching for the door handle. Kelley withdrew the .38 from his cargo pocket, placed the barrel against Lester's temple and fired. Luckily, the rather soft, low velocity round failed to pass completely through his skull.

Kelley opened his door, pulled Lester's lifeless body from the driver's seat and left it in the street. He backed up and turned the wheels to the left to get out of the parking space and inadvertently drove over Lester's body while driving away.

Now, it was just a matter of collecting his bill and he would disappear into the night. He knew that the car was well known on Duval—so he would park and walk around until he found who he needed to find. Then, he would collect his fee and disappear into the night.

He shot up in the car and nodded off for a couple of hours. It was about 9:30, and he knew that the hunting would be good at the late night happy hour they held at Dirty Mary's. He had been told that the tourist ladies get drunk on cheap Mojitos and sometimes flash their tits at other patrons.

He staggered down Duval, looking like a slightly older and more inebriated tourist on a bender. He walked towards the water until he found the club. Kelley entered and found what he was looking for—almost exactly where he pictured the man would be—dead center of the bar, buying a round of shots for three women—all slightly past their prime, but seemingly intent on trying to recapture that old magic of their younger days. And Flynn was intent on trying to help them.

"Hello Flynn," said Kelley.

Flynn looked at him in obvious shock, but tried to play it off. "Kelley, how the hell are you? Ladies, I'd like to introduce you to an old friend of mine, Ken Q. Kelley."

They all greeted him with alcohol-induced enthusiasm, but one regarded him with a slightly puzzled look.

"What's the "Q" stand for?"

"Quinton, like the boat captain in *Jaws*," said Kelley with a slight grin.

Chapter Nineteen - Marco Ramos

Michael and his father sat in the cab of the black Chevy Suburban parked at one end of the runway and watched the Gulf Stream G550 pass overhead at an altitude of about sixty feet. It nimbly touched down with squeak of the landing gear a short distance down the tarmac and taxied towards a small complex of hangers and administration buildings at the far end of the taxiway. A sign announced the business to be Conch Republic Air, an aviation maintenance company that provided ground support activities to transiting aircraft.

The Congressman and his party had been given expedited diplomatic clearance to enter the U.S. "Apparently, they are skipping customs clearance today," said Michael.

Michael had enough of being treated like an invalid. He

wanted to get on with the process, and perhaps it would serve some cathartic purpose—escorting his fiancée's body back to her homeland. His mother and Char had visited with him that morning in the hospital. He awoke in the early morning hours, at first convinced that it had all been a terrible dream. But, the intravenous drip attached to his arm seemed to indicate otherwise and he began to tremble with fear, in that he wasn't sure he could live without Sofia.

The only thing that brought some semblance of order to his mental state was the need for closure. He spent the rest of the time working through the remaining stages of grief by focusing on the need for finality and through it; he would accept the new reality that Sofia was dead.

Some resolution would come from dealing with the funeral and more still would come from killing the bastard who had robbed him of a chance for happiness in what had been a strife filled and bloody existence. In the meantime, he would put on a brave face for her family and then set about the very real task of finding Kelley and killing him.

Char wheeled the big vehicle back on the road, down the access ramp towards the airport and exited when he saw a sign for the aviation company. He drove into the parking lot just as a group of men started to disembark from the business jet.

Michael recognized the tall thin frame of his friend Ramos climbing down the boarding ladder. Two older, distinguished looking men followed; Ramos's father, Carlo, a senator and his uncle, Tito, Sofia's father—a wealthy emerald merchant. They were all dressed in dark suits, despite the tropic heat. Following them was a stocky, bald man with Popeye-like, hair-covered forearms. He wore a dark blue Guayabera that did not sufficiently conceal the semi-automatic pistol on his hip.

Michael had spent nearly a year in Bogota as Marco Ramos' guest in Carlo's resplendent mansion. Char had visited from Cartagena on occasion. He had decided it provided the perfect place to dock the boat as fees were less expensive than in other ports like Aruba or Curaçao and close enough to visit Michael when he wanted. Therefore both men knew Carlo and Tito Ramos fairly well—although those meetings were during happier times.

Marco went to Michael, and they embraced. Michael wanted to groan due to the pain from his still fresh wound, but suppressed the desire. He really didn't know what to say—they had witnessed the death of a few comrades together, but this was different. Marco found the words. "Don't worry, Michael—she's in God's hands now."

Michael nodded, afraid to talk lest it come out a sob. He and Ramos had shared much—a few months in Iraq during the invasion and just over a year ago when he had served as Liaison Officer to the Marine Special Operations Team Michael had been detailed to. Ramos had coordinated the medevac of several grievously wounded Marines from the Venezuelan jungle and for that Michael would be eternally grateful.

They walked back to the SUV. Char opened the rear passenger doors and helped the two elder Colombians into their seats. "Where is Sofia?" asked Marco.

"She's at the medical examiner's office. He can suggest a funeral home, and they can prepare her body for burial and place the casket in a flight container," said Char.

"No, there is no time for that. They can prepare my daughter for travel, and we will take her body back for burial in the family plot," said Tito Ramos.

Char drove the SUV onto Route 1 and headed for the medical

examiner's office located in a hospital on Marathon Key—about 45 miles away.

Little was said—the gravity of the occasion discouraged any small talk. Char turned the radio off, and they rode in silence during the long miles to the hospital. As if to match their mood, traffic was heavy and the weather threatened a thunderstorm.

Michael stared out the window at the surviving remnants of the Old Florida Overseas Railroad that once ran from Miami all the way to Key West—destroyed by the Labor Day hurricane of '35. Much of the arched stone bridgework, concrete viaducts and steel trestles of the railroad still remained—perhaps as a testament to what had been. They had built the first road to the Keys on its remnants. He found it strangely analogous to his life with Sofia. She was the railroad, and his life had been the hurricane that destroyed it.

***

Marvin Ralston, the medical examiner, had been in the position for over fifteen years. He loved living in the Keys—having a home on stilts located right on the canal in Key Colony Beach. The hours weren't bad, and he made extra money teaching forensic pathology at Florida International University in Miami and Florida Keys Community College. But, right now, he was in a bit of a pickle as he was wont to say.

The body of a young woman had been picked up yesterday. He was chagrined to learn from the Hospital Corpsman on the Mohawk that she had also been a doctor. *Such a waste*, he thought. He had taken possession of her personal effects and gave them a cursory identification, sure as shit finding an ID card from the International Red Cross that listed the deceased's address in Bogota.

He had conducted a very thorough wrongful death autopsy on the woman and determined with a high degree of certainty that the cause of death was a gunshot wound to the woman's chest, damaging the heart and causing cardiac arrest. He had recovered the bullet and sewn up the chest cavity. *That should be that*, he thought.

For all intents and purposes, the woman's remains were ready to be released to the funeral home, except the case was in federal jurisdiction because the crime had taken place in a national park. He was told to hold onto the body until an FBI agent could be dispatched from Miami to examine the evidence in the case, but he had thoroughly examined the deceased and transcribed his findings in the pathology report. Therefore, there was no need to maintain custody of the body.

Adding to this frustration was the fact that he had been summoned to a telephone and verbally accosted by a deputy marshal during the conduct of the autopsy. He suspected the deputy was the cause of the involvement of the FBI. Sure the case had to be investigated, but life also needed to return to a semblance of normalcy and that meant that a body should be released for a funeral.

Ralston had received a call from a friend of the family who stated that they were in route to see the body. It was Sunday evening and he had plans to catch the Dolphins on a big screen at a local sports bar, but the family had flown in from Bogota, the caller had explained. Normally, he would have told them to call during office hours, but knowing that they had come so far, he instructed them to come right over to view the body.

He arrived at his office in the Fisherman's Community Hospital with a thermos of coffee, a corned beef sandwich and the Sunday edition of the Miami Herald. For practical purposes, his office was located near the rear of the hospital next to the loading dock.

He retreated to his desk, spread out his snack and began reading the front page of the paper. He had finished reading the national news and was about to turn to the sports section when the door opened and six well-dressed men ranging in age from mid to late twenties to early sixties, filed into his office.

For some reason, Ralston thought of the scene from the movie, *True Romance*, when the mobsters entered Clifford Worley's trailer to find out the whereabouts of his son and their cocaine. The feeling was a fleeting one, however and dissipated when one of them held out his hand in greeting.

"Doctor Ralston, I'm Char Blackfox and these folks are Sofia's father, uncle, cousin and fiancé."

Ralston shook the man's hands and then started to mouth the typical platitudes, "So sorry for your loss," but found that the words seemed inadequate for the somber group of men before him. Best to show them the body and get them out of his hair—he might still be able to squeeze in a little football. "Please allow me to show you the deceased," he said finally.

Ralston walked outside and across the hall to the morgue cold room, withdrew a set of keys and unlocked the grey steel door. A subtle sickly sweet odor emanated from the room—some of the occupants had been there for a long time. He walked to a wall of stacked stainless steel drawers— resembling a giant filing cabinet that an abstract artist might create and label as art.

The men filed in behind him. Ralston walked to the first row and grabbed the handle of the hermetical sealed drawer and slid out the carriage containing Sofia's body. It was inside an opaque body bag with a zippered closure. Ralston, grabbed the large rubber tab of the zipper and addressed the men. "Gentlemen, I caution you, there is an incision from the cause of death autopsy that has been sutured shut, but the appearance is somewhat off-putting."

"Please just uncover her face," said Tito, "I want to know that it's her."

"Very well," said Ralston. He unzipped the bag so that Sofia's face and neck were visible—revealing a young and beautiful face, tinged blue by the near freezing temperature of the cooler.

"Now leave us. We want to be alone with her," said Tito.

"Sorry, I can't do that—state law," protested the coroner.

"That wasn't a request," said Carlo. He turned toward the burly man in the Guayabera. "Luiz, take the doctor back to his office, and pour him a cup of coffee. We'll be there in few minutes."

Luiz patted the medical examiner on the back and lightly shepherded him towards the door. "Muévete." The doctor understood, but turned toward the men gathered around the corpse.

"I warn you gentlemen, this is a violation of state law. The body has not been released due to a pending investigation. Do not touch the deceased or you will be held accountable."

"Una otra cosa—tome las llaves," said Carlo. Luiz reached into the doctor's lab coat, retrieved the key ring and then tapped him on the back.

Tito looked at her for a moment and then turned away. He turned to Michael and grabbed his arm. "Look, fucking gringo, look at what you have done to my beautiful daughter!"

Michael stood in front of the drawer and said nothing. He couldn't make himself turn from Sofia's father's righteous stare. Carlo grabbed his brother and pulled him away—offering soothing words in Spanish. "Tranqilo, mi hermano. No vale la pena."

Michael moved closer to Sofia's body, bent down and lightly kissed her lips. He turned to address her father. "I asked you for her hand in marriage. You made me vow to take care of her and I failed you, but no one could have anticipated she would be killed by a mad man whose life she saved. I can't bring her back for you or me, but I will kill the son of a bitch that took her life."

"Big talk, fucking gringo. This man almost killed you as well. What makes you think you can find him and execute him?" said Tito.

"Because I'm going to help him," said Char.

"And so will I," said Marco.

"Okay, everyone wants to be a hero, that's good. The Lord might have claimed vengeance for himself, but he never lost a daughter to a sniper's bullet," said Tito. "So, Michael, you find this son of a bitch—you kill him and we are even. But, if you don't— you'll have to sleep with one eye open for the rest of your life."

"So will you old man," said Char.

"Then we understand each other, no?" asked Tito.

Char locked eyes with the man. "Like two roosters in a cock fight."

"Good, now we are going to take my daughter out of this place and home to Bogota where she belongs."

"That might be a tall order. When I was in the senate," said

Carlo, referring to his eighteen year tenure in the Colombian legislature, "we drafted numerous measures to speed the repatriation of our people from the U.S., because it was always a lengthy process—in best of times it could take up to five days."

"Ah well my brother, you made your fortune talking, while I made it digging emeralds out of the mud and rocks of the earth. We will make this happen today," said Tito.

Chapter Twenty - Repatriation

Ralston sat at the round wooden meeting table he had in the corner of his office—as Luiz didn't want him within reach of a phone. He had finished two cups of Emeril's Special Dark Roast from his thermos and felt jazzed from all the caffeine.

The men filed back into the office, and Ralston jumped to his feet. "Gentlemen, I warn you. You're dealing with an open investigation into the death of Sofia Ramos, and I cannot release the body without written authorization from the FBI."

"We are taking my daughter out of here and you can either help us and profit from it, or I can have Luiz see if he can get you to qualify for an early retirement," said Tito.

Ralston stared directly at Tito, "I warn you, sir, you are

threatening an officer of the state."

"Calmate, doctor, calmate," said Carlo. He was used to dealing with his aggressive and impetus brother. Carlo pulled out a passport from his inside coat pocket and showed it to the man. "That's a Colombian diplomatic passport given to me as the soon-to-be-named ambassador to your fine country. You misunderstand us. I need the services of a consultant to plan the repatriation of my niece's body to Bogota and for that, I would happily pay a consulting fee."

"In emeralds," added Tito. He withdrew a leather pouch from his suit pocket, opened it, and poured the contents into his hand. "These are all a little less than one carat oval cut Colombian emeralds. I guarantee you that your wife, your girlfriend—both of them, are going to love you forever. Or you can just sell them and retire a little earlier."

"Do I have to ask what you want in return?" said Ralston.

"Doctor, I just want to take my daughter home to bury her in our family plot, next to her mother," said Tito.

Ralston slowly shook his head. "As I said, that's impossible. Even with a release from the bureau, it will take a few days."

"Are you a father?" asked Carlo.

"Yes, I have four children."

"All alive, I presume?" asked Tito.

Ralston grew quiet as if in thought. After a moment he answered. "Yes, and it would probably kill me if one of them died."

"And yet I am alive still," said Tito. "We are all stronger than we think."

Ralston nodded. "Keep your emeralds—I'll help you. You just have to make it look like I didn't."

"Just leave that to me," said Char. He had found a box of zip ties in the morgue and was holding up a few foot long specimens. "These should do nicely."

***

Davis pulled up in front of a teal colored condominium complex at the north end of Miami Beach. He was driving a GSA-issued Chevrolet Malibu as he was damn sure not going to use his own car on a long drive.

The condo complex was the kind of place that might have been a slightly upscale boutique hotel back in the its heyday—around the time Jackie Gleason broadcasted from here. It was now a faded gem that someone had converted into condos. It was easier to do that than compete with all the modern and obscenely luxurious hotels that dotted the beachfront.

The passenger side door opened and a tall, tan, dark-haired man got in. "This better be good—I'm giving up my Sunday to drive to Marathon exactly why?" asked Jason Reynolds.

"And good morning to you too," said Davis. "The Medical examiner called me. He has the body of Sofia Ramos on ice. She was engaged to a Michael Blackfox, son of Char Blackfox. He has an eighty foot Hatteras yacht that I have a seizure order for."

"Sofia Ramos? That name sounds familiar," said Reynolds.

Davis shook his head. "It should—she's the woman who was shot in the chest at Fort Jefferson. Don't you read your email?"

"Oh, right," said Reynolds. "It's early and I haven't had my coffee yet. I tied one on last night. I need a cheeseburger and fries to soak up the stomach acid—hit a drive-thru will you."

"Sure," replied Davis. "Blackfox is bringing the next of kin to see the body. We need to get him to give up the yacht in exchange for releasing it." said Davis.

"Jeez, you are a cold-hearted motherfucker," replied Reynolds.

Davis and Reynolds had been classmates while attending the federal fraud investigations and forensic accounting course at the Federal Law Enforcement Training Center (FLETC) at Glynco, Georgia. One of the portions of the course that Davis had found to be of great interest dealt with asset forfeiture.

They were both divorced heavy drinkers with a penchant for sexual encounters with easy women. In both cases, these proclivities for over use of intoxicants and sex with floozies resulted in disciplinary action. Davis got talked into a tryst with two prostitutes in the Dominican Republic while executing the arrest of Char Blackfox on a fugitive warrant and a seizure order for the *Good as Gold.*

They had seized the boat from an island off the coast of Colombia and had stopped to refuel in the D.R. Char had arranged the ménage à trois and had one of the hookers dose Davis' drink with what was later determined to be a generic version of Rohypnol. Char and his boat had slipped away into the night, and Davis had been suspended and transferred. Since then Char had made a deal with the government and received a pardon for a heist and assorted other transgressions.

Reynolds had a similar tale of woe involving the misuse of a government issued credit card to pay for lap dances at a Hialeah strip club. He had almost been fired, but made restitution and was ordered by his supervisor to seek help for his twin addictions— booze and pussy. Now, he was given every shit detail that was assigned to the field office and luckily for Davis that involved the investigation of the murder of Sofia Ramos.

"Sandwich Qbano all right?"

"I wanted a burger and fries," protested Reynolds.

"So get the ropa vieja and patacones—it's almost the same thing."

"Whatever," said Reynolds. "Just as long as I get some food in my stomach ASAFP."

"Roger that," said Davis. He made a few quick turns and located the Cuban chain restaurant that he favored because they gave a rather healthy policeman's discount. He pulled up to the drive-thru and ordered two of the Cuban specialties, along with a couple large Diet Cokes. He had been drinking last night as well and while he found that Gatorade was the best drink to curb a hangover, Diet Cokes were a close second.

They drove in silence as each agent ravenously wolfed down their meal. Davis drove with one hand—easily navigating through the mid-morning traffic while chomping on his barbeque beef sandwich. He drove west on A1A and then south on the interstate until it flowed into the Taylor Highway. They passed a strip joint in Homestead causing Reynolds to stir from his semi-slumbering state. "Hey, let's say we stop on the way back, have a few libations to put us back to equilibrium and talk to the ladies?"

"You mean get a few lap dances. I thought that one of the conditions of your probation was no strip clubs?" asked Davis.

"Yeah, but the other one is no booze," said Reynolds.

"Right, so let's say you pay for it with your G-card," said Davis, referring to his government issued credit card, "and we'll make it a date."

"Nope. I'm pretty sure that's how they caught me in the first place," said Reynolds.

Davis laughed. "Ya think? That's some first rate detective work there, Clouseau."

"Okay, no G-card. We'll figure something out. If it's happy hour and I'm late with my rent payment, I can probably afford it. Don't forget, first round is on you for getting me to lean on the M.E. a bit," said Reynolds.

Davis shrugged his shoulders, noncommittally. "Right, well I suppose I could short my alimony payment or something."

Reynolds slapped the dashboard with his palm. "That's the spirit—think outside the box!"

"You know, if we manage to seize this asshole's yacht, I'll get a bonus of up to one percent of the value—which is in the neighborhood of $40, 000," said Davis.

"So, that's the deal!" said Reynolds. "I knew you weren't doing this out of the kindness of your heart for some poor murdered Colombian chick."

"Oh, fuck no! She was engaged to the son of the guy who fucked me over in the D.R. We need her body as collateral to get the boat, capiche?" said Davis.

"Okay, hotshot, so I'm risking my job—which as you know is already on thin ice, to help you. What's in it for me?"

"Is my undying gratitude not enough?" asked Davis with a

smile.

"I'll take half," said Reynolds.

"You'll take ten percent—that's a finder's fee and my official limit for such low brow activities," replied Davis.

"Make it twenty-five or you can turn this G-rod around and drop me at 660 at Angler's," he said referring to a popular Miami watering hole. "I'll be in plenty of time for happy hour—two for one drinks."

"Twenty-five percent then," said Davis.

Reynolds smiled. "That's my boy."

Davis knew the way to Fisherman's Hospital. A few years ago, he had cut his foot on some glass while walking on a nearby beach with his second wife. It was a nasty cut that required twelve stitches to close. That time they stumbled on the emergency room by sheer luck. He pulled into the covered entranceway of the modern one story concrete block building and parked in the no parking zone. He took out a placard that said 'U.S. Marshal' and placed it in the windshield.

"So, we play bad cop, good cop?" asked Reynolds.

"I prefer bad cop, insane cop," said Davis.

They entered and followed the signs directing them to the medical examiner's office. Davis knocked and waited for a moment before bursting in, badge in hand.

The man he assumed by the white lab coat to be Doctor Ralston was securely tied to his high backed leather desk chair. His forearms were strapped to the arms of the chair with locking zip ties and he was bound with duct tape on his chest and lower torso.

Finally, a gag had been fashioned with duct tape and placed over his mouth.

Davis swore under his breath, knowing that the body, his collateral, was probably gone. He placed his credentials back into his pocket, approached the bound man and ripped the tape from his mouth. "Let me guess—a man named Char Blackfox was here?"

Chapter Twenty-one - Alabama Bound

"Excuse us ladies. Me and me mate here got some business to talk over," said Kelley. He grabbed the taller man by the arm and bum-rushed him to the door of the bar.

"What the hell, Kelley?" said Flynn.

"Where the fuck is my money?" asked Kelley.

The two men stood inches apart arguing loudly while late night partiers flowed around them.

"I don't have it."

"You promised me fifty grand if I took care of your dirty

laundry and now I want my money," said Kelley.

"It's not as easy as all that. The insurance company has thirty days to adjudicate the claim," said Flynn.

"Stop talking like a fucking barrister, you toad. I got no money and you need to make that right!"

Against Flynn's better judgment, he decided to get the obviously high man off the street—if he didn't, he risked the guy wandering into a bar and sharing his dilemma. "Let's go back to my boat and see what I can advance you."

Kelley had enjoyed smacking Flynn around, that fancy lace curtain Irishman got on his nerves. Flynn had promised him fifty thousand dollars at the conclusion of the job and he had tried to welsh on the debt. Kelley followed him back to his boat and collected twelve hundred dollars that Flynn kept hidden in has cabin as a rainy day fund.

He was reluctant to part with that much money—he'd offered three hundred, but Kelley said bollocks to that and popped Flynn a good one in the eye—causing the drunk to fall and hit his head on a tie down cleat. Kelley would have gladly killed him right then, had Flynn not owed him money.

Kelley had also gotten the address of the woman who had contracted for the hit on her husband. He figured he'd take up the debt with her personally and perhaps toss her a fuck.

He drove the stolen Chevelle SS to Miami, turned down Alligator Alley and up I75 to Route 10, going west. The car was a slag on gas mileage, and Kelley decided he would dump it in favor of something more economical.

The drive from Key West knackered him, and he was so hungry he could eat a farmer's ass through a blackthorn bush.

Kelley had some fond memories of time spent in Gulf Shores a long time ago. He decided he richly deserved a side trip and figured he'd find a nice place to have a few pints, some fried fish and a bit of a kip.

It was late afternoon by the time he got to Gulf Shores—just over the Florida-Alabama state line. He was hungry, tired and in need of a couple of pints of the black stuff. A place on the side of the road beckoned him with the promise of all three. The Stateline Bar and Grill sat just off the side of the road. Across the street, a vacancy sign on the similarly named Stateline Motel promised fulfillment of his need for sleep.

The restaurant was a one level cement block structure, originally painted a rich sky blue that had been washed out by years of exposure to the elements. Kelley entered and was momentarily blinded by the dark and cool interior. He waited a moment for his eyes to adapt to the darkness, and he was able to make out a long bar that ran the length of the back wall. He approached and a tall blond bartender wearing a red and white checkered shirt tied into a halter top and Daisy Duke Shorts looked at him expectantly. "What'll you have?"

"A pint of the black stuff."

She went to the tap, removed a dry 20-oz. tulip-shaped imperial pint sized glass with Guinness spelled out on the side, titled it to a forty-five degree angle, filled the glass to the bottom of its bump and then set it aside to settle. Once done, she filled it the rest of the way, set a coaster before Kelley and placed the pint upon it.

"Ta da," she said.

"Well poured lass," said Kelley.

"My name's Kim. That's a very sexy accent. Where you from?"

"County Kerry, Ireland. Ken Q. Kelley."

She offered her hand and he shook it. "What's the 'Q' stand for?" she asked.

"Anything but quick," he said with a smile. She laughed and smiled mischievously at him.

He ordered fish and chips and they turned out to be surprisingly good. Nice, firm white fish that she said was Dover sole served on a bed of thin, crispy chips. He finished the meal and ordered another beer.

She presented it before him. "Just passing through?" she asked.

"I was thinking of renting a room in that motel across the street, but I couldn't find the office," said Kelley.

"That's because this is it. How many nights do you need it for?" said Kim.

"That depends, Kim. Are you going to play hard to get or are we going to get right to it?"

She laughed and slapped the back of his hand. "Why I can't believe you said that Mister Ken Q. Kelley. How very naughty of you." She walked to the register, printed out his tab, placed it on a small clip board and placed it before him. "Here—you're on the bottom and I'm on the top."

"One night then," he said with a smile.

She laughed again. "I'll give you room five—it's got a new king mattress and a Jacuzzi tub. Go check in and wash up. I'm off in two hours. Then we can have a few drinks and if you're a good boy—I'll personally give you a tour of the mattress."

He chatted with Kim until his beer was done and excused himself. As promised she gave him a key with an elongated green diamond-shaped tag with a white 5 embossed upon it. He entered the room, stripped off his clothes and walked into the bathroom. There was a shower stall next to the heart shaped Jacuzzi. He turned on the water and waited for it to heat up before stepping inside. He let the water run over his body—relaxing his shoulder and back muscles after twelve hours behind the wheel. He stepped out of the shower, wrapped himself in a thin terrycloth towel and regarded himself in the mirror—His body was a topographical map of scars, bruises and stitch marks. He lay down on the bed and dozed until it was time for his date.

At the appointed hour, he returned to the bar. They started doing shots of Jameson, which she chased with a Corona. She ordered a cheeseburger for dinner and devoured it while he munched on Buffalo Chicken Wings. Finished with dinner, she packaged up six beers and a bottle of Jameson and escorted a very drunk Kelley towards the door.

He hadn't had sex in a while, but the amount he had imbibed counted against him—until he saw Kim naked. She was clean shaven and had pierced nipples sporting gold rings. Added to this was a serpent tattoo that ran down her side to her pelvis where its venom dripping mouth surrounded her vagina. A gold belly chain hung loosely from a tan midriff. "I'm a bit of a freak—I hope you're up for that," said Kim.

They had sex multiple times during the night and he awoke to find her head buried under the covers—fellating him. Once she got him hard, she straddled his manhood and began riding him. "Come on Kelley," said Kim. "Fuck me like the mad Irishman you are!"

She rode him hard for a while and then he rolled her onto her side and finished. "Come on, let's get dressed and you can buy me breakfast, but we have to hurry—they stop serving at 10:30," said Kim.

He rolled off the bed and pulled on his shorts. It was getting consistently colder as he drove north and he didn't have a pair of long pants with him. He figured he'd have to invest his dwindling advance on a pair of jeans and some heavy work boots—in case he had to kick someone's face in.

They held hands as they crossed the road, but Kelley was suddenly uncomfortable with the intimacy of the situation—it was one thing to have a night of wild sex, but quite another to have someone he actually cared about.

"So, where you headed, Kelley?" She asked him over a breakfast of banana pancakes and apple wood smoked bacon.

"Enterprise, Alabama," he said before digging into a short stack of hotcakes.

"May I ask why?"

He thought about it as he chewed the moist, flavorful cakes, "I've got a debt I need to collect."

"Must be a lot of money," she said, attempting to draw him out.

"To some, it may be," he said before taking a sip of coffee.

She picked up a thick piece of bacon and slowly chewed as if contemplating something. "So, what can I do to help you, Ken Q. Kelley?"

He placed the last of his pancakes into his mouth, considering how much he should share with his new lover. "I'm glad you asked—what kind of car do you drive?"

Chapter Twenty-two – Flynn

Tito withdrew a satellite phone, dialed the pilot and ordered him to fly the plane to the Marathon Airport. The pilots had been standing by in the Conch Republic Airways waiting room for just such a call and were airborne a short time later and on the ground in Marathon in a little more than a half hour.

Tito waited for Char to finish binding the man to his office chair before stuffing the emeralds into the pocket of his lab coat and pinching the man's cheek. "A man with four kids could always use a few extra pesos, am I right?"

Doctor Ralston had proven to be very helpful. He furnished them with an air tray—basically a lined shipping box for bodies and directed them to a vending machine where they procured bags of ice to keep the body cool in transit. Michael rented a pickup truck from the airport rental agency and they loaded the air tray into the back.

Char drove the SUV onto the tarmac and up to the idling jet. The men loaded the air tray into the aft baggage hold and then entered the passenger compartment. Char grabbed Michael's arm as he exited the pickup. "Make my apologies, but I can't go. I've got to take care of a few things here."

"Dad, they're expecting you to come with us," said Michael. He was not expecting this and was disappointed he wouldn't have his father's imperturbable confidence to rely on.

"I want to ask Flynn about a few things, and I have do before it before he leaves for his next fishing charter on Wednesday.

"Why? What's up?" asked Michael.

"Remember Dennison's dive computer?" asked Char.

Michael nodded. "Yeah, the guy was a real gear guru—he had everything but a set of artificial gills."

"He could have used those," said Char.

"True that. I believe it was a high end air-integrated computer that tracks the airflow through the regulator. I've used similar units. Flynn has it stowed in his cabin."

"Will it track depth?" asked Char.

"For that amount of money, I would hope so. The one I used detailed the dive just like a flight computer—except in this case it records depth instead of elevation and how much time spent at each level. It may also note any catastrophic events—such as the purge of the air tank.

"Or someone shutting off the air valve?" asked Char.

"I don't know—maybe," replied Michael. "We have to get our hands on that device. I don't think Flynn knows what he's got."

"Could be—he still dives with an old U.S. diver's rig from the '70s, when they were good. But he deals with divers with newer gear every day. If we take it, he'll know it's missing," said Char.

Michael thought for a second. "Replace it with another rig. Hopefully, he'll never know the difference."

"I'll take care of it," said Char, suddenly anxious to change the subject. "Watch your ass down there, kid. Some more of Sofia's relatives may want to take out their frustrations on you."

Michael nodded. "Yeah, I'm pretty sure we haven't seen the last of that. But I've been through worse."

"You and me both, kid. Don't worry about the pickup. I'll take care of it."

Michael hugged his father and walked towards the jet. He had neither a toothbrush nor a passport, but matters ranging from the trivial to the illegal didn't concern him. He would put on a strong face as the grieving fiancé and try not to get stabbed by any relatives mad about his part in Sofia's death.

***

Char returned the pickup and headed back to Key West. He watched a steady flow of tourists streaming out of the Conch Republic now that the weekend was coming to an end. He had a standing offer to stay at his ex-wife's apartment above the gallery—on the couch, but he could work on that. Even after all these years, he was still attracted to her. Yet, he doubted that letting all the skeletons out of the closet had improved her opinion of him.

It was long past sunset by the time Char arrived downtown. He parked the behemoth in a lot, took the ice pick from the glove box, and walked to Duval Street. Flynn was a creature of habit imparted with a strong taste for the drink. Char had passed many evenings with Flynn and he knew the man was a fan of Irish whiskey, Guinness, and any female below the age of fifty—that number slipped by ten years as it got later.

Flynn always raved about an Irish bar with a Caribbean theme and Char headed straight there. After it opened in the late sixties, O'Sullivan's Caribbean Bar and Grill quickly became a minor institution. It was housed in an old white clapboard building that had originally served as the Pan Am ticket office of the first airport in Key West, whose closeness to Cuba made it the logical choice for the fledging airline industry. The building's open patios and atriums were cooled by large antique belt driven ceiling fans that dated back to the building's construction in 1927.

According to Flynn, O'Sullivan's had all the ingredients for a successful watering hole—music, decent food, women, craft beers, and cheap drinks—at least during happy hour. He found Flynn seated at the bar alone, a half full glass of Guinness sat before him. Char slid onto the empty barstool on Flynn's right. He took the ice pick from the cargo pockets of his shorts and placed it in front of him. "Seen this before?"

Flynn turned to look at Char. He had a badly swollen black eye and a cut on his forehead that was closed with a butterfly bandage. "No, should I have?"

"What the hell happened to you?" asked Char.

"The husband of one of my regulars got suspicious and followed her to a rendezvous and then I rendezvoused with one of his fists—for a banker, he was a pretty tough guy," said Flynn.

"Sorry to hear about Sofia—what the hell happened?"

"Somebody shot her," said Char. *Probably the same somebody that killed the owner of that ice pick.* He looked at the bartender and pantomimed pulling down a tap.

"Guinness and a shot of Jameson. Set my friend up as well."

"Thanks Char, I'm a little short. I appreciate the kindness," said Flynn. Char nodded, remembering that Flynn had once confessed that he was one or two payments away from losing his boat. If his charter business dried up even a little bit, the bank would repossess it. "Ah well, it sucks to drink alone and you look like you could use a few drinks. When are you heading out?"

"Not until the end of the week at the earliest. We are going to get hit with a tropical storm late Tuesday, so I delayed the trip a bit. Aside from the lack of cash flow, it's not a problem," said Flynn.

The bartender, Conor, a Dubliner over here on work visa to add authenticity to the Irish Pub, poured the draughts with the precision of a soufflé chef and delivered them each with a four leaf clover imprinted in its thick head.

Char picked up his glass and tapped it to Flynn's. "To better times."

"Yeah, better times," replied Flynn.

They drank the round and ordered another. Char found Flynn to be little more than politely curious about Sofia's death and not curious at all about the ice pick.

"It has initials carved into the handle. What was the name of the diver who died on your boat?"

"Harold Dennison of Enterprise, Alabama," said Flynn. He finished his shot and followed with a deep sip of beer. "Why?"

"The initials are the same. Did Harold Dennison use an ice pick when he spearfished?" asked Char.

"How the fuck would I know?" exclaimed Flynn.

"Settle down, old son. I'm just trying to get to the bottom of who killed my boy's fiancé."

"Yeah, well it sure the fuck wasn't me—I've got my own problems. I don't put together a good season and the bank will foreclose on my boat!"

"Where has his body been shipped?" asked Char.

"I turned him over to the State M.E., called Dennison's wife and told her where she could find his body. I assume he's been shipped back to his home by now," said Flynn.

"What about his dive gear?" asked Char.

Flynn turned to look at him. "What is this—a fucking interrogation?"

"No Flynn that will come later. Just tell me where the gear is."

"Still on my boat—I'm supposed to box the stuff up and send it off to his wife, Victoria. I think she's a trophy wife. He brought her down here once. They stayed in a suite at the Casa Marina—what a gorgeous piece of ass!"

"Did you meet her?" asked Char.

"Yeah, back when I had the cash, I would always host a party on board my boat the night before we'd head out on a trip. I did it up right—lots of top shelf booze and hors d'oeuvres that I had a local Greek restaurant make. I even had a guitar player strumming Jimmy Buffet tunes," said Flynn. He stared off in the distance as if remembering the event.

"One more question, amigo. Did you ever slip it to her?" asked Char.

Flynn's face reddened. He jumped off the bar stool and turned to Char "I've had enough of your bullshit line of questioning." He said it loud enough so that most of the occupants of the bar looked at him.

"All right, easy now, let's have another drink." Char signaled Conor, who nodded, but seemed in no hurry to serve them.

A few minutes later, he delivered the boilermakers and looked at both men. "Gentlemen, let's keep it down to a dull roar. You're scaring the other customers. I'd hate to cut you off—it's bad for my tip."

Char reached into his pocket, brought out a roll of bills and peeled off a twenty. "Here's a down payment."

"Bad form, mate. You should always tip at the end of your service," replied Conor. Nevertheless, he took the bill and retreated to the far end of the bar.

"Everybody's a critic," said Char.

They finished their drinks, ordered another round and some bar food. The conversation turned to other subjects—fishing, the benefits of a luxury yacht versus a convertible and whether Key West had gotten too touristy—it had.

Eventually, they hit the cobblestone streets, looking for the next bar. Flynn walked like a man braving wave-tossed seas. Char watched him stagger down the street, hit a telephone pole with his shoulder, bounce off and trip on a curb—then fall to his knees. Flynn didn't seem to immediately notice.

Char helped the man to his feet, "Come on Flynn—let's put you in a cab. Still got that bottle of Pappy Van Winkle on board?"

"Yup," said Flynn. "I was saving it for a special occasion." He fished out a cigarette and then searched his pocket for a match. Char pulled out the Zippo he had carried since Vietnam and lit Flynn's smoke.

"Well, if this isn't a special occasion, what is? Let's toast a farewell to my would-be daughter-in-law and one of the finest people I've ever met."

Flynn sat down on the curb, looked down at the cobblestone and inhaled deeply. "Sure, Char why not?" Char flagged down a cab.

"Charter Boat Row off North Roosevelt Boulevard," said Flynn. The driver nodded and accelerated up Truman Avenue—in a hurry to unload the two drunks. The taxi pulled onto the causeway and Flynn directed them to his sixty foot Hatteras Convertible.

"Pay the man," said Flynn as he drunkenly climbed out of the back.

Char gave the guy a ten on a $6.50 fare and didn't wait for change. He followed Flynn to the gangplank and climbed on board the stern. Flynn opened the sliding glass doors that lead to the main salon.

"Take a seat, I'll get the Pappy," said Flynn. He disappeared down a short hallway to his cabin. Char looked around the interior and remembered the last time he was here—watching Harold Dennison receive CPR.

Flynn staggered into the main salon with a bottle of very expensive twenty year old bourbon in one hand and two short glasses in the other. "Here's Pappy!" he slurred. Flynn filled the glasses with about four fingers of the brown liquid, and clicked his glass against Char's.

Char drank slowly, taking time to savor the oak mellowed, well-aged, amber liquid—while Flynn gulped his down like it was cheap liquor.

"Got to take a leak," said Char.

"There's a head in every cabin, but the closest is the first one on your right," said Flynn.

Char turned left instead of right and entered Flynn's cabin— sure as shit the high end SCUBA equipment sat piled in the corner. Char switched on the light and examined the Buoyancy Compensator. On one shoulder strap, mounted so the handle would be pointed downward was a custom made neoprene scabbard. Char removed the ice pick from his pocket, slipped it in and fastened a short bungee cord like retention strap—it fit perfectly. He removed the ice pick, placed it back in his pocket.

Next he turned to the air integrated dive computer. It was installed on the regulator assembly by an air hose quick connect fitting. He pulled down the outer ring until it snapped free from the air hose. Char removed the computer console and placed it in his pocket. He retrieved a similar one he had bought at Diver's Warehouse and snapped it back in place.

There was a compact desk in the corner of the room. Char went to it and perused the documents scattered about its surface. There was a letter tucked between a row of weathered paperback books on a shelf above the desk. He picked up the envelop and read the return address.

There was no name on the envelop—just a return address in Enterprise, Alabama. He opened it and withdrew several photographs of a petite naked, brunette on a beach—judging by the white stone buildings and deep blue water, it was probably taken in Greece. *Flynn was right—she is a piece of ass*, thought Char. He opened the letter and read it.

He exited the cabin and found Flynn sitting on the stern, looking up at the stars. "What were you doing—taking a dump?"

"No, long piss—had a lot of beer to get rid of," said Char.

Flynn had the bottle nestled in the chair next to him. He poured himself another four fingers of bourbon and offered Char a refill. "I'm fine, but we should probably make that toast we talked about."

Flynn looked at Char blankly. "What shall we drink to?"

"How about Sofia and the part you played in her death?"

The proposal had the desired effect—even in Flynn's inebriated state, his face flushed red and his jaw dropped.

"I had nothing to do with it," said Flynn.

"You were fucking Dennison's wife."

"Guilty as charged, but that does not make me a killer."

"No, arranging the murder of Dennison makes you a killer," said Char.

"Nonsense—the death certificate says he died by drowning—accidental death."

"I'm confident that the M.E. can be convinced to reopen the investigation into his death."

Flynn gulped down the rest of his drink and poured himself another one. "Go ahead—he did drown. They'll find water in the man's lungs—case closed."

"Flynn, let's just cut out the bullshit, shall we?"

Flynn looked at Char and smiled. "The fact that I had slipped it to Mrs. Dennison does not make me a killer, Char. You've got no proof other than an ice pick that fits into a scabbard. It does fit—does it not?"

"Oh yeah, like a glove."

"He could have found it scuba diving," said Flynn.

"Who are we talking about?" asked Char.

"Whoever killed Sofia."

"This is getting tedious," said Char. He leaped to his feet, walked to a stowage compartment, opened it and searched around and retrieved what looked like a small aluminum baseball bat. He removed the fishing billy, slapped it against his open palm three times and walked over to Flynn. Without hesitation, he brought the club down in a powerful swing and struck Flynn across the knee.

Flynn screamed in pain. "Son of a bitch!"

"That's to show you that I'm serious. Every time I ask you a question and you don't answer, I will hit you at different pain points until you tell me what I want to know," said Char.

Flynn started to protest and drunkenly tried to stand, but Char swung the club into Flynn's ankle in a powerful arcing blow. Flynn crumbled to the deck.

Char squatted down in front of the man. "Who gave you the black eye?"

"I told you—some banker. I was slipping it to his wife."

Char stared down at the man. "Wrong answer," said Char. The aluminum fishing Billy came crashing down against his ear. Flynn grabbed the wounded ear and screamed out in pain. "I got all night Flynn and I'm going to start fucking you up for real."

"No, please stop. No more," pleaded Flynn.

"Tell me," said Char.

"I never wanted this. It was Vicky's idea. Dennison had one of the biggest dealerships in Alabama. The wife convinced him to take out an insurance policy that paid double indemnity for accidental death. She is set to inherit the dealership and get a ten million dollar payday from the insurer."

"Who is Kelley?"

"He's a guy who hung out at a bar I used to go to in Key Largo. He was always going on about his experience in the Real IRA. I thought he was full of shit, but aside from you, I didn't know anyone else who had claimed to have killed people," said Flynn.

"Yeah, he's a killer all right," said Char.

Flynn shook his head in agreement, "Yeah, he's as crazy as a shithouse rat."

Char was sick of staring down at the man and his knees were starting to ache from squatting. "Come on, get up." He offered Flynn his hand, pulled him to his feet and helped him to sit back down in a deck chair.

"So, Dennison's wife paid you to arrange the death of her husband."

Flynn shook his head slowly up and down. "Sorry, Flynn, but I got to hear you say it."

"Yeah, she said she would give me a million dollars—enough to pay off my boat and more," said Flynn.

"How much did you offer Kelley to kill him?"

"$50,000 and he wanted another $50,000 for shooting Sofia and Michael. I didn't tell him to do that. Michael found the ice pick and Kelley decided that both of them had to die as some twisted form of risk management," said Flynn.

"Where is Kelley now?"

"Headed to Alabama, I think," replied Flynn.

"Why?"

"He wanted payment. I gave him what money I had—about $1200 and he is headed to Enterprise to get the rest from Vicky, but she won't be there."

"Where will she be," asked Char.

"They have a place on Indian Rocks Beach, I called her and told her she better hole up there for a while until I get a handle on things," said Flynn.

"Get a handle on things? Flynn, you and Vicky are going to jail." Char pulled out the microcassette recorder from his pocket.

Flynn's eyes widened when he saw the recorder. "What about Kelley."

"Very simple, Flynn, I'm going to track him down and kill him before he does any more damage."

Chapter Twenty-three - The Prodigal Son

Ann had performed a minor miracle in converting what had once been a warehouse above her gallery into very comfortable living quarters. The living room sported a large lead paneled industrial style window that overlooked the street. She had salvaged it from an old boat yard that was being razed to make room for high-end homes. Ann's bedroom and the kitchen were in the back of the living quarters.

It was Wednesday morning, and Char was becoming concerned about his son. Michael had left for Bogota Sunday evening, in the company of Sofia's relatives, and Char hadn't heard from him since.

Char's smartphone vibrated on the wood coffee table and

woke him. He fumbled with it for a moment and then remembered how to answer it—Michael had bought the damn thing for him in an electronic store in the Colon Free Trade Zone for his birthday. Char was convinced Michael had done so more as a gag gift for the technologically challenged than a heartfelt token of a son's good wishes.

"Dad, I'm coming in this afternoon. Where do you want them to land the plane?

Char sat up on the couch, rubbed his head to shake the sleepiness from his thoughts and tried to formulate a response. Ann saw that he was awake—walked in from the kitchen and handed him a cup of coffee. He mouthed his thanks, took a sip and replied, "Meet me in Marathon. I'm going to have a short meeting with Ralston. See if they wouldn't mind flying us up to Saint Pete from there. I'm thinking of meeting with the FBI in Tampa."

"Why Tampa?" asked Michael.

"Let's just say we'll probably have better luck there and leave it at that. How was the funeral?"

"About what you'd expect—several hundred friends and relatives loudly grieving in Spanish. Followed by a family gathering where everyone drank too much—including me. All in all, I'd rather be back in Fallujah."

"Anyone threaten you?" asked Char.

"No, they knew I loved her and cut me some slack. Everyone was very cordial," replied Michael.

"Is Ramos coming back with you?" asked Char.

"No, he used up all his leave for the funeral and his Commanding Officer wants him back in the saddle. If we need him, he said to call and he'd come running."

Ann stood in the kitchen doorway looking at Char and pantomiming flipping an omelet. Char nodded affirmatively. She disappeared into the kitchen and he heard plates being rattled. One of the things that he sincerely missed was his ex-wife's cooking—she was an artist with a spatula as well as a paint brush.

Char ended the conversation, reclined on the sofa and closed his eyes. He awoke sometime later to find a perfectly formed, lightly browned omelet and two slices of wheat toast resting on a square white stoneware plate in front of him.

He examined the plate, "Ham and cheese?"

"No dear, that's an actual Denver omelet," said Ann. "I went shopping this morning while you slumbered."

"Well, well," said Char. He sat up, grabbed the silverware and commenced eating. The omelet was the right mix of hot, spicy and meaty. She had loaded it with chunks of ham and bacon, as well as plenty of peppers and onions.

She refilled his coffee mug and then retreated back into the kitchen—returning a few seconds later with her own plate. She sat down beside her ex-husband. "Rough night last night?"

"No more than most," he said while chewing on a piece of toast. "Why?"

"You stumbled in here and passed out on the sofa without as much as a word. Oh, yeah, and you slept in your clothes," said Ann.

He cut off a large piece of the omelet, shoveled it in his mouth and chewed it as if considering an answer. "You've heard me talk about a guy named Flynn?"

"Isn't he the charter boat captain from here—fifty something and perennially on the make for younger women?" she replied.

"That would be him," said Char. "I had to rough him up a little last night to get him to confess to his role in the death of a diver on his boat."

"Oh gosh," said Ann. That was the other thing he missed about his wife—she hardly ever swore. Even the most God-awful problem barely engendered a curse word.

"There's more. He hired an ex-IRA hit man to kill the guy while making it look like an accident. That same hit man shot Michael and killed Sofia because they found evidence that proved he killed Dennison."

Ann stopped eating her omelet and looked at Char. "And Flynn confessed to all this?"

"I had to beat a confession out of him." He picked up the microcassette recorder from the coffee table. "I'm going to take it up to St. Pete and give it to the FBI. Dennison had a double indemnity insurance policy and his wife stands to receive ten million—not to mention his other assets," said Char.

"Why St. Pete?"

"Dennison's wife was pulling all the strings and she is currently staying at Indian Rocks Beach." Char didn't bother telling his wife that he had a deputy marshal out of the Miami office looking to seize his yacht.

Ann put down her plate on the table, clasped her hands together, turned and looked at Char. "After knowing you for over 35 years, I can read you like the funny pages."

"That's book, my dear."

"If the shoe fits," said Ann. "It's clear you're not telling me everything, but that's okay. Just take care of our only son. Don't get him killed or I'll ask you to never darken my door again. Do we understand each other?"

Char nodded.

"I have to hear you say it, Charles."

Char stood up realizing that he needed to get moving towards Marathon. "Honey, please don't worry. Nothing bad will happen to the kid that doesn't happen to me first."

"Sounds right," said Ann. Then she did something she hadn't done in years. She bent over, put her hands on either side of his face and kissed him on the lips. "Take care of yourself, you old goat."

Shocked by the kiss, Char considered what to say and decided he needed to ensure she understood the gravity of the situation. "Flynn knows I have enough evidence to put them all away and there's a lot of money in the mix, greasing the wheels of bad decisions. The man that killed Sofia and the diver is still on the loose. If they can exert leverage to make me go away—they will. Flynn knows you are here and may decide that you are just the collateral he needs," said Char.

"What's he look like?" asked Ann.

Char was prepared for the question. He pulled a piece of newspaper print from his pocket that he had ripped out of a Key West Angler's Guide after leaving Flynn's boat. He handed her the ad.

Ann examined the newsprint for a few seconds, "Not a bad looking guy."

"Yeah, if you like philandering alcoholics with orange-tinged, precancerous skin, he's your man."

"Why, Charles Blackfox, you sound jealous," said Ann.

"No, definitely not. Just keep the ad and if he shows up, skedaddle and get somewhere safe."

There wasn't much more he could say and he hoped that his advice sank in. He and Michael would be far away—eight hours by car and he could not afford to have anything happen to her—for various reasons.

He drove the 45 miles to Marathon in light traffic—the storm that Flynn had forecasted was pushing good weather east as it blew in. The day was sunny, but he could see storm clouds in the rear view. He was glad he would be heading north.

***

Ralston had found a donut shop in a sun bleached strip mall. Ray's Donuts had definitely seen better days and now was mostly kept alive by a steady flow of old timers who found the sugar-covered fried dough irresistible. Ralston had never been in there before and that was the draw.

He didn't want to meet with Char at his office—in truth, he didn't want to meet with the man at all, but he felt powerless against the rising tide of events that had taken on a life of their own. He sat down at the counter and ordered a couple of old fashions with a cup of coffee and texted the address to Char's cell phone while he waited for his order.

The agents had bought the story of some unknown Colombians absconding with the woman's body. He had offered no names, including that of Char Blackfox and had recently discovered the emeralds he was given were of a very high quality—he planned to have one of them mounted on a ring as soon as this whole thing blew over.

He dunked the old fashioned style doughnut into his coffee and chewed the moist cake before washing it down with a sip of the steaming hot beverage. He finished the first one and turned his sights to the second, unsure whether to devour it now or ration it should his meeting be delayed.

The waitress, a gal in her early forties, wore a large multicolored nameplate that announced her name as Doris. She stood in front of him staring, presumably at a figure in the doorway. Ralston turned around to see the tall, lanky figure of Char stride into the shop and slide onto the stool next to him.

"Hello honey, how about a cup of joe and a chocolate covered?" said Char.

"Sure, Sugar, right away," said Doris. She deftly bounced around the food prep area and returned with the beverage and pastry. "You want sugar for your coffee, baby?"

Char cast a sly smile at the waitress. "No, Doris, they tell me I'm sweet enough already."

She laughed as if no one had ever said that before and Ralston realized it might have been a mistake to sit at the counter. She smiled broadly at Char. "You need anything else, sugar?"

"No, darling, I'm just here to converse with my friend." He tapped Ralston on the shoulder, hoping she would get the hint.

"Well, just make sure to give me a shout if you do." She slid the tip of her middle fingers slowly across the top of his donut—covering it in frosting and then placed it in her mouth. She smiled at Char, slowly turned and retreated while accentuating the swing of her hips. Both men sat there bemused by the display.

"I wish I had that effect on women," said Ralston.

"It only works with certain women—normally the ones who work in donut shops. I thought you were married?"

"Divorced—two time loser."

"Just once for me," said Char.

"Did she divorce you?" asked Ralston.

"Yeah," said Char. He decided to offer a clue about his break-up with Ann—so few knew the real truth about why she had left him. "I got into a little trouble with some guys wearing silk suits and pinkie rings—not to mention having lots of vowels in their last name.

"I get the picture."

Char nodded. "I kept one step ahead of them by moving around a lot and she got tired of life on the run." Char took a sip of coffee and shook his head as if considering something. "But, it all worked out. We're still friends and we managed to raise a wonderful boy who grew into a fine young man."

"You should write a book," said Ralston.

"Maybe I will. And you?"

Ralston took a bite of his doughnut and a sip of coffee. "My first wife left me because of my second wife—the latter being a young student in a medical forensic course I taught. One day she woke up and I wasn't her sexy professor anymore—just some fat old man she had to sleep with. Now, I just go fishing a lot."

"Yeah, me too," said Char.

"So, what do you have for me?" asked Ralston.

Char reached into his cargo pocket, retrieved the microcassette recorder and a placed it on the counter in front of the man. He withdrew a set of ear buds from his shirt pocket. "Here, use these or we'll have the cops here in a few minutes."

Ralston was familiar with the device as he often used one to record the autopsies, which would then be transcribed into a written report. He listened to the recording and was shocked at what he heard. He rewound the recording and listened to it again. Once satisfied, he removed the ear buds and regarded Char. "Who is the man on the tape?"

"The captain of the charter boat that Dennison was on," said Char.

"He admits conspiring to kill the man, but he did so under duress—you beat him—didn't you?" said Ralston.

"I incentivized him to tell the truth—will there be a problem with that?"

"Well, you're not a cop. He could have you arrested for assault and I'm guessing here—battery, but the testimony can't be directly suppressed. Still, it will be problematic," said Ralston.

Char had a padded shipping envelop with him. He placed it on the counter in front of him. "How about if I had Harold Dennison's dive computer and it tracked the time, date, location, his depth during the dive and annotated when someone shut off his tank of air?"

Char opened the envelop and removed a sheet of paper with a sharply undulating line written across its length. "This line represents the dive telemetry of Harold Dennison's last dive. It's generated by an air integrated computer. These dots here," said Char, pointing to a long line of periods joining the otherwise unbroken line, "corresponds to when the air supply to the computer is off."

Ralston took another bite of his donut, chewed it slowly and studied the paper. "So, it appears that Harold Dennison's air supply was turned off sometime during the dive—while he was at depth. Not an approved dive practice, said Ralston. "What else do you have?"

"This sharp upside down V shape here represents a sharp ascent towards the surface and an equally sharp descent during the period that the air was off—as if he was making an emergency assent and someone stopped him," said Char.

"You might have something, but electronic evidence is like any other—subject to scrutiny by the defense. They'll try and prove that it's tainted. It's less of a problem if the source is a private citizen rather than the police, but they'll still try. The more evidence you have, the harder all of it is to debunk," said Ralston.

"What do you recommend I do?" asked Char.

"Give it to the FBI. I know the agent investigating Sofia's death. He works out of the Miami office."

"I'd rather deal with a guy I know up in Tampa. He's a retired cop and private investigator. I can hire him to work as an intermediary."

"What the hell are you worried about?" asked Ralston.

"Let me ask you this, did the FBI agent have another guy with him when they found you tied to your chair?"

"Yeah, a deputy marshal."

"Carl Davis?" asked Char.

"That sounds right." Ralston reached into his pocket, retrieved his wallet, searched through it and withdrew a business card with a gold shield embossed on it. "Yep, that's it. Asset forfeiture division."

"That's what I was afraid of. That guy is trying to seize my boat because it was once owned by one of the gangsters I didn't mention....specifically," said Char.

"Well, that is a different matter entirely. Let me give the FBI agent the recording. It will get the ball rolling."

Char deftly retrieved the recorder before Ralston could object. "Sorry, Doc. No can do. I'm going to work this my way."

"Fair enough, but keep me in the loop. You might need my help," said Ralston.

Char got up, retrieved a bill from his wallet and threw it on the counter. "I'll be in touch. Please give my regards to Doris." Char retreated to his vehicle, slipped behind the driver's seat and headed to the airport to await the arrival of his son.

Ralston watched Char drive out of the lot, withdrew his cell phone pushed a number and waited. "Agent Reynolds, this is Doctor Ralston, the Monroe County Medical Examiner. Got a few minutes?"

Chapter Twenty-four - Enterprise

Kim had lent him her five-year old Mazda Miata and offered to park the Chevelle in her garage. A cold October wind chilled him as he walked across the motel parking lot to the borrowed Miata. Kim leaned against the hood with her arms provocatively crossed under her breasts, pushing them against the thin cotton of the tube top.

"Checkout time was 11, ace," said Kim.

"I know the owner, perhaps she'll cut me some slack."

"She already has. Just bring my car back with no dings or dents and I'll cut you some more. Call me when you hit the county line and I'll be waiting for you in room five, wearing nothing but a smile."

"Being the boss does have its privileges." He wrapped his arms around her and kissed her, thrusting his tongue deep into her mouth. She kissed him back while gently sliding her hand down the front of his shorts. She lightly caressed his crotch and felt something stir within.

"No time for that my love. I need to get cracking while it's still daylight."

She pulled away from him, grabbed the door handle and held it open for him. "By all means, Mister Kelley, please allow me to assist you."

He kissed her once more and then slid into the small red sports car. "I'll be back tonight or I'll call you if I'm delayed," said Kelley. He turned the key in the ignition and the engine roared into life. Luckily, he had been raised driving a manual transmission. He put the stick shift into first gear, spun the rear tires and sped out of the parking lot towards Interstate 10.

He exited onto a state route that eventually took him into Enterprise, which turned out to be adjacent to the large Army aviation base at Fort Rucker. He located the address with Kim's GPS and followed the directions to the outskirts of town—where suburbia gave way to farmland. He turned onto a narrow and nameless, but numbered country road. The GPS announced that he had arrived and Kelley cursed loudly. He stared at a Tara-like mansion situated at the top of a small ridge about a hundred yards from where Kelley sat. It had two wide porches that ran the length of the house on both stories, complete with white Greek columns supporting an arched portico. Most troubling of all was a high white stone wall that ran completely along the large yard and ended in an electric gate. There was an access control station complete with a keypad, card reader, camera and speaker phone—it seemed that Harold Dennison liked his security—not that it had done him any good.

Clearly, this situation would call for some planning. His stomach rumbled and Kelley figured that a dose of protein would jump start the thinking process. Remembering he had passed a burger joint, he wheeled the vehicle around and headed in that direction.

He shivered as the late November wind cut through him during the short walk to the door. Kelley noticed a Ford F150 with Enterprise Building Inspector painted on the door. It even sported a revolving caution light atop the cab. The vehicle had an official look to it that would ally suspicions and hopefully, open gates—he could eat later.

It was a little past eleven and the lunch time crowd was yet to arrive. Kelley studied the restaurant's few patrons and tentatively identified the driver of the pickup—a heavy set, red faced man sat in a booth against the far wall, busily consuming a huge burger and a large order of fries. He wore a blue, short sleeve button down shirt with what appeared to be an identification badge clipped to his pocket.

Kelley returned to his vehicle and pulled it to the rear of the parking lot. He opened his kit bag and retrieved a Walther PPK automatic from a side pocket. He checked the magazine, pointed the rearview mirror towards he exit door and waited for the man to exit. He didn't have to wait long—a few minutes later, the man exited carrying his beverage. The building inspector reached into his pocket to retrieve his keys, while Kelley leaped from his car and trotted towards him.

"Excuse me sir, I couldn't help notice the lettering on the side of your truck, Can you answer a question for me."

The building inspector turned towards him with a look of

tolerated annoyance plainly displayed on his face—figuring he'd get a question about what voltage wiring to install for a stove. "What's the question, chief?"

Kelley closed to within a few inches, thrust the short barrel into the fat man's stomach and fixed him with a wild-eyed look. "Do you want to live?"

The inspector looked at him with wide eyes and started to stutter a reply, but Kelley shushed him, "All right, now be calm. We're just going to go for a ride—then I'll let you go, okay?" the man nodded. Kelley knew he better speak calmly—lest this bogger throw up and that would make bags of the job.

"I'm going to slide past you and sit on the passenger side. Then, I want you to get in and off we go," said Kelley. Kelley did so, making sure to keep the pistol pointed the man. The building inspector hesitated getting in—making it look like he was going to run for it. Kelley fixed the man with a stern look and pointed the barrel at his hip. "Get in or I'll shoot you in the leg and then pull you in. If you're lucky you may not bleed to death. You've got three seconds, one, two…." The inspector climbed in and looked at Kelley.

"Well, what are you waiting for Bowsie? Start the bleeding truck."

"Where to?" asked the man.

"Country Road 113," said Kelley

"Where on 113?"

"Number 145," replied Kelley.

"Harold Dennison's place?"

"Yeah, that's it. Have you been there before?" asked Kelley.

"Harold's a friend of mine or he was—he's passed."

Kelley cracked a slight grin since he was the one who 'passed him.'

They road along a circular route past a Walmart Super Center and Kelley made a mental note to stop back later and get some chinos and a couple of shirts. "Tell me about his wife," said Kelley.

"You mean Vicky? She's an ex-stripper from Birmingham who sunk her fangs into him and it looks like she'll get everything— the house, a beachfront condo in Florida—even the dealership. That's it off to the right. It's the biggest in Southern Alabama."

"How'd such an upstanding citizen end up with a stripper?" asked Kelley, suddenly curious.

"We had a bachelor party at the club. A bunch of bikers crashed the party and tried to abscond with the stripper, whose name happened to be Vicky. Harold put a couple of them in the hospital."

"How's that?" asked Kelley.

"Harold is a nationally ranked judo champion. He was an alternate in the 1996 Olympics. It's lucky he didn't kill someone."

Yeah, thought Kelley, *real lucky*. Kelley looked to where the man pointed. The large oval shape blue plastic sign outlined in white piping said 'Dennison' in big white letters. It was mounted high enough for anyone driving the circular bypass to see. The lot took up over a quarter mile of frontage on the business route and it looked to have close to a hundred new cars on it.

"What's your name, mate?" asked Kelley.

"Why do you want to know? You know my name you'll have to kill me, right?"

Kelley smiled. "Naw, it's the other way around. The better I know you, the less I'll want to kill you—in theory, unless of course you're a real tool."

The guy laughed nervously. "It's Clarence, but everyone calls me Bubba."

"I'm not sure that's much of an improvement, but here's the deal, Bubba. I'm here to collect a bill. You help me do that and I'll send you on your way unharmed. Try to bollock up the deal and I'll put one in your forehead, fair enough?"

"Not really," said Bubba

"Well, it's the best deal you're gonna get. I need to get in the house and speak with Vicky. Can you make that happen?"

"She hates me. I used to go fishing with Harold, but she put a stop to that."

"Yeah, crazy bitches do that. Can't take the chance that a buddy would be a sounding board for some of their bizarre behavior. Your mates, if they are true mates, will call bollocks on a floozie like that," said Kelley

Bubba grew quiet, thinking he should have done more to convince his friend not to marry the stripper and just maybe that would have saved his life. He also came to the realization that his life was suddenly in play. He drove back on the main state highway and accelerated for the three or so miles until they reached rural country road 113.

Bubba pulled the truck up to the gate and stopped short of the access control station. He turned to Kelley and smiled, as if under duress. "They just installed the gate and I haven't closed out the building permit yet. I could say I'm here to do a final inspection."

"Good thinking there Bubba," said Kelley.

He pulled the truck forward lowered the window and touched the call button. There was no immediate answer—Bubba pushed it again. "Maybe no one's home," said Bubba.

"Ring it again," said Kelley.

He did so. A voice with a Latin accent answered. "Hello?"

"Lupia, it's me, Bubba Hendershott. I'm here to do a final inspection of the gate. Is Vicky here?"

The speaker cackled, "No Mister Hendershott, Misses no here. She went to Florida. She told me to let no one in. Sorry."

"Address," said Kelley.

Bubba nodded. "When will Vicky be back?"

"I don't know Mister Hendershott—she left in a hurry and told me not to let nobody in."

Fucking Flynn, thought Kelley.

"Address," said Kelley.

"Okay, Lupia, I'll come back another time."

Bubba raised the window. Kelley smacked Hendershott across the nose with the barrel of the small automatic. "Ouch! Why did you do that?" He reached up and rubbed his nose.

"I told you to get the address," said Kelley.

"I know it. I went bone fishing with him once. We stayed at the condo. It's right on the water in Indian Rocks Beach."

Kelley smacked him again. This time across the cheek. Bubba cried out. "That's not an address."

"Stop hitting me, it's called *The Sand Dollar*."

"All right, that's almost as good as an address. Let's head back to the restaurant."

Bubba felt relief wash over him. He might yet get out of this alive. *He would drop this crazy man off, head to the police department and report him. With any luck they would catch him driving to Florida.*

They drove back down the long country road, past a long stretch of undeveloped wooded lots dotted here and there with for sale signs. "Pull over here," said Kelley.

"Why?" asked Bubba. He felt the cold rush of adrenaline inundate his bloodstream. He pushed the pedal to the floor. The large V8 that Harold Dennison had included at no extra cost when he sold the pickup to the city thundered. The gravity generated by the acceleration pushed Kelley back in his seat.

"Pull over!" yelled Kelley over the roar of the engine.

"Fuck you, limey bastard," said Bubba.

Kelley swore—*why the fuck does everyone think I'm English?*

Bubba continued to accelerate. A farm truck loaded with hay turned on to the road less than a mile away. Bubba felt exhilarated—he hadn't felt this way since hooking onto that hammerhead shark last year in the gulf. He pulled the truck onto the wrong side of the road. "Hey, limey boy, you drive on this side of the road in London, don't cha?"

"What the hell are you doing?' said Kelley.

"Taking you in bloke. Give me the gun or I'll ram this truck into that one."

Fucking hell, thought Kelley. *There was no way this wasn't going to get messy.* He reached up and placed the barrel against the side of Bubba's head and fired once. The sound was deafening in the confined space. The smell of cordite and burned flesh filled the cab. Bubba had a death grip on the wheel—the truck careened off the narrow road and flipped over into a drainage ditch. The airbags erupted braking Kelley's forward momentum and knocking him unconscious.

He awoke to the smell of vaporizing gasoline wafting into the enclosed space. He tried to lower the window, but it didn't work. Kelley attempted opening the door, but it only opened a few inches due to the slope of the hillside. The windshield had caved in, but failed to break. He tried kicking at it, but the angle made his kicks ineffectual. Kelley suspected he didn't have a lot of time before the truck would catch fire. As if on cue, flames puffed up from under the hood.

"You in the truck, can you hear me?"

"Yeah, please help me," said Kelley.

"I'm going to break the window. Watch the glass."

Kelley turned away from the side window. He heard something heavy strike the glass. It shattered and showered the cab in glass shards. "Crawl out to me," said the voice.

Kelley put the pistol into his cargo pocket and crawled out the hole—cutting his stomach on the few shards left in the window frame. He crawled up the hillside and got to his feet.

Three men were busily engaged in fighting the fire with large fire extinguishers. One of them turned to look at Kelley, "You okay?"

Kelley nodded—too shocked to speak.

"Is there anyone else in the cab?" Kelley didn't know how to answer and said nothing. "Well, is there?"

"No," Kelley said finally.

There was a Dodge Charger parked on the side of the road with its trunk open. A placard on the front announced the owner to be part of the Enterprise Volunteer Fire Department. *Apparently, that's where the fire extinguisher came from,* thought Kelley.

The fire smoldered out. One of the men—most likely the owner of the Charger circled the vehicle and located Bubba's body. "Hey, there's someone else down here. It's Bubba Hendershott. I think he's dead."

Kelley ran to the Charger. The keys were still inside. He turned the ignition and heard nothing—the engine was already running. He popped it into drive and the tires kicked rooster tails of dirt into the air. He heard a shout and looked back. The guy who had saved him was waving his hands over his head.

Kelley looked ahead expecting to see the stop sign at the end of the road and instead saw Dennison's house in the distance. He skidded to a stop, spun the wheel and attempted to turn the vehicle around on the narrow road. The right wheels started sliding down the hill and he pushed the gas to the floor. The wheels spun and shot the Charger onto the pavement.

The firefighter stood in the middle of the road—blocking his escape. Kelley accelerated and pointed the center of the hood directly at the man. *Move, bastard move*, he thought. The man dived to the right just as Kelley thought he had hit him. He sighed and exhaled in relief. Now all he had to do is get back to the burger joint, get in Kim's Miata and drive away as if nothing had happened.

Kelley dumped the car in a vacant lot a short distance from the restaurant, tossed the keys onto the passenger seat and exited. He drove out of town making sure to obey the speed limit and headed for the interstate as a line of police cars and emergency vehicles passed him going in the other direction.

Kelley badly wanted a fix, but would have to go back to the motel before he shot up. He opened his aged flip phone, hit a number on speed dial and waited for the other party to answer. When he finally did, Kelley had to search for the appropriate words to convey his disappointment.

"You lied to me Flynn," said Kelley. "Oh and my fee just increased. I want five hundred thousand or that bitch will go straight to the chair, or whatever these sod gobblers are using these days," said Kelley.

"Where are you headed?" Flynn asked.

"Well Flynn, I'm either headed down to Key West to take care of two problems, or to see the merry fucking widow to take care of one."

Flynn felt a cold shiver run down his spine and his stomach felt queasy—like he was going to vomit. He was sure that Kelley wouldn't kill Vicky, at least before he collected his retroactively raised fee. "Don't hurt Vicky—we'll pay what you want," said Flynn.

"Damn right you will. Call Vicky, tell her I'm going to come see her and suggest she let me in. She's gonna have me as a houseguest for a while. You get some leverage on that crazy bleeding wild man and then meet me at Vicky's place—I'll be there late tomorrow."

"She's pretty independent—she may not let you in."

"It's either me or the bleeding Sheriff's Department. Make sure she understands that." Kelley killed the connection and sighed deeply. *In two and a half hours I'll be back at the motel. I can beg off seeing Kim, shoot up and nod off for the night. Things are definitely looking up,* thought Kelley.

Chapter Twenty-five - Leverage

It was a little before seven. Flynn sat in his pickup parked down the street from the Blackfox Gallery attempting to ferret out a plan. He sat sweating in the cab—the ancient pickup's AC unit had stopped functioning about the time Jimmy Carter was attacked by a killer rabbit. The heat of the day hadn't yet dissipated to be replaced by a slightly less punishing heat of twilight. Even with both window's open, the humidity enveloped him like a soggy blanket.

He had originally put some thought into the situation—otherwise he might have waltzed right into her gallery and given her a story about wanting to buy an expensive painting and then lure her away on a pretext. Something like 'I'd love to see how it looks over my fireplace.' But there were a few problems with that—he didn't have a home—let alone a fireplace and Ann would immediately suspect it was a ruse to perpetrate a theft.

So he settled on waiting for closing time when he would force his way inside and take the woman hostage. She lived upstairs so it would be easy for her to lock the front door and then retreat up to her apartment before he could muscle his way inside.

Observing the shop was difficult as traffic was still heavy—the street served as a secondary thoroughfare for reaching the heart of downtown Key West and he had been forced to park about ten parking spaces down and across the street from the gallery's glass front door.

There was also a host of unknowns—whether there was an alarm, or that she might be armed or know what he looked like. He sat perplexed but not paralyzed with indecision when an amazing thing happened—the lights inside the gallery's glass picture windows snapped off and a few moments later a lithe feminine figure appeared at the front door. He watched in amused disbelief as she locked the antique wood frame door and walked in his direction

"Fucking hell," said Flynn. He slid his lanky body lower on the seat–ensuring that he could still observe her as she transited the street. He waited for her to pass, reached into the glove compartment and removed a combination stun gun and flashlight. He counted to fifteen in his head before exiting the cab and trotted after her.

He bought the device last night, a few hours after his conversation with Kelley—the man's threat was still fresh in his mind. The salesmen who sold him the stun gun told him it generated 80,000 watts—which he assured Flynn was enough to drop the biggest thug. "Hell, if he doesn't go down on the first stun—feel free to juice him again."

Flynn laughed, but didn't quite believe the salesman so he decided a test was in order and he knew the perfect subject. The owner of a boat yard down the street from where Flynn docked his Hatteras had a Rottweiler guard dog that he let roam the yard after closing. The big bastard loved to patrol the fence line next to the street and terrorize unwary pedestrians with spittle spewing, snapping jaws.

Flynn walked by several times until he heard the unmistakable sound of the heavy chain collar the beast wore around its horse sized neck and the snapping of the dog's jaw signaling his approach. Flynn boldly walked up to the chain link fence and gripped it with four fingers of his left hand just as the black and tan animal launched itself at the dangling treats. He pulled his fingers out of the hole, pushed the stun gun through and touched it against the beast's exposed midsection. It let out a whimpering cry and collapsed into a quivering mess at the base of the fence.

"Well, I guess it works after all," said Flynn.

Shit, did I kill the fucking beast? He waited for a few moments, more curious than concerned until he saw the it begin to stir. It slowly got to its feet and shook as if wet—looking none the worse for wear. *Pity*, he thought. He returned to the boat and recharged the battery to ensure it would be fully ready for his upcoming encounter with Ann Blackfox.

Flynn picked up the pace and closed the distance between him and Ann until he had to slow his footfalls—lest she hear him. He was still about three parking spaces behind her and he knew that she would hear him if he drew any closer.

He pulled the stun gun from his back pocket, turned on the power and ran towards the woman—closing the distance in seconds. She started to turn to confront whoever was chasing her.

He was running so fast that when he struck her with the stun device, he collided with her and knocked her off her feet. A black object flew from her hand and clattered onto the sidewalk about a dozen feet away. He left her shuddering on the pavement and walked to recover the object. He reached down and picked up the small, five-shot revolver and put it in the pocket of his shorts. He returned to where Ann's body lay and pulled her to her feet— surprised at how light she was. She moaned. He deftly threw her over his shoulder and started walking back to his truck.

About 50 feet from his cab an elderly couple stopped in front of him. Both appeared to be in their late seventies and the look on their faces said they were having none of it.

"What are you doing with that lady?" said the woman.

"She's my wife," said Flynn, "we had one too many mojitos at Sloppy's."

The old man repositioned himself so that he was standing directly in front of Flynn. "I guess you're going to have to prove it, son."

"Oh hell, I don't have time for this, said Flynn. He pulled the stun gun out of his pocket, switched it on and ran at the old man with Ann still hoisted on his shoulder. The old man threw a punch at Flynn and it landed somewhat ineffectually on the side of his head. "Ouch, that hurt, you old bastard!" said Flynn.

"There's more where that came from," said the man.

The old geezer was dancing around like a bantam weight fighter, but a slow one. Flynn feinted to left, the old man came in to land an uppercut and Flynn thrust the electrodes into the old man's chest.

"Ah, argh, aaaaahhh," moaned the old man as he collapsed

onto the sidewalk.

The woman screamed and ran to the prostrate figure. "You son of a bitch—he has a bad heart!"

"Then he shouldn't stick his nose in other people's business," said Flynn. But she probably didn't hear him—she was rummaging through her husband's clothes for his nitroglycerin pills.

Flynn thought briefly of calling an ambulance, but discarded that idea—they might bring the cops and that was the last thing he needed right now. He ran to his truck—his captive was awake and writhing, so he shocked her again in the buttock.

He got to the truck, opened the passenger door and shoved Ann inside. He ran around the other side of the truck, climbed in and withdrew his cellphone. He thumbed through recently dialed numbers, selected one and pushed send.

"Yeah?"

"Derrick, it's Flynn. I'm going to need to take a week or so off. I need to go up north for a while. Family emergency."

"Jesus, Flynn, we got a charter starting tomorrow. What with the weather and the dead guy, we haven't gotten paid in a while." replied the first mate.

"Can't be helped. You've captained before. Just take them out and do your best. I'll pay you when I get back—trust old Nicky, there may even be a bonus for you. I got to go."

He ended the call and patted Ann's behind. *Hmm, pretty taut butt for an older broad.* She moaned and he thought he would have to shock her again, but didn't want to risk killing the gal. "Be quiet or I'll have to shock you again." The threat apparently worked— she immediately quieted down.

Flynn drove to the marina where Kelley had left his boat and parked as close to the berths as possible. He slapped Ann on the butt a couple of times to wake her.

"Wakee, wakee," said Flynn.

He pulled the gun from his pocket, opened it, removed one of the bullets and examined it. They were made entirely of copper with a hollow point surrounded by eight pointed fleshettes meant to break off after impact to inflict maximum damage. *Must have been Char's idea*, thought Flynn. *Hopefully, I'll get the chance to use it on him.*

Ann moaned again and laboriously sat up. "Where am I?" she asked.

"A marina, we're just about to take a boat ride."

"Flynn?" she asked.

"Yes, my dear. Nicky Flynn at your service."

"You're an ugly motherfucker—you know that?"

"I've been told. Now, I'm going to get out of my side of the truck. I want you to slide over to me and get out. Then, I'm going to put my arm around you and we're going to walk down the dock like a slightly drunk couple having trouble finding their boat, got it?"

"I'd rather kiss a snake," said Ann.

"Shut up and do as I say or I'll put a couple of these nasty fucking bullets in you."

She nodded, remembering what the salesman had told her about the lethality of shredder bullets.

"Okay, I'll do as you say," said Ann.

"Good girl. If you behave, we might even stop somewhere for a meal," said Flynn brightly.

"Wonderful," said Ann. *I'm being kidnapped by some asshole who thinks he's taking a date on a sea cruise.*

Chapter Twenty-six - Johnnie and Earl

Char had learned Eddie had taken up the PI trade after retiring from Pinellas County Sheriff's Department. A few months ago, Flynn mentioned the name Eddie Doyle while making conversation over a poker game. They were both tied up off Ambergris Cay, with the intention of heading northeast—Flynn was heading back to Key West, while Char was considering the western tip of Cuba for a while. A squall had kicked up, and both crews were waiting it out.

They were talking boats and conversions. Char knew of a guy in New Orleans who had converted a patrol torpedo boat made by Higgins into a beautifully restored and custom sport fisherman. Flynn was trying to one up him and mentioned an article he had read in the Tampa Tribune about the restoration of a 100-foot former Navy tugboat by a retired Pinellas County Sheriff's Detective nicknamed Eidetic Eddie Doyle.

Char waited for Flynn to leave, a few dollars richer—since

Char was distracted. He used the boat's satellite phone's data kit to connect to the internet where he browsed through the archives of the newspaper. Given the molasses-like speed of the modem, it took over an hour to find the Sunday supplement detailing the restoration of a Vietnam-era Navy tugboat by a former Robbery Homicide Detective and his lovely wife, Carla.

The happy couple was pictured standing arm in arm on the back deck of the *Fond Memories*. He was surprised Eddie had resisted the urge to call it *The Busted Flush*. Char was holding a glass of bourbon in his hand and was just about to take a sip when the picture finally appeared on the laptop's screen. "Holy shit— she's alive," he said aloud. Char instantly forgot about the drink— it slipped from his hand and shattered on the deck. That was over a month ago and since that time, he had thought a lot about Carla. Now that Char was headed back to Madeira Beach, the thought occurred to him that he might see Carla again.

Char called Johnnie and Earl on his cell—the *Good as Gold* was still an hour south of Tampa Bay. Char instructed them to tie up at the only marina in Madeira Beach big enough to moor an 80-foot yacht. Johnnie knew of a nice marina in St. Pete Beach that could easily handle the boat, and had a decent bar restaurant, but he learned a long time ago that the boss, while not necessarily always right, was the guy who paid his salary.

"Look for an old Navy tug about 100-feet long. On it will be a man by the name of Eddie Doyle. Tell him that Char Blackfox would like a consultation with him. Assure him that it's not a joke," said Char.

"You're the boss. Anything else I should know? Is he armed? Did you sleep with his wife?" asked Johnnie.

"Yes on both counts, but don't worry about it—I can always

get another mate."

Johnnie ended the call. "Funny motherfucker," he said and then slapped the phone loudly back into the cradle.

He was at the helm, piloting the boat while Earl slept after navigating   through the night. Johnnie checked the *Good as Gold's* position on the Northstar GPS/plotter. He figured he'd keep his eye out for the most visible landmark on the horizon, the 431 foot tall, Sunshine Skyway Bridge, and then dead reckon up the coast to John's Pass, which would allow him access to the Intercostal Waterway and the aptly named Mad Beach Marina. He hoped they had dredged the boat channel recently as he remembered that it had been really shallow.

He spotted the bridge a little after three and they arrived at John's Pass a short time later. Earl was up by then, but Johnnie was better turning boats in tight spaces—something that he learned in the Navy's Special Boat Squadrons. Johnnie heard him down in the galley rattling pots and pans—then there was nothing. He heard Earl's footfalls on the stairs that lead up from the galley. Earl shuffled into the pilot house, naked except for a pair of threadbare board shorts he usually slept in

"Dinner ashore Johnnie?" asked Earl.

"Why not? We can stop by and see this guy Char wanted us to speak with."

"Whatever, dude, cuz we are down to the last of the vittles in the food locker and I would love to get me a cheesesteak and fries at the Bamboo Grill."

"Sounds like a plan," said Johnnie.

"What guy, compadre?" said Earl. He had a severe bed head, an unlit cigarette dangled from his lip and he regarded Johnnie through partially closed, sleep-snot encrusted eyes.

"Never mind, dude. Just go grab a shower and be ready to help me tie off the boat. I need you on deck in ten minutes."

"No hay problema, amigo, can do easy." Earl disappeared down the stairs to his quarters and Johnnie concentrated on staying in the narrow boat channel.

Even in the fading sun of the fall afternoon, he couldn't have missed the Vietnam-era tugboat if he tried—it was big and naval grey in a fleet of smaller, white boats. The only thing that rivaled it in size was the yacht Johnnie was piloting, but the tug was still longer and wider than the sleek Hatteras.

The larger yachts were tied up along a long wharf adjacent to the channel separated at certain intervals by rows of berths that ran perpendicular to the wharf. This allowed the less maneuverable yachts to more easily dock. Smaller boats were relegated to maneuvering into the inner berths near the center of the marina. As luck would have it, the slot they had reserved was immediately behind the tug. It appeared to be the only one left big enough for the *Good as Gold*.

Earl busied himself on deck dropping fenders over the side and adjusting their height so the roughhewn timber bumpers on the wharf wouldn't damage their hull. Once that was done he readied the lines as Johnnie painstakingly brought the boat in dead slow at a 45 degree angle and eased slowly towards the wall. Once he was within a few feet, Johnnie eased the throttle into reverse while Earl jumped onto the wharf and tied off the yacht at fore and aft. Once that was done, he waited for Johnnie to shut off the engines, so they could hunt down the office and pay for a week's berthing.

The Hatteras Motor Yacht was so streamlined it lacked a hatch amidships—access was most usually made via the stern. Johnnie locked the sliding glass door, spent a few minutes securing various lines and hopped onto the weathered wooden dock. "Come on boy, I've got serious eating and drinking to do," said Earl.

"Go without me if you want—I've got a few errands to take care of. It's better if I go see this retired cop by myself—he might be less jumpy," said Johnnie.

"How about this—give me the company credit card, I'll pay the docking fee, and then we'll meet up at the Bamboo Beach Club. Char can buy us the first round."

"Hell, he's buying dinner as far as I'm concerned," said Johnnie.

Johnnie handed him the yacht's credit card—issued from an offshore bank, and Earl departed for the marina's office, located toward the center of the complex. Johnnie walked up the dock and regarded the 100-foot long Navy grey, ocean-going tug. He walked up to the gangplank—which looked to be original equipment and called out, "Ahoy, *Fond Memories*, I'm here looking for Eddie Doyle." He waited and then called out again.

"And who would I refer to?" said a male figure. The man looked to be about Char's age, but of medium height and build. He was dressed in a tropical shirt, dark shorts, and sandals -- he certainly looked relaxed.

"I'm Johnnie from the yacht to your stern."

"The *Good as Gold*," said the man. It wasn't a question.

"The very same," said Johnnie. "Are you Eddie Doyle?" The man nodded affirmatively. "May I come aboard?"

"Not just yet. Why did you come?" asked Eddie.

"I've been instructed to give you a retainer in furtherance of your representation in a difficult matter requiring your particular brand of expertise," said Johnnie.

"Jeez, son. That's a lot of bullshit in one sentence, perhaps you should come aboard. I'd rather be bullshitted in comfort," said Eddie.

He ushered Johnnie towards the stern and followed him down the open passageway to what could only be described as an outdoor lounge adjoining the rear of the superstructure. Someone had painstakingly transformed the rear of a Spartan navy tug into a comfortable and relaxing grotto.

The stern had been transformed into a lush oasis—tropical bamboo plants screened it off from the casual observer. There was an alfresco dining area—complete with an outdoor kitchen and adjacent lounge area that looked like it would be at home in a five star hotel. In it sat a set of matching dark rattan couch and chairs surrounding a long teak coffee table. A bamboo tiki bar with matching wooden stools sat off to the side. The aromatic smell of smoking pork wafted up from a barrel shaped smoker set off to the side of the grilling station.

"Drink?" said Eddie.

"Beer?" asked Johnnie.

"Sure, we can do that, "said Eddie. He pointed to one of the rattan arm chairs. "Have a seat."

Eddie went behind the tiki bar and returned with two cans of Coronas—still coated with chips of ice. He handed Johnnie the beer, opened his and took a sip. "Okay, so we don't have a lot of time. My wife is due home from work and I'm preparing dinner for her. She works in a law office and all day she's dealing with asshole attorneys. The last thing she needs is to hear the name Char Blackfox—got it?"

"Roger that," said Johnnie. He took a sip of his beer. *What the hell had Char done to piss off this guy's old lady?*

Eddie sat down in the other arm chair, took a long swig of his beer and looked directly at Johnnie. "Let's get down to cases shall we—what the fuck does Char Blackfox want with me?"

Johnnie thought for a moment as Char had not shared that piece of information with him. "He didn't tell me exactly, but it involves the death of his son's fiancée. He knows who the killer is and needs your help to act as..."

"Intermediary?"

"Yeah, intermediary," said Johnnie. "He also would like to keep his involvement secret."

"There's no specific confidentiality privilege between a private investigator and a client, but in the past I've used a lawyer from my wife's law firm to get that. It should work in this situation as well," said Eddie.

"All right, it sounds like we are agreed in principle."

"Not so fast," said Eddie, "I have a couple of conditions of my own. I normally charge $250 an hour or $1000 a day. But, I have a special fuck you price for Char Blackfox. Four hundred dollars an hour or $2000 a day. I want a retainer of $10,000 delivered to me in cash." Eddie thought for a minute and added. "Gold is also acceptable."

Johnnie stood up—sure that the conversation is over. "Come on, Eddie, no one would pay that. It's just dealing with the FBI not robbing a bank.

"Funny you should use that expression. I'm doing this for many reasons kid. One, Char Blackfox caused me a lot of grief at one time. Feel free to ask him what he did because I'm tired of telling the story. And two, if it involves that crazy lunatic there is bound to be more to it than just talking with the cops. And three— based on past experience it will probably involve gunplay and lots of it."

Eddie looked at his wristwatch and then jumped to his feet. "That's it kid, the wife is due here and so you've got to be going. I'll trust you to show yourself out and give Char the message."

Eddie walked over to the beer cooler behind the bar, grabbed a bottle of Jameson and poured two fingers into a short glass and knocked it back. *And four,* thought Eddie, *if it wasn't for Char being such a shit, I would have never met my wife or solved the case of my life.*

Chapter Twenty-seven - Duck-Tape

The first thing he did was to tie her up. He then rifled through her purse—finding approximately twenty four hundred dollars that were proceeds from a recent sale she had neglected to deposit. She had screamed as loudly as she could through lips taped shut until he ripped it off her face. "I can't breathe asshole. And by the way, It's called duct tape, not duck tape, because it was used to tape up ventilation ducts, you moron."

"Now you see, we're not going to get along well at all if you keep talking like that. I'll leave your mouth untapped if you promise not to scream out. When we're out to sea you can scream all you want," said Flynn.

They were in the cabin of Kelley's boat. Flynn had thrown her down on the bunk, climbed on top of her—straddling the woman as he wrestled her hands together in order to tape them up. After they were in open water, he untied her, but made her sit at the dinette in the cabin while he piloted the boat towards Marco Island.

Flynn docked at a marina on Marco Island during the early morning hours to grab provisions, fuel up and get a meal. Miller's Hideaway Marina had everything he needed—a fueling station, dockside bistro and even several well-appointed motel rooms where he had stayed on previous occasions. The bistro had dockside seating that overlooked the inner coastal waterway. They had reached the refueling station while it was preparing to open and after a short discussion with the attendant, Flynn left the boat tied there while they dined. He had vetoed eating on the outdoor deck in favor of a more controlled environment inside the small dining room—just a half dozen tables and a small bar.

He would also invite her to a nice meal, drinks and then who knows—perhaps a quick trip to one of the marina's motel rooms for a little slap and tickle. Hell, she was still a good-looking woman—although Flynn usually preferred them younger—desperation can be a force multiplier.

Ann hadn't acted up until they had eaten. She had made sure to get plenty of protein down her throat—a ten ounce New York Strip with a couple of crab legs. She barely touched her wine, claiming a sour stomach that in retrospection should have alerted Flynn that she was up to something.

Ann had a plan of sorts—she was going to make a scene—douse him with wine, kick him in the balls—whatever it took and then run like hell for help. She wanted a glass of wine to calm her nerves, but drank water instead.

Flynn had eaten ravenously. He started with shrimp cocktail, which was followed by a Caesar salad and a twenty ounce ribeye. By the time dessert was ordered, Key Lime Pie for him, coffee for her, Ann figured it might be time to execute her plan.

The coffee arrived piping hot. The waiter filled her cup and before Flynn could react, she flung it into his face. Flynn screamed out in pain, but the scream was largely reactionary as in her rush, she had missed most of his head—the mass of airborne coffee had splashed harmlessly on the wall, while Flynn launched himself on an intercept course to catch his fleeing captive. He thought something like this might be in the making so he had closed his check immediately after they had ordered dessert.

He grabbed her arm as she reached the slatted wooden door sporting a porthole shaped window. He let her get outside and then flung her into the door, causing it to slam closed. He pulled her pistol from his pocket and pressed the barrel into her ribs. "I'll shoot you right here, bitch."

"I doubt that, I'm your hostage—you need me alive," said Ann. She felt she had already lost.

Flynn brought his mouth closer. She could feel his hot malodorous breath on her cheek. "Okay bitch, how about I go back inside and put a bullet into our waiter's forehead. You know the newly married young kid you seemed to like so much."

The door was pushed open. The waiter stuck his head through the door and regarded them both, "Folks is everything all right?"

"Sure Mike, everything is just fine," said Flynn reassuringly.

"It's Matt actually and I need to hear it from the lady."

Flynn twisted the muzzle into her ribs to insure she understood the bullet's proximity. "I'm fine Matt—it was just a lover's quarrel." The thought of being Flynn's lover suddenly appeared in Ann's mind causing her to partially retch. Flynn smiled and nodded in agreement. There would be nothing left to do but police up his hostage, mutter an apology to the waiter with a folded twenty in his hand and depart the area.

After he taped her up, he pulled his cellphone from the pocket of his shorts, searched through his list of recent calls and pressed send. He waited for Char to pick up. "Char, old buddy, how you doing? Shut up and listen. I have someone here who wants to talk to you."

Flynn held the phone up to Ann's mouth and looked at her. She stared at him and said nothing. He pulled the phone away and spoke into it. "She's being quiet right now—which is surprising for a woman. I just want you to know I have Ann here. If you want me to prove it I suppose I can burn her with a match to get her to cry out or something." He smiled at Ann while he said it.

"Give me the phone, asshole," said Ann.

"Excuse me Char, it seems the lady has decided she wants to talk to you after all." Flynn held the cellphone to her mouth.

She spoke quick and loud as she was sure he would stop her. "Char, we are in Marco Island on a Mainship 30…"

Flynn pulled the phone away and brought it up to his ear. "We were just leaving. Involve the police and I'll throw Ann into the gulf with as much ballast as I can find. But not before I have some fun with her. You read me old son?" said Flynn. He listened for a moment and then spoke, "Just let me clear up some financial obligations to Kelley and everyone can walk away happy from this deal—some of us more happy than others. But, go to the cops, and I can assure you that Ann will die."

She felt her heart sink and she sobbed openly before chastising herself—*if I'm going to act like such a coward I should probably just wait until we get into deep water and jump overboard. No sir. I'm going do everything I can to spoil this party—even if I have to throw a turd in the punch bowl to do it, thought* Ann.

Chapter Twenty-eight – Carla

Eddie had cooked his and Carla's favorite meal—a large rack of baby back ribs he bought at Publix on sale. He had seasoned them with a rub he had developed through years of trial and error, and smoked them over indirect heat of apple wood chips until the meat was in danger of falling off the bone. He had roasted some potatoes on the grill with garlic and cheese and made coleslaw from red cabbage, carrots, pineapple and plain yogurt. He had a ready supply of beer—Corona for him and Corona Light for her.

They had spent most of Carla's modest fortune restoring and updating their tugboat. It was of World War Two vintage, but had been mothballed and then overhauled to serve in Vietnam. Whoever said a boat was a hole in the water into which you poured money was not lying. So far, they had sunk over a half-million dollars into the restoration, with the end barely in sight.

She was forced to take a job as a paralegal for a law firm that practiced criminal defense. It was stressful work and the clientele was often disreputable, but wealthy enough to hire a mouthpiece to keep them out of jail.

She reported to the senior partner—a not unattractive, distinguished looking attorney, who was also a lecherous serial womanizer. He had taken a couple of halfhearted passes at Carla when she was first hired, but after discretely rebuffing them, he upped the ante to a full court press by calling her into his office and trying to force himself on her. Bad mistake. She waited until the appropriate moment when his pants were down and kneed him in the balls—since then, things had calmed down and he had even managed to display the requisite amount of professional decorum around her. He was still a notorious slave driver and kept Carla late during an evening when Eddie would be working miracles with the smoker.

So, she was in a rush to sit in their outdoor lounge, drink a cold one and watch the sunset. She parked their ancient Jeep Wagoneer in the marina's resident parking slot, and hurried down the weathered wooden boardwalk that divided rows of boat berths on either side.

There were numerous other residents on the walk, some just pulling into a berth for the evening after a day spent fishing or sailing. She greeted a few people she knew to be long-term residents when a tall angular figure caught her eye at the wharf where her tug was moored. There was something strangely familiar about the man. He walked purposely forward and she noticed a slight limp in his left leg.

Sonofabitch, I can't believe it's him, she thought.

He strode forward engrossed in a cellular call and didn't notice her approach. She wondered what she would do if she would ever meet the man who had left her for dead because she had jilted him for a better man—well, at least a wealthier one. She needed calmer waters after the tumultuous sea that was Char Blackfox.

He continued to advance and Carla wasn't sure he would notice her. Her heart was beating a furious and staccato rhythm in her chest. He walked towards her, thoroughly absorbed in a heated conversation and oblivious to her presence. She could have easily walked past, but she stopped in midstride and then stepped in front of him. He finally noticed her and stopped before colliding. Char looked down at her and started to smile as Carla placed one leg behind him, pushed both arms into his chest with as much strength as she could muster and propelled Char off the dock and into the water.

"Remember me, asshole?" She didn't wait for an answer, but broke into a run that didn't end until she reached the gangplank of the *Fond Memories*.

She ran to the stern to find Eddie at the guardrail watching Char swim towards a ladder at the far end of the row of berths. Someone tossed in a circular life saver—possibly as a joke, which Char promptly ignored. Eddie turned to look at her, "I probably should have told you about him."

"Ya think?" said Carla.

"I figured you'd find out soon enough."

Carla put her hands on her hips. Eddie knew that stance well—she wanted answers. "What the hell is he doing here?"

"He hired me for a job. Ten grand upfront. He was delivering it," said Eddie.

"Why the hell would you offer that criminal your services?" said Carla.

"He's been pardoned—he's not a criminal anymore. At least in the eyes of the law."

She shook her head as if not believing the words coming out of her husband's mouth. "He sure the hell is as far as I'm concerned."

"We need money honey—otherwise we'll soon be sharing a studio apartment in Pinellas Park."

"Just keep him away from me," said Carla.

And you from him, thought Eddie. "Can I get you a drink my dear?"

"Yes dear—I would love a shot of Don Julio and a Corona Light. Why not join me?"

It's gonna be one of those nights, thought Eddie.

Chapter Twenty-nine - IRB

"Who is it?" asked the disembodied female voice emanating from the intercom.

Kelley had given this lots of thought. Who do you inexplicably open your door for? Cops? Not necessarily—especially in her current circumstances. He was sure he would get a referral to her attorney. No, in her present circumstances she would be receiving lots of correspondence about her late husband's estate.

Kelley had seen the FedEx courier parked at strip mall in St. Pete—eating a late lunch at a Jersey Mike's. He waited at the rear of the FedEx van for the guy to finish his submarine sandwich and clubbed him on the back of his head when he opened the door. He must have hit him too hard as he smelled shit when he pushed the body into the back. He drove a short distance towards the beach, but the smell became intolerable.

He pulled off into the mangroves that bracketed the inlet near the VA Hospital, removed the man's shirt–forgoing his shit-stained pants and disposed of the body in the tall vegetation. It would soon be discovered by the birds, which would draw in the alligators and eventually the police, but by that time he would be happily ensconced in Victoria's high-priced condominium by the sea. He hadn't met her—but, according to Flynn she was a hot piece of ass. He would have plenty of time alone with her to sample her wares, before Flynn was due to arrive.

"FedEx," said Kelley, hoping he had stifled his accent enough to add the proper amount of plausibility to the ploy.

"Stand in front of the camera," said a female voice.

Kelley took a step forward to better align the logo on his shirt with the camera lens and expose the cardboard envelope addressed to someone else. He waited a moment—thinking perhaps that he had blown it, when he heard the reassuring electronic buzz of the door lock being released. *Easy peezy,* thought Kelley.

He knew the subterfuge would fail once the door was open and she got a better look at his work books and jeans, so the moment after he rang the doorbell, it opened a crack and he pushed his way in. She started to yell, but he punched her in the stomach causing her to double over and collapse.

"The bill collector is here," said Kelley—employing his normal baritone Irish brogue. "I'll take the first payment out in trade."

She awoke on the bed with Kelley on top of her. She was naked and vulnerable. She tried to scream, but he had taped her mouth shut. She screamed anyway.

***

Flynn had piloted the boat throughout the night and had reached Indian Rocks Beach a little bit before sunrise. He watched the false dawn and felt pessimistic—there were too many chess pieces on the table moving against him. Still, maybe he could have Vicky pay off Kelley and get rid of him. He was kidding himself to think the madman would just take his lump of flesh and go away. But that was exactly what he would propose.

He steered the boat through John's Pass and into Boca Ciega Bay and then turned north in the gulf inner coastal waterway. Vicky's condo was a pink-colored, eight unit high rise with expansive views of the gulf and the mainland. It sat at the end of a tear shaped landmass that projected out into the waterway

He passed the expansive Bay Pines Veterans Complex off his starboard side, but missed seeing Char's yacht docked just a few hundred yards away. It would be doubtful he would have recognized it in the still twilight of the early morning.

Vicky's condo complex had twelve boat slips and Flynn could hardly wait to tie up Kelley's boat, run upstairs to envelop himself into the soft feminine folds of Vicky's sumptuous body. He licked his lips in anticipation as he passed under the Tom Stuart Causeway. There was still the matter of how he would transport a tied up Ann into the building. There were several four-wheeled push carts that the complex owned to allow boat owners to transport gear between condo and boat. He just needed some type of sack to stick her in, and he would be able to sneak her into the building.

A short time later he tied up at the dock and ran to the intercom. He buzzed. "It's Flynn, let me in." The lock clicked open and Flynn ran past the bank of three elevators in favor of running up the eight flights of stairs.

He rang the doorbell, and Kelley answered. His shirt was open, exposing a topographical map of various scars covering his torso. "So how is she?" asked Flynn.

"You mean how was she? As good as you said she would be," said Kelley.

Bastard! thought Flynn. *If given the chance, I would kill this miserable Mick.*

"She's sleeping now. She was upset at the likes of me having a go at her, so I shot her up with a little H to quiet her down."

Flynn fought the urge to shoot the son of a bitch where he stood. When this was over, it might just do that—in the meantime, he would play nice. "Well then I guess we aren't going to be talking with her lawyers about getting her husband's assets freed up."

"She'll be fine in a few hours. Maybe we can still do some business," said Kelley.

Flynn shook his head. "It'll be too late in the day and this place is known. It's better if we relocate tomorrow morning."

"Where to?" asked Kelley.

"Every heard of Steinhatchee?"

"No."

"Neither has anyone else. It's a four hour drive north of here. I inherited a fishing camp there." Flynn walked into the bedroom and checked to ensure that Vicky was breathing. She was naked beneath the sheets—softly snoring.

He found the linen closet outside the bathroom and rummaged through it until he found an old mattress cover—it was translucent, and shaped like an oversized body bag, and it would be close to perfect for concealing the petite female. He grabbed the cover and headed to the door. "Come on—give me a hand."

Chapter Thirty – Wet Char

Earl regarded Char in disbelief as he clumsily hopped on to the stern of the *Good as Gold*, wearing soaking wet clothing and carrying his deck shoes. Earl was reclining on a chaise lounge, drinking an oil can sized Fosters while catching the sunset. "What the hell happened to you?" he asked.

"An old girlfriend appears to be a bit pissed off at me," said Char.

Earl shook his head, "Every women you've ever been with appears to hate you. What's your secret?"

Char regarded him with an amused look. "That's funny coming from a man whose longest relationship is with a wispy long haired lad named Johnnie."

Earl looked pissed for a moment and then laughed, "Touché. What say, I get you a towel and a fresh set of cloths, so you can dry off and change without fucking up my nice clean salon."

"Yeah and after that, I want you to go over to that tugboat in front of us and tell the owner I want to see him in an hour for an initial meeting. Assure him that it has nothing to do with his wife pushing me into the water."

Earl nodded and disappeared into the cabin. Char stripped down to his shorts, sat down on the other chaise lounge and fished another oil can out of the cooler. He popped the top, took a big gulp and didn't put it down until he emptied it.

Carla had looked good for a women who was just three years his junior. He remembered that last time he saw her was when he was robbing the *Star of Tampa* as it sat in the gulf about thirty miles off shore. She had left him for the owner of that floating casino and he had exacted his revenge—robbing the patrons and stealing what they thought at the time was a million dollars in gold. One of the robbers had shot the owner when he tried to thwart the robbery. Char and the other thieves escaped in a yacht they had borrowed—without the owner's knowledge—and headed for land. A rogue wave on the leading edge of a hurricane hit the casino boat as they got underway and it went down with all hands, sans Carla. Char had no idea how she saved herself, except for the fact that Carla Rogers had always been a survivor.

The same huge wave hit the robber's boat as they landed and beached it. One of the robbers, a friend named Jimmy O'Brien, buried the gold moments before he was captured. The loot sat unmolested for thirty years until Jimmy, Char, and Michael returned to recover it. Char drank the last dregs of the beer as Earl returned with a dry set of clothing.

"Nice, you took my beer while I'm doing you a solid," said Earl.

Char picked up his wet shorts from the deck, withdrew his wallet and handed Earl a soggy five dollar bill. "There, we're even. Now go tell Eddie I want to see him."

"Sure thing boss." Earl hopped off the stern and trotted towards the *Fond Memories.* Char reached into the cooler and took the last oil can. He popped the top and reclined on the chaise lounge. *Thirty years after the robbery the guy who had bankrolled the job, an exiled Mafia capo from Providence, had sat lying in wait for them to return and dig up the gold. This time however, Michael, a newly separated Marine Force Recon officer, had tipped the odds in their favor. Eddie had investigated the case and that led to investigating Carla. Interesting the way the world turns sometimes*, thought Char.

Earl came back down the dock. "He said he'd meet you here in two hours. I'm meeting Johnnie at the Bamboo for happy hour. I'll catch you later." Char nodded. He was soon asleep on the lounge chair, snoring quietly and dreaming of Carla. He dreamed she was being sucked down by the undertow of a ship— presumably the *Star of Tampa* and he was trying to save her, but try as he might, he could not reach her hand. He watched helplessly as she plummeted toward the bottom of the gulf. He must have been talking in his sleep as he awoke to find Michael shaking him.

"You were hollering in your sleep. It was starting to annoy the neighbors," said Michael.

"Bad dream. What time is it?" asked Char.

"Quarter of eight. Want some dinner?"

"Not right now—I'm expecting Eddie Doyle any minute. I invited him over so we could sketch out a plan."

"This should be interesting—mind if I sit in?" asked Michael.

"I insist—you are integral to the conversation," said Char. "It shouldn't take that long—we can swing over to Harold Seltzer's for some prime rib after we're done."

"Sounds like my kind of warning order," said Michael. "I just hope he gets here soon—I could eat the ass out of a goat."

"Well now, I'd hate to keep the goat waiting. "Caught by surprise—a flutter of adrenaline coursed into Michael's system. He turned around unsure what to expect, only to find a middle-aged man of medium height wearing a dark linen shirt over light cotton pants and deck shoes smiling at him from the dock.

Char sat up in the lounge chair, "Eddie Doyle?"

"One and the same."

Char gave him a beckoning wave. "Come on aboard. We've got lots to talk about."

Eddie entered the spacious main salon and took in the luxurious surroundings—the long teak dining table, corner sofa unit and matching lounge chairs of white glove leather and whistled. "This is Sally's boat correct?"

"Was would be the operative word," said Char.

"Gangster plush," said Eddie.

"I'd like to think I've added a few touches here and there," said Char.

"Yeah, we cleaned up the pools of blood," said Michael.

Char pointed towards one of the lounge chairs "Have a seat. Want a drink?"

Eddie selected the other lounge chair and slowly sank into its deep recesses—he smiled at the surprising level of comfort it provided. "No thanks, I was working on a few Coronas back on my boat"—*not to mention a shot of Patron,* thought Eddie. "I'd like to keep what's left of my wits about me."

"Fair enough. So, should we run down the situation for you?" asked Char.

"There's a little matter of a retainer," said Eddie.

"Right, I was coming over to pay you when Carla intercepted me." Char walked over to the bar, picked up two stacks of bills and tossed them to Eddie. "It's still a little damp."

"No bother—damp money still spends." Eddie gave each bundle a cursory inspection and placed them on the arm of the chair. "So tell me Char, why do you need my services?"

"My ex-wife has been kidnapped by two maniacs, and they'll kill her if I go to the FBI."

Eddie looked puzzled—thinking maybe he hadn't heard Char correctly. *Who cares about their ex-wife?* thought Eddie. "Isn't that like the old joke about your lawyer going over a cliff in your Ferrari?" he asked.

"There are no mixed feelings about this, dickhead," said Michael. "One of these assholes killed my fiancée, shot me, and is holding my mother hostage—we want them dead."

"Settle down son," said Char.

Eddie looked at both men. "Perhaps you guys should start

from the beginning—don't leave anything out."

Michael went behind the bar and poured himself a bourbon—neat. He was going to need this to steel his nerves and keep him from breaking down. "I met my fiancée in Bogota, after sorting out a nasty piece of business in Venezuela," said Michael.

"I heard," said Eddie.

Michael regarded the detective with a skeptical look, "You heard? It was classified TS/SCI."

"A detective I used to work with, Marilyn Ramirez, is dating a Marine from MARSOC."

"I guess he upgraded her clearance," said Michael.

"Yeah, in a manner of speaking," said Eddie. He paused for a moment as if considering something. "It just occurred to me that you both know Marilyn—or at least you've been acquainted."

Char had to think for a moment and then it occurred to him—Marilyn was the young female cop who had surprised them four years ago. They returned to the park to retrieve gold that had been looted from *Star of Tampa* and hidden by Jimmy O'Brien years before. She had gotten the drop on the four thieves and would have put an end to their raid—had Jimmy not grabbed her ankles and pulled her legs out from underneath her.

"Fort Desoto?" asked Char.

"One and the same," said Eddie.

"If it makes you feel any better, the guy who tripped her is dead."

"It does," said Eddie. "But, that's ancient history. Whatever maneuver you pulled off in Venezuela got you pardoned and I'm just here to do a piece of business, so please continue."

Michael told the tale. He started at the late afternoon dinner that they had hosted in this very room. He told Eddie of the futile lifesaving efforts employed by Sofia, finding Kelley with a collapsed lung, their fatal trip to Fort Jefferson and then he passed the baton to Char. When he finished, talking, Michael looked at his watch—it was half past nine. Any hope of making a late seating at their favorite steak house was rapidly diminishing.

Eddie considered his words for a moment—wanting to avoid garnering another outburst from the younger man, who obviously still grief-stricken over the death of his fiancée. "It sounds like both these fuckers are past their sell-by date."

"Some men just want to watch the world burn," said Char.

Michael stared at Char, trying to recall where he had heard that line. "Who said that?"

"Alfred. You know—Alfred on Batman."

Michael let out a short derisive snort, "So now we're quoting cartoons?"

"Actually, it was the movie I watched last night—couldn't sleep, but if the shoe fits..." said Char.

Michael pantomimed shoving something with an abrupt motion of his hand. "Stick it up the motherfucker's ass?"

"First light it on fire—then stick it up his ass and watch him burn," said Char.

"For some people at some point—either a judge, a jury or some ad hoc group says your shit's over—you're too fucked up—we're going to have to kill you," said Eddie.

"Judges are for people with shitty parents and a bullet is the only judge these fuckers are going to get," said Char.

"Spoken like a member of that ad hoc group," said Eddie. "What's the guy's name?"

"Nicky Flynn is the charter boat captain. The one who killed Sofia and shot me calls himself Ken Q. Kelley," replied Michael.

"What's the 'Q' stand for?" asked Eddie.

"Fuck if I know," replied Michael.

Eddie sat forward in his seat. "Son of a bitch! In '87 I investigated three murders that that occurred on Treasure Island. One was a double homicide of a paddle boarding couple taken out by one shot, and the other was of a guy shot through a pillow with a hollow point slug from a .38 special. We named the killer the PBK which stood for Paddle Board Killer."

Michael stared at him. He felt a cold flood of adrenaline course through his system. "How do you know it was the same killer?"

"The apartment where we found the corpse was registered to one Ken Kelley. We found no identification on the body or in the apartment. The guy was a petty criminal with a few priors—mostly for dealing in stolen property."

"So, whoever this guy is—it isn't Ken Q. Kelley," said Char.

"Better still—whoever this guy is, he's already wanted for a triple homicide. The woman who was killed had a husband who disappeared at the same time. The guy used a different pseudonym on the lease and their marriage license—he was basically a ghost. We interviewed various associates of his wife and a few mentioned that he was rumored to be a member of the IRA or a splinter group.

One of them told us that he was sent here to buy guns. We recovered a few prints in the apartment. It's a long shot after all these years, but it's enough to get the Pinellas County Sheriff's department involved," said Eddie.

Char smiled. He was beginning to think that ten grand was a wise investment. "What about the fact that he killed Sofia and shot my son?"

"Bird in the hand," said Eddie cryptically. "You have two hostile Feds on your tail who would rather seize your yacht than cooperate in getting an arrest warrant. Not to mention the fact that it would be a federal indictment—which is harder to get. The alternative is to dust off an old arrest warrant in the murder of the actual Ken Q. Kelley, a woman named Kiley Reilly and an Australian known as Ricky Barnett.

Char was amazed by Eddie's eidetic memory. "So, where do we start?"

Eddie locked eyes with both men. "Right now these scumbags are trying to figure out how to milk enough money out of the lady who hired them to make it worth their while. To do that, they need a safe place to hunker down while they liquidate her husband's assets. We go in early tomorrow morning—with SWAT and catch them with their pants down."

"We can't go to the police or they kill mom," said Michael.

"Most criminals are motivated by a few things—greed, lust, revenge, feeling no pain—that about covers it. They don't have a lot of self-discipline. Over time, they tend to fuck up—get drunk, do some drugs and want to sleep."

"Yeah, Kelley or whatever his name is has a penchant for morphine," said Michael.

"Great—we'll swoop in while he's nodding." Eddie leapt to his feet. "I'll take that drink now—tequila, neat."

"I thought you didn't want to cloud your thinking," said Char.

Eddie clasped his hands conspiratorially. "Done thinking—so let's get to drinking—we're in for an early morning wake-up call."

Michael withdrew a short brown bottle from beneath the bar and poured three fingers of the liquid into a short glass.

Eddie picked up the glass and smelled the contents—he nodded approvingly. He swallowed the shot and placed the glass back on the bar top. "I got a call to make, but before I do tell me more about this condo in Indian Rocks Beach."

Eddie told them to stand by for a call and departed back to the *Fond Memories*. Carla had gone to bed, still a bit piqued that Eddie had taken a job from an old adversary. He went to the grotto on the back deck, opened a can of Corona, took a seat on a bar stool and pulled out his smartphone.

"What was it that Kojak used to say—who loves you baby?" said Eddie.

"Jeez, Eddie, who the hell is Kojak?" asked Marilyn. She had drifted off to sleep after her boyfriend had left—dawn came early for MARSOC, often before daylight. He had knocked one out of the park, they had a quick dinner of pizza and a couple of beers and then there was an encore. She looked at the clock radio—it was ten seventeen.

"Never mind kid, how long would it take to get a no knock warrant at this time of night?"

"Longer than you've got. I wake a judge now and it better be good or the sheriff will call me in for a counseling session. "

"Is that like an ass-chewing?" asked Eddie.

"Yeah, but with less curse words—the effect is the same."

"Oh, it's worth it kid—remember the Paddle Board Killer?"

"Just barely—I was in the third grade. I remember my mom wouldn't take us to the beach for a year."

"I think I've found him," said Eddie.

"I'll wake up Judge Garcia—I think he has a thing for me."

"What is he like, eighty years old?" asked Eddie. "It might be a pleasant respite from the twenty-five year old Raider currently jumping your bones."

"Two words—yuck and ick!" said Marilyn.

"That's three words—ah, the things Judge Garcia probably knows about pleasing a woman."

"He's long forgotten," said Marilyn. "So, what makes you think you've got the PBK?"

Eddie ran it down for her and Marilyn jotted down the highlights on a legal pad she kept next to the bed when she slept. She thought he would have enough to at least get the judge to sign off on the warrant. He told her to call if she got it approved and to call Captain Trevino from the Pinellas County SWAT.

"If things go as planned, we'll be breaking down a door and taking down one of my last open cases," said Eddie.

"Yeah, Eddie as long as it's all about you." Marilyn ended the call. She picked up her clothing from the floor, pulled on her shorts and slipped a too large MARSOC t-shit over her head. She padded into the kitchen to make some coffee—she doubted she would be getting back to sleep anytime soon. *Eddie should know better*, she thought, *who was it that said everyone has a plan until you punch them in the mouth?*

Chapter Thirty-one - Steinhatchee

The door was reinforced against hurricane strength winds, but it didn't stand a chance against the thirty pound tactical entry tool employed by a sheriff's department deputy. He spent every free moment either in the weight room or in a judo dojo and took every door that stood against him as a personal affront. The door lock shattered and fell to the transom and the door flew inward.

The six deputies spread out in a one hundred eighty degree circle around the entry point, shouted "Clear!" when they found no one and rushed into the two bedrooms to do the same. The whole operation took less than a minute.

Per Eddie's guidance, Char and Michael stayed away from the site until told to move up. This was standard operating procedure—no civilians in a law enforcement operations area.

There was also the uncomfortable fact that both Char and Michael had been the suspect of just such an operation four years previous.

Cops, especially SWAT operators, had notorious short tempers and one of them might want some payback. Eddie needn't have worried—word had filtered out of the raid Michael had led against a terrorist group armed with an Iranian electromagnetic pulse tipped ICBM. Trevino, a former Army Ranger, had nodded at Michael and Char when they entered the condominium. That was a ringing endorsement as far as Eddie was concerned—he wished Trevino gave him that much respect.

He approached Eddie and regarded him while shaking his head from side to side, "Well, it looks like you struck out again, Doyle."

"Looks like it. Mind if we look around?" asked Eddie.

"Knock yourself out. I need to leave a man behind until the locksmith gets here, but have at it," said Trevino. He stopped in front of Michael on the way out the door. "I heard about Venezuela—good job. Sorry to hear about your fiancée—stay strong."

Michael nodded, afraid that his voice would crack if he tried to speak.

"Looks like you dodged a couple of bullets," said Eddie.

"How so?" asked Michael.

"It appears Trevino is letting bygones stay gone and the other member of your nascent fan club is chasing stiffs in the mangroves this morning. Marilyn Ramirez was supposed to be in on this raid, but a kayaker spotted a body floating in the mangroves off of Bay Pines this morning, and she's conducting the investigation," said Eddie.

"So, what now?" asked Michael.

"We look around—try and get a clue as to where they've gone."

Char opened the sliders to the wrap around balcony and took in the expansive view of the sea. The rising sun was still shaded by the building casting long shadows on the tranquil waters of the gulf. He walked around the side and viewed the boats tied up to the rear of the complex. He studied the row of boats for a moment to be sure and then walked back into the living room. "His boat is tied up out back in the canal," said Char.

"Okay, so they probably didn't go by boat. Go have a look up close just to be sure. I'll call the management company to see what kind of car is registered to this condo and what parking space it's assigned," said Eddie.

Michael walked into the open kitchen and looked at the granite countertops. The condo was relatively new—probably built for the top of the market as the features were well-made. All stainless steel appliances, including a large Wolf four burner gas stove that was probably wasted on an ex-stripper turned trophy wife. There was a granite-topped island in the center of the kitchen on which sat three objects—a ceramic beer stein, a framed photograph, and a key.

"Hey Eddie, I think I've found something," said Michael. He picked up the photograph and examined it. It was yellowed with age and faded. A man stood in front of a ridiculous looking car. It was wider than a normal car, the edges were rounded and there were expansive areas of glass. There was a gold-colored plate at the base of the frame that read

"January 5, 1975, William Dennison takes delivery of the new American Motors Corporation Pacer."

"What do you make of this?" asked Michael.

Eddie picked up each of the objects and then turned to Michael. "Your mother left us a clue—I think it means they've gone to Steinhatchee."

"How the hell did you figure that out?" asked Michael.

"Easy, the AMC Pacer was a hatchback," said Eddie. He pointed to each of the three objects; "stein, hatch, key."

Michael smiled. "How long does it take you to do the Jumble?"

***

When word reached her of Harold's death she waited as long as she could before breaking down and buying a new silver Jaguar XJ, a turbocharged luxury car with a final price of just under a hundred thousand dollars. She now sat in the back seat, next to a man who had raped her and then shot her up with something that had made her sick and then caused her to pass out. She was still feeling lethargic from the after effect of the drug and secretly longed for another dose to keep her from feeling her plans had exploded in her face.

Kelley had survived in the Real IRA because he had grown eyes in the back of his head. Twice they had tried to off him in prison and he prevailed both times. He hadn't liked the condo. It was on a high floor and there was basically two ways out—the elevators and the stairs. Both could be easily secured by the police. It was also known that Vicky was in residence there. It was only a matter of time before they were found out. It was best to keep moving until they could pay him off—he had now settled on a figure of two million dollars.

Flynn drove the car. He was motoring north up Route 19 in the light traffic of the early morning heading through long uninhabited rural stretches of Citrus County. The route was dotted with car dealerships, swamp land, and small towns. Flynn planned to follow the route until he reached the turn off for Route 51, which would take him to his family's fishing lodge on the Steinhatchee River. The resort was the oldest on the river, being built with a VA loan by his father in the aftermath of World War Two.

The old man had built a main lodge with a dormitory for single fishermen and ten small rustic cabins for families. It had thrived at first, as it was the only place on the river. Slowly, modernity crept into the rural area. Better, more comfortable lodges were built that siphoned off business from Flynn's Angler's Camp. Eventually, all that was left were the regulars—those too poor or too set in their ways to seek better accommodations. Ultimately, even these fishermen stopped coming, and the lodge was forced to shut down.

His father passed at the turn of the millennium, and Nicky inherited the lodge. Flynn entertained ideas of reopening a refurbished facility, but the truth was that most of the buildings were beyond saving. Termites flourished unchecked in the untreated wood structures, but the main lodge was built of block construction and was still habitable.

The facility was within the river's floodplain and would occasionally be inundated with river water. The moribund complex was overgrown with dense fan palms, red banana leaf, river birch, and tropical palm trees. Creeping ivy threatened to devour several of the cabins. At dawn and dusk, ground fog hovered along the low-lying river frontage giving the complex a foreboding aura.

Flynn had done the best he could to keep the main building in a good state of repairs, but infrequent visits, an oppressive subtropical climate, and the host of opportunistic rodents made this an uphill battle. He hired a couple of caretakers to further arrest the process, but he suspected the two brothers had ulterior motives.

Josiah and Jairus Gibson were both rail thin, jittery, and had missing teeth. What teeth they had were green and rotten. But, they worked cheap and that was definitely a consideration. He allowed them to live there rent free, store their boats and only paid them $400 a month. He heard that they had done time for cooking meth and threatened them with immediate termination should he discover them doing so, but he wasn't there enough to give the threat any more teeth than the brothers had in their head.

It was a little after five a.m. by the time they arrived in Steinhatchee. Flynn pulled off Route 51 onto an overgrown dirt road that lead to his camp. He got to the gate and was annoyed to find it chained shut. The chain was a new touch—the last time he was here the gate was secured by a loop of wire.

He hit the horn for several long blasts causing Vicky to cover her ears and hunker down in her seat. "Stop it, you're hurting my ears." She had felt this whole scenario had gotten badly out of control and she vainly tried to gain some of it back. She had Flynn wrapped around her little finger when she was allowing him to slip it to her in Key West.

Now that the deed was done, she should be more in control as she didn't really need him for anything. Kelley forcing himself on her didn't bother her as much as Flynn probably thought it did— she had to have sex with lots of loathsome men on her rise out of the sleazy backroom of Tattle Tales Strip Club to the coveted place beside a wealthy local businessman. She counted Harold among those repugnant characters.

Now, the Irish asshole wanted more money as he knew she was loaded. A nice fat insurance policy that offered double indemnity for accidental death and the biggest dealership outside of Birmingham made her worth conservatively about twenty million dollars—so she supposed she could part with a couple hundred thousand, but that's where she would draw the line. She would contact her lawyer in Birmingham and get him to arrange a short-term loan to tie her over until the death benefits were paid—a half million should be enough.

She supposed she might be able to get Flynn to kill Kelley and when that was done, she would find a way to get rid of Flynn. After that, she could sell the dealership and head to the South of France or wherever newly rich 27-year-old women would want to hang out. When she burned through her money, she would just look for another rich old man.

Vicky hadn't concerned herself with the identity of the other woman in the car, but picked up from the way they treated her that she was not there by choice.

Flynn waited outside the car. An early morning mist hung close to the ground, obscuring the ramshackle buildings and reflecting halos of light off several high intensity lamps strategically located around the property's perimeter. It would be a gross understatement to describe the place as gloomy.

A light in the main building clicked on and a short time later a flashlight illuminated on the porch. A lone figure slowly shuffled down the dirt road to the gate. He walked beneath one of the lights and Flynn saw that he was armed with a shotgun. The figure approached within ten feet to the gate, stopped and pointed the shotgun and light at Flynn. "Who's there?"

"It's Nicky Flynn. Which one are you?"

"Josiah. Jairus is off taking care of some business."

At this time of night? Must have a paper route, thought Flynn.

Josiah leaned the shotgun against the gate, wrestled with the lock for a moment, unlocked it and pushed it open. Flynn got back into the sedan, slowly pulled into the complex and parked in front of the main building.

Kelley looked at the ramshackle cabins, one with a collapsed roof, and another whose walls had fallen in and exhaled loudly, "Shit, what a fucking dump! Tell me it has a telephone."

"Yeah, we even have cable TV and internet access. All via satellite."

"Flynn, I'm hungry," said Vicky.

"Don't worry, Baby, I'll send one of the caretakers out food shopping."

Flynn placed the Jag into park and the locks automatically popped open. Ann didn't waste a second—she launched herself out of the back seat and broke into a run. In a panic, she ran back down the entrance road, instead of breaking for the woods or the river. Flynn slammed the shift lever into reverse and then into drive. He floored the Jag and the throaty V6 turbocharged engine roared into life—kicking up twin rooster tails of dirt as he pursued Ann. She panicked when she saw the car, assuming that Flynn was trying to run her over. He pulled along her and lowered the window— thinking he would threaten her with bodily harm. Instead, Kelley flung open the back door and hit her with it—the forward momentum of the car striking her back had force sufficient enough to throw Ann off her feet.

She hit her shoulder on the hard packed dirt road with an audible crack and she cried out in anguish. Something wasn't right—she couldn't move her arm. Flynn stopped the car and ran to her. "That was a stupid thing to do," he said. He gingerly helped her to her feet and into the back seat. She cradled her arm and stared at Kelley, "You son of a bitch."

"Do that again, and I'll kill you," said Kelley. Ann didn't doubt his veracity. Flynn skidded to a stop in front of the steep set of stairs that lead into the main lodge. Kelley jumped from the front seat and roughly pulled Ann from the vehicle, causing her to wince in pain. "Get up the stairs, bitch," said Kelley. She stumbled up the stairs and nearly fell, but Kelley none too gently grabbed her upper arm and near carried her up the steps.

They entered a surprisingly well maintained fishing lodge that hadn't been materially changed since it was originally furnished. The main room sported cedar plank walls giving way to high ceilings hosting several antique belt driven fans. The lobby was furnished with a collection of white painted wicker furniture with faded flowered cushions. Ann felt like she had stepped into a postcard from Florida in the 1940s.

Josiah had followed them into the lodge. He eyed Flynn apprehensively.

Flynn peeled off ten twenties from a roll he retrieved from his pocket. "Go to the Publix in Live Oak and get some supplies for the week—nothing fancy; bacon, eggs, burgers, bread, lunch meat some steaks and potatoes—enough for a couple of days. Take Vicky with you and get anything else she wants."

"Get me a bottle of bourbon and some Guinness," said Kelley.

Josiah looked at Flynn skeptically, but the man nodded his assent—a drunk Kelley could be useful or at least less harmful. "Call your brother and get him here, I want to hire some of his buddies for security for the next couple of days." Jairus had a gang they used for distribution and it would be easy enough to press them into service as security. One thing Flynn knew about Char Blackfox was the man didn't quit—there was considerable evidence to suggest the son was the same.

Vicky's lawyer would probably get to the office at nine and Birmingham was an hour behind them, so they would have a nice breakfast and then she would make the call. After that, it was a waiting game—dependent upon how liquid her assets were.

***

"We gave your way a try and it didn't work, now we do things our way," said Michael.

Earl had opened the weapons locker. It had grown exorbitantly since Venezuela. He had five 2 1/2 pound blocks of C4, a dozen fragmentation grenades, three M4 carbines, and one M32 multi-shot grenade launcher. He picked up his M4—it was tricked out with a Trijicon Advanced Combat Optical Gunsight that allowed Michael to gain a quick sight-picture and place accurate rounds on target—even in low light conditions and at maximum range.

The explosives were expendable items—they didn't account for them and the other weapons had been damaged during the mission and forgotten about by everyone but Char when they evacuated from the Venezuelan jungle. Those weapons and a host of others were laid out on a tarp laid down to protect the thick pile carpet of the main salon. Michael picked up the M4 carbine, slid the bolt open, and locked it to the rear. He examined the barrel for carbon, slid a loaded magazine into the magazine well, and released the bolt—causing it to chamber a round. "I'll take this, five magazines, and equal number of frag grenades. I'll also take a block of C4."

"Why do you need C4?" asked Eddie.

"There's no problem in the world that can't be solved through the proper use of high explosive—plus I like blowing shit up," said Michael.

"I'll stick with my Smith & Wesson Model 10." Eddie had used the same weapon since he was a CID agent. The .38 caliber, six-shot revolver was originally designed in 1899 and had been a military mainstay for much of that time. It was simple to operate, didn't kick much, and was easy to keep clean, but the common wisdom was that it lacked stopping power.

"We've got a spare M9 Beretta we could let you use, said Char, thinking that Eddie would be more comfortable with the military's standard sidearm. "We can hook you up with some hollow points, as well."

"I'll stick to what I'm used to. I'll take a couple of grenades, however. I like blowing shit up as well," said Eddie. Michael laughed.

"If it's our marriage you're talking about, I would say you're doing a fine job."

Both men looked towards the stern. Carla stood inside the glass slider silhouetted in the dock lights—her legs were spread shoulder-width apart and her fists were balled at her side. "Marilyn called me—what in the name of all that's holy are you doing with these criminals!"

"I've been hired to go after them," said Eddie.

"I'm not talking about them, I'm talking about this asshole," she said while pointing an accusatory finger at Char.

Eddie approached her tentatively and lowered the tone of his voice to a whisper. "Honey, we talked about this. I don't do this, we miss a loan payment, they seize the *Fond Memories,* and we're renting a one-bedroom apartment is South Saint Pete."

"I thought you said Pinellas Park?" said Carla.

"It's worse than I originally thought," said Eddie, trying to elicit a smile.

"Getting killed will also solve that problem, Eddie. You've still got your life insurance from the Sheriff's Department," said Carla. She hadn't meant it to sound callous, but she was past the point of caring. Every time Char Blackfox entered her life, pandemonium ensued, and he wrecked whatever chance she had for happiness—even this late in the game.

"There's a lot at stake here," said Char.

Carla locked eyes with Char as if she could incinerate him with her stare. "I'll get to you in a minute—for now, just do us all a favor and shut the fuck up!"

Char looked at Michael and grimaced—she hadn't changed that much. Michael shrugged his shoulders in response.

"Eddie what I'm telling you is that if you risk your life for this miscreant—you deserve what you get and if that's death, then so be it—I'll move on."

"Touching," said Eddie.

Carla didn't hesitate, "That's the same amount of consideration you are giving our marriage."

"Carla, if you find a quicker way of making thirty thousand dollars, then I'd like to hear it, otherwise, I have to do what I'm being paid to do," said Eddie. Char had recently sweetened the deal to keep Eddie engaged.

"So, it's all about the money?" asked Carla.

"No, but knowing your feelings about Char, I thought I'd leave any sentimentality out of it," said Eddie.

Carla shrugged and made an offhanded gesture towards the weapons. "What else is there to all of this?"

"They have my wife," said Char.

"And they killed my fiancée," said Michael.

Carla shook her head. "Why not let the police handle it?"

"In Taylor County? There is a Sheriff's Department, but no SWAT. Hell, they have to call out reserve deputies for anything bigger than a bar fight," said Eddie. He knew it was an exaggeration, but he was anxious to wrap up the discussion. They had to move fast if they were going to catch Flynn and Kelley with their pants around their ankles.

"Alright, it seems like you have your mind made up, and you know the stakes, but before I leave, I want a word with him," she said, pointing at Char.

Michael looked at Char with a feigned look of concern. "Fine, Eddie and I have some planning to do on the bridge." He signaled Eddie with a pointed thumb and the detective nodded. They both retreated up the short stairwell and Char heard the door click closed. He wondered if they would hear him if he screamed.

"Long time," said Carla.

"Funny, I felt like you and I just rekindled our relationship when you pushed me off the dock," said Char.

"Oh, I owed you that...and more, but I'll settle for that for now."

Char crossed his arms. "Okay, so tell me that I'm a scumbag

and that I ruined your life and all the rest of the things I imagined you'd say to me if given the chance."

"What happened, happened a long time ago. I lived through it—it made me stronger. It's just a part of my life now—whether I like it or not," said Carla.

Char nodded his head slightly. Just like the bullet that passed through his leg and the friends he had lost due to war and other misdeeds, those events haunted your thoughts long past their manifestation.

"I hated you for years for what you had done. But when everything is said and done, it all turned out for the best. I met the man of my life—trust me, Char, he's twice the man you are in every conceivable way," said Carla. He had expected worse, but she wasn't done. "It took me a long time to realize that. You're like a hurricane that blows through here every few years. It clears out all the weak buildings and trees—leaving only the strongest in its wake. I'm one of the survivors."

"I've changed," said Char quietly.

Carla regarded him for a moment and then nodded her head slightly, "I heard, but do people like you ever really change? Maybe you just directed your winds at another target."

He nodded. "Maybe so. I'll bring him back to you alive, Carla."

"You can't promise that," she said quietly. "But do yourself a favor, Char. Don't come back without him, because if you do," she carefully considered her words, "there'll be hell to pay." She turned, walked out through the open sliders to the stern and she was gone. He went to the bar and poured himself a short glass of Gentlemen Jack, brought the glass up in a toast. "There always is," he said before downing the contents.

Chapter Thirty-two - Sons of the South

Jairus was the leader of the two brothers. Whether it was because he was born three minutes before Josiah didn't really matter—he was a boss of men—albeit criminal men—his brother was merely a follower. Both men were tall and gangly, with almost identical receding hairlines, worn long in back. Their penchant to wear cut-off overalls and wife-beater t-shits, rotten teeth, and taciturn demeanor could have gotten them cast as heavies in a teen slasher movie—should one ever be filmed in Steinhatchee.

Both men had grown up as sons of the south—in that they believed in all the mythology perpetuated about the War Between the States. It went way beyond just having large Confederate battle flags attached to the roll bar in the back of Jairus' F250 Super Duty pickup.

When inebriated, on drugs, or liquor, Jarius openly targeted vehicles with northern plates for harassment up to and including running them off the road and beating up their occupants. Both brothers had done time for a particularly grisly beating of a bunch of drunken Spring Breakers who'd had the misfortune of canoeing in the river that passed where they had hidden his cooking operation.

Among the Spring Breakers were two teen girls who had originally accused the brothers of rape, but they had recanted sometime afterward—perhaps because they feared having to return to Taylor County for a trial. The brothers got off with just over six months served. Since then they had sworn off meth cooking and busied themselves with the importation and, to a lesser extent, growth of high quality marijuana.

Josiah stood at the antique cook stove in the voluminous kitchen. It was a gas stove that Flynn's father had bought in 1947—when the nascent tourism industry was just starting to awaken.

He cooked a dozen eggs and a pound of bacon—unsure whether it would be enough. The double swing doors to the kitchen flew open—Jairus burst into the kitchen looking like he hadn't slept for days. Actually it had been closer to a week, but that's what meth did for you. He used marijuana to alleviate some of the drug's detrimental effects with limited success.

"Where's Flynn?" asked Jairus.

Josiah motioned to the right with his spatula. "He's in the private dining room with some guests. You best straighten up before talking to him—he gets the idea you're high, he ain't gonna like it."

"You're right brother—give me some of that chow you

cooking—that will straighten me up," said Jarius.

"Can't do it bro—it's for the guests," replied Josiah.

It was too late. Jarius grabbed the spatula from his brother's hand, shoved him out of the way, and grabbed a plate from the stack Josiah had staged on a side board. He helped himself to at least half the eggs and an equal portion of bacon. He tossed the spatula on the stove and scurried out the doors to the lobby.

"Asshole," said Josiah. He began plating the remaining food and delivered it to the dining room. The long mahogany dining table had been damaged through neglect—water stains and vandal's etchings lay scattered on its surface. "Sorry, Boss. I'm gonna have to cook up some more food."

"What happened?" asked Flynn.

"Jarius."

"I see," said Flynn. "When he is done scarfing down my food, have him come see me in my office. You can serve the plates to the ladies."

"Feck that," said Kelley, "Let that bitch wait," he said pointing at Ann. Kelley grabbed a plate from Josiah and retreated towards the sideboard to gather cutlery. "Jaysus, I'm so hungry I'd eat the horse and run after the jockey."

Flynn took the other plate and handed it to Vicky. She looked at it and feigned interest. "Scrambled eggs and bacon?"

Flynn jutted his chin toward Ann "You don't want it, I'll feed it to her," said Flynn.

She grabbed her plate away from Flynn, "No, I'll take it," said Vicky. "You," she said pointing at Josiah, "get me some toast—

wheat if you have it, whatever if you don't."

"And bring me a beer," said Kelley.

Josiah cooked the additional meals, and they all settled in to eat. Kelley retrieved the Guinness from the cook, popped the top and painstakingly poured the black liquid into a tall glass. Once it settle, he sampled it and smacked his lips, "Ah, that's the stuff! I feel like I'm on holiday."

"Well, don't get carried away—we've got work to do," said Flynn.

"Right you are," said Kelley. He jumped to his feet and clapped his hands together. "Here is the deal—I had the chance to look over your properties when I passed through Enterprise looking for you. You're regular landed gentry you are. You got the house in the country, the condo at the beach and one of the largest dealerships in between Birmingham and Mobile." Kelley retrieved his glass of Guinness from the table and took a sip. "I was saving the best for last—a ten million dollar insurance policy on your dear departed husband. A death that I facilitated and during which I received grievous wounds. You also failed to mention your husband was a judo expert—which contributed to me being wounded. Therefore, my fee for performing this service has increased—I require one half of your insurance settlement or five million dollars."

Vicky looked at Flynn, but he made no motion to speak. She stared at him with wide eyes, imploring him to intervene and put this handyman in his place, but Flynn remained silent. "Flynn, say something," said Vicky.

Flynn smiled warmly and looked at Vicky. "I suggest you pay the man." Flynn had long given up on the thought of the two of them together. He had made a deal with Kelley for one half of his inflated fee—figuring that once the money was in hand it would be a race to see who double crossed who first. But, he had given it some thought and decided that two separate wires to two different bank accounts could provide him at least some level of surety. The last time he was in Belize, he had traveled to Belize City and opened up an offshore account.

During a brief period of time, Flynn had been able to market the fish camp as a corporate retreat. He had equipped the resort with rudimentary tools—a projector, screen, some speaker phones, a laser printer, and a couple of workstations. He received a few corporate bookings—mostly from small companies with avid fisherman among their senior leadership, but there was never any return business. All the equipment however, remained in place and ready to be placed into service to complete the various transactions.

Flynn pulled the speaker phone out of a cabinet under the sideboard and plugged it in. He pulled out the card from Vicky's lawyer and punched in the number.

"Morrison, Kirland and Associates," a soft, but business-like feminine voice emanated from the speakerphone.

"Carland Morrison, please," said Flynn. "Tell him Vicky Dennison is calling."

"One moment please." Flynn, pushed the mute button, walked over to Vicky, grabbed the back of her chair, and rolled her in front of the speakerphone.

"Just like we discussed Vicky— tell him that you are taking an extended vacation overseas and want the money sent to two accounts—I'll give him the numbers."

Kelley approached the woman and she visibly shuddered. "Do

like he says, lassie, and I'll be out of your long, dark hair in no time—screw up and we'll be bunk mates for a long time to come," said a smiling Ken Q. Kelley.

"This is Carland, Mrs. Dennison." They exchanged pleasantries and got down to the matter of the insurance payment. "The insurance company has thirty days to adjudicate the claim and another two weeks to issue a check. If there are issues surrounding the death, it can take longer," said Carland.

Vicky looked at Flynn who pantomimed a question. "What issues?" she asked.

"I'm not sure, Mrs. Dennison. I have an appointment this afternoon with two federal agents to discuss the death of your husband. Hopefully, they will clue me in." All color drained out of Vicky's face, she swallowed hard and looked at Flynn with pleading eyes. "Mrs. Dennison—are you there?"

She said nothing—Kelley kicked her under the table, causing her to cry out. "Ah-ouch! I'm still here."

"One other thing, Mrs. Dennison. I represented your husband and him alone. Against my advice, he decided not to enter into a prenuptial agreement between the two of you. I now feel that had I been more persuasive, he might still be alive. Good day to you."

The connection ended and was replaced by a dial tone. Flynn reached over and tapped the power button on the speakerphone. "So, now what?"

"Simple, we bleed off the five million from the dealership," said Kelley. Vicky began to sob loudly. She cried out and pounded the table. Kelley looked at Flynn, "Shut her up, or I will."

Flynn slowly got to his feet, walked over to Vicky, and touched her shoulder. "Come on sweetie, this isn't helping anything. I'll take you somewhere so you can rest."

"I've got a better idea," said Kelley, jumping to his feet. "I'll take her—I need a little relaxation."

"Noooo," said Vicky, "don't let him take me."

"Kelley, come on. Let's keep to the task at hand," said Flynn.

"Is that an offer, Flynn? Because I have a task for someone. So, who is it going to be?"

"Fine just have her back in a half-hour. We've got to call the GM at the dealership." Flynn placed both hands on the young women's slender shoulders and helped her to her feet. He spoke soothingly to her, "Vicky, go with Kelley. Pretend you're taking him to the Champagne Room. Kelley will take a hundred bucks off your tab."

Ann stared incredulously at Flynn. "You're both filthy scumbags!"

Flynn smiled at Ann, "Keep it up old girl, and I'll let him have a go at you," said Flynn.

***

Carl Davis and Jason Reynolds stood before the large antique dark maple desk of Carland Morrison. The room was paneled in similar dark maple interspersed with six columns of book shelves holding legal tomes. Behind Carland's high backed leather chair hung his ornately framed undergraduate and Juris Doctorate degrees—both from Auburn. The space radiated confidence.

They had flown in this morning and driven down from the Birmingham Airport. Pleasantries had been exchanged, the offer of refreshments was made and declined, and the agents got down to the subject at hand.

"How long had she been married to Harold Dennison?" asked Reynolds.

"About a year. She was a stripper from Birmingham. Would you like to see her picture?"

"We would," answered Davis. Carland opened a file and approached the agents.

"Here is one from her agency." The eight by ten color photograph captured the image of a petite raven haired woman in a sequined G-string leaning against a chrome stripper pole. She was bare breasted and had a sly, but slightly wanton looking smile upon her pouting lips.

"A beauty," said Reynolds.

"Yeah, I'd tap that," said Davis.

The lawyer nodded slightly in the affirmative, "Harold had good taste, but poor judgment."

Reynolds held up the photo. "Mind if we keep this?"

"I'll have my secretary make you a copy. How did you say Harold died?"

"A drowning. At least, that's what the death certificate says," replied Reynolds.

"And you have reason to believe otherwise? May I ask what that might be?" asked Carland.

"Allegedly, he had a dive computer that recorded his dive profile—how deep he was at each phase of the dive. We have hearsay evidence that it would show that he did not drown, but that someone shut off the air to his regulator, choking off his air and drowning him. Once that was done, the air was turned back on," replied Reynolds.

"Making it look like he suffered a heart attack and drowned?" said Carland.

"That or a stroke," said Reynolds.

"I used to go spearfishing with Harold. In fact, I was trying to join him on that trip but I was in the middle of a trial. He was going to fish by himself and he preferred it that way," said Carland.

"Because another diver, spearfishing fish near you can be dangerous?" asked Davis.

Carland nodded. "Exactly—most experienced spear fishermen hunt alone. Vicky knew this—we all did. It sounds like an open and shut case. Why not just arrest Vicky?"

"We don't have the dive computer and would like to have it in hand before we do," said Reynolds.

"Who has it?" asked Carland.

"A fly in the ointment," said Davis.

Carland returned to his desk. "My IT guy talked me into getting a high-end PBX with a lot of very cool, gee-wiz features I never thought we would need. He demonstrated one such feature this morning." Carland withdrew a sheet of paper and handed it to Reynolds. "Maybe this will help."

On the paper was a typed telephone number and a JPEG image of a small map of Steinhatchee with a red push pin sticking in the map near a deep bend in a river.

Chapter Thirty-three - Leagan Reonard

Under the curtain of a starless early morning sky, a Boston Whaler towed a kayak through heavy surf—headed for the mouth of Steinhatchee River, across the ironically named Dead Man's Bay. The towed boat was a folding Keppler kayak, built by the same company that supplied MARSOC, the Marine Corps Special Operations Command. The low profile, lightweight frame was perfect for approaching locations clandestinely. Michael was dressed in a lightweight wet suit, impact helmet, and neoprene booties. The Whaler would get Michael past the river's outflow and disengage before they approached within hearing distance of the fish camp.

Johnnie was at the helm of the Whaler, while Char and Eddie occupied the bow. Earl waited offshore on the *Good as Gold*, which had traveled through the night to reach Steinhatchee before dawn. The plan was as straightforward as it was simple.

They had located the fish camp through various websites, including one from the business itself—or what was left of it. The pictures and map on the site gave Michael, Char, and Eddie an idea of the place's layout and where it was located on the river. What they lacked, however, was current information about the amount and disposition of what Michael would call 'threat forces' occupying the objective. Michael's job was to fill in the blanks. The years he spent first in Battalion Recon and later in Force Recon were excellent preparation for what lay ahead.

Johnnie let go of the tow line once they were past the tidal basin and Michael began paddling in an aggressive and practiced motion. He hadn't been in a kayak in a few months, but his muscles seemed to remember the routine. His plan was to approach the bend in the river that hosted the camp's docks, exit the kayak, and swim upriver. He had a snorkel, mask, and swim fins and figured he could remain clandestine enough to exit the river within sight of the fish camp's wooden dock. He chose the spot because that was where an intermittent stream entered the river. He could paddle the kayak up the stream until it petered out and then low crawl the rest of the way up. The stream passed a short distance to the west of the ring of largely abandoned cabins and main building of the camp.

Michael paddled the kayak towards the left side of the slow moving river, hoping the dark starless night and thick overhanging foliage shielded him from casual observation. It was a shame that he wasn't here during better times as the tall Cyprus trees shrouded in hanging moss and Kentia Palm trees would have made an idyllic scene.

He paddled upriver for about a half an hour, fighting the slight downstream current. His shoulders burned from the repetitive motion, but it was a good feeling and he welcomed it. It was good to be doing anything physical—especially if it brought him within striking distance of the man who had killed Sofia.

Michael touched his paddle to what he took to be a large tree branch—only to have it erupt into life and try to strike his oar. He had startled an adult alligator from its slumber and it propelled itself toward Michael's kayak with a swift flutter of its powerful tail.

Michael smacked the gator across the nose twice quickly, but felt all he did was anger it. The beast continued to approach—Michael thought it was going to launch itself against the fragile boat and collapse it, when the gator unexpectedly disappeared beneath the surface. He braced himself for what he felt was inevitable—thinking for sure that the reptile would breach his kayak from underneath.

He sat frozen for an interminable moment waiting for the beast to strike as sweat careened down his face in a cavalcade of warm rivulets—and nothing happened. Relieved, Michael felt his butt unclench and he let go a long sigh of relief. Anxious to put some distance between him and the alligator, Michael paddled powerfully for several minutes.

He passed numerous wooden docks—many were long abandoned and in various states of collapse. Given the tropical climate, if left to the elements, a dock didn't stand the test of time. Most modern docks were made of treated tropical hardwoods such as red cedar, but that was expensive and Flynn couldn't currently afford such luxuries. Flynn's dock, while serviceable, was a patchwork of repairs with various pieces of scrap wood salvaged from an old factory procured by the Gibson brothers.

He rounded a bend in the river and caught sight of a light in the distance. Michael stopped paddling, reached into the kayak's forward storage compartment, and withdrew a pair of low light surveillance binoculars. A curved light pole projected over the river a less than a hundred yards upriver. The single yellow light bulb under a saucer-shaped porcelain shade cast a surreal glow upon the water. A freakish looking man with a corpse-like pallor and a receding hairline that descended into a mullet sat upon a plastic chair with a compact assault rifle laid across his lap.

Michael wondered who he was waiting for. As if in answer, the sound of an outboard motor reverberated downriver a few moments later. *Incoming*, thought Michael. He needed to get off the river as the approaching boat was sure to see him. The mouth of the creek was still a good twenty five or so yards away, but if he paddled for it, there'd be a risk the man on the dock would see him.

Michael pulled the dive mask over his eyes, slipped out of the cockpit and into the murky water. He grabbed the flippers from the storage compartment, reached for the tow line, and began slowly towing the kayak to shore. He reached for the bottom and sank beneath the water. He softly frog kicked with his flippers— knowing that the more natural movement would make less of a disturbance in the water.

Something hit his thigh with the violent impact of a sledgehammer, but spread over a larger area. He felt multiple razor like incisions into the flesh of his thigh and realized with grave clarity that the gator he startled had stalked him until he entered the water. The gator shook Michael in its jaw and began to drag him into the deeper part of the river. *What if the gator started to turn me over and over until I become so disoriented that I would gasp for air and be rewarded with a lung full of water. Don't they call it a death spin?* thought Michael. He realized that the feeling this created was the exact reverse of that you get when a dream turns violent, but you realize it is only a dream. This felt like a nightmare—but it was real.

He gasped for a last breath as the beast pulled him under the murky water and reached for the eight inch Ka-Bar-style bayonet that hung from a scabbard secured to his chest. He heard of a Marine who got attacked by a crocodile during jungle training in Thailand who got it to let go by sticking a thumb in its eye. His Ka-Bar was a lot better than a finger—if he could only find its eye. He wasn't certain that he could find the same vulnerable spot, but he was sure he knew where to find the top of its boney skull—it was clamped to his leg.

Michael pulled the bayonet from its sheath, and traced the blade of the knife along the hard, scaly ridge of the creature's massive head. He ran the blade along the ridge until he felt it peak and then jammed the knife into the armored skin underneath. The knife struck something hard, and glanced off the creature's skull. He brought his arm back up over his head and tried again and this time the blade found purchase, but penetrated a mere fraction of an inch. The gator powerfully shook his thigh, causing Michael to almost drop his knife.

He lifted the Ka-Bar up high over his head and forcefully brought it down directly into the gator's skull, but the water deadened the force of the descending strike. Nothing happened, so he did it again. The beast started spinning him in the water, and Michael knew he was in trouble as he was losing his ability to hold his breath—one way or another, this would end soon.

With all the force he could muster, Michael plunged the knife into whatever flesh he could find, withdrew it and plunged it down again. He repeated the hectic attack until near exhaustion. Finally, the blade sank to its hilt into something that felt soft and gooey— his knife thrust had found the beast's eye. The jaw opened and released his thigh. Michael kicked hard towards the surface, realizing he was about twelve feet away from air.

He surfaced and gasped for breath just as the roar of a large outboard loudly announced its proximity. Michael turned to his left and bow lights headed right for him. He plunged back into the water and felt the roar of the propeller as it passed overhead. He turned toward shore and swam back to the ruined dock that sheltered his kayak.

He waited several tense minutes in the deep recesses of the dock, unsure whether he had been seen or not. He slid the mask down off his face and brought the binos up to his eyes. Michael could see three or four men illuminated by the dock light. Two figures stood on the boat throwing bags up on the dock while a man with a mullet and another man watched. There was the low murmur of conversations and one loud commanding voice that dominated the others.

Michael was bleeding and he badly needed to treat his wounds. He had an Individual First Aid Kit (IFAK) in the cargo compartment—he rarely traveled without one. He had a QuickClot bandage, cloth tape, antiseptic spray, oral antibiotics, painkillers and plenty of rolls of gauze. He heard gators had filthy mouths that often contained fecal remnants of the animals they preyed upon, but he wasn't going to curtail the op while he still had the ability to carry it out. He made a mental note to see a doctor when morning came.

Michael retrieved the waterproof bag that contained the IFAK, along with his weapon and climbed out of the water. Where there was once a dock there was probably also the ruins of a house. He just wanted a place where he could turn on a light and treat the wound. Michael followed an overgrown path from the dock and found an old picnic table that still looked like it would support some weight. He spilled the contents of the bag on the table, retrieved a headlamp and turned it on.

He opened the IFAK, took out a small spray bottle of antiseptic, reached behind his back, grabbed the lanyard attached to the wetsuit's zipper and lowered it. He pulled the suit down beneath his shoulders, and then tried to pull it down to his ankles, but it seemed to be stuck to his thigh and buttocks. He winced in pain and cursed, withdrew his knife and began cutting away the thin neoprene material of the wetsuit.

There were was a butterfly-shaped patch a foot long that corresponded to where the gator's teeth had bitten through the wetsuit and into the flesh of Michael's thigh. There was no spurting blood flow, so the gator hadn't severed any blood vessels. He slowly peeled the neoprene from the wounds and grimaced in pain as it tore loose. Then he got to work treating the dozen or so puncture wounds. He was in too much pain to sit down and searched through the kit until he found a small bottle of pills that Sofia had given him a long time ago—he hoped they were still good.

Michael heard a rustle of brush behind him, slowly turned to confront a bearded man slowly walking towards him carrying a shotgun. He was shirtless in coveralls and rubber boots. The man jacked a round into the chamber of the shotgun, pointed it at Michael's head and tightened his grip. "My name is Leagan Reonard. I figured you should know the name of the man who kilt you."

He was a crusty old semi-vagrant who worked for the Gibson brothers offloading marijuana from smuggling boats offshore and then moving them into short-term storage at the fish camp prior to their redistribution. When he wasn't drunk or high on pilfered grass, the man slept in one of the fish camps abandoned cabins.

"Why you want to do that?" asked Michael. "I have no quarrel with you."

"I seen you in the river. You kilt my gator. Been feeding him since he was a pup. So I'm gonna fuck you up. Now get your hands up over yur head."

Michael slowly raised his hands, looked down at the Ka-Bar resting atop the weathered picnic table and silently cursed. It would take him seconds to grab the knife and attack the shotgun-toting swamp-rat and that was too long. He looked up at the tree-shrouded grey morning sky and lamented his bad luck—bit by an alligator and shot by a swamp-rat did not strike him as a particularly meaningful epitaph.

"What's that you got in your hand?" asked Reonard.

Michael had forgotten about the pills and figured he might have something the swamp-rat wanted. "This? Nothing, about twenty five or thirty tabs of extended-release capsules of Kadian."

"How many milligrams?"

The question surprised Michael as he didn't expect to encounter a swamp-rat with expertise in appropriate pharmaceutical dosage for recreational use, but who was he to question a man with a shotgun. "One hundred milligrams."

Reonard smiled a toothless grin, "Ah-yup—them's the good ones—got to crush em up, but they'll get you high all day long." He motioned with the shotgun. "Toss em over here."

Michael tossed the pill bottle directly over the man's shoulder. Reonard instinctively turned to watch the small brown bottle as it arced over him. The bottle landed under a short palm and was lost in the diminished light of the early morning. Reonard made a move to retrieve the bottle and then realized his mistake.

Michael grabbed the Ka-Bar from the table, ran after the man with the knife held low. Reonard spun around to bring the shotgun up, but he was a second too late. Michael parried the shotgun with his left arm while he stabbed Leagan Reonard in the stomach, withdrew the knife and slashed his throat. The man dropped the shotgun to the ground and grasped his throat as blood spilled from severed carotid arteries in his neck. Leagan Reonard collapsed to the swamp floor and died.

Michael looked down at the corpse with disdain.

"The gator bit me and died. How do you think a coony ass swamp rat was gonna fare?" He stuck the knife into the ground, and retrieved the pill bottle, opened the cap and swallowed a couple. He knew they weren't a hundred milligrams—more likely twenty, but they would ease his pain.

He expeditiously treated the wounds, pulled up his wet suit, retrieved the shotgun, and headed back to his kayak. Disaster had been averted, but his recon mission had been compromised. Sooner or later someone would go looking for Leagan Reonard. Still, he had a mission to accomplish and that meant risk. He had managed some of it, but if he were to walk away now, it would amount to a failure. He had to get eyes on target and to do that, he needed to install the pin microphone and audio transmitter he had purchased from a surveillance technology store in St. Pete.

Michael followed the path that Reonard had approached from. It was little more than a game trail that traveled along the intermittent creek until it opened up into the parking lot in front of the main lodge. Michael retreated back into the brush and took a knee, curious to see if this vantage point would help him locate a place to put the audio bug.

One of the screen doors flew open and three men Michael didn't recognized walked out of the door. A voice hollered after them. "And don't come back until you find that asshole."

The men approached one of the pickups, an old F100 Ford, and piled in. The antiquated engine sputtered to life in a cloud of noise. After a few seconds of revving the engine the entire lot was covered in thick black smoke. The driver dropped the vehicle into drive and it lurched to the gate.

The cloud of dense smoke provided Michael a great opportunity to surreptitiously approach the building. He ran through the dense cloud across the parking lot in a sprint. His wounded thigh throbbed in protest, but there was no time for pain. He slid under the raised structure and looked for the most effective place to install the microphone. It didn't take him long to locate the retrofit communications conduit installed underneath the conference room.

The contractor had used PVC piping to protect the fiber cables from the elements. The line ran from the middle of the floor up the side of the building to a parabolic antennae installed on the roof. Michael examined the piping. It was sealed to the building with a plastic collar secured to the wood with four long screws. He listened for a few seconds and heard a voice he didn't immediately recognized and another that sounded almost like it was coming over the radio. *Speakerphone,* he thought. He withdrew a utility tool and started to unscrew the plastic collar.

Chapter Thirty-four - Fire Sale

"It's the biggest dealer in the state," said Calvin Henshaw, the GM of Enterprise Autobama. "They sense an opportunity, Mrs. Dennison and they want to move." Henshaw suspected that he was on speakerphone, but he nonetheless continued talking. Crimson Automall had a great profit-sharing program, matching 401K and three weeks of vacation. They sniffed around continuously, but Harold never wanted to sell. Harold wanted to own the dealership until he died. *Well, he had it his way*, thought Henshaw.

"They are offering us seven point five million for the real property and we can sign over the inventory to them. It's a low ball offer, but it's a conversation starter," said Henshaw.

"And ender," said Vicky. "Harold confided in me that he could sell it for ten million if he wanted."

"Yes, that may be true, Vicky, but Harold's dead, and they sense that you want to rid yourself of his assets. They also offered that they would be able to close immediately. We can do the entire sale via electronic signature and wire the funds anywhere you want." Henshaw had made a blatant attempt to appeal to her sense of greed.

Flynn reached over to the speaker phone and pressed the mute button. "Dammit, Vicky, take the money. You can settle your debt with us and still have plenty left over to go chase young male tail on Ibiza or San Tropez."

She looked at Flynn and smiled as if to a small child—"Nicky, if I settle too easily, they might suspect something—like Harold's attorney. If I pay you and him," she said making a gesture with an outward turn of her thumb, "I'm down to just two and a half million. I'd be better off with a few million more. So, please let me handle this." She turned off the mute button.

"My counter is nine million dollars. I'll give them until two p.m. eastern time to make their last best offer," said Vicky. She reached out and touched the off button on the speakerphone.

"That's fookin grand," said Kelley. "We're holed up here like sitting ducks waiting for two crazy Indians to cut our bleeding necks, and you thought it would be a great fookin idea to add a few more hours to the process."

Vicky visibly cowered whenever Kelley spoke and this time she seemed to shrink in her seat. She thought giving herself up to him would engender some good feelings toward her, but up to this point they had failed to materialize.

One of the Jairus' men was found with his throat cut and his belly splay open while his innards were being consumed by some of the smaller gators in the river. The younger gators had since moved up a little further on the food chain when Michael killed their main rival. The discovery that someone had gotten so close to the compound caused both Kelley and Flynn a great amount of sphincter-tightening concern.

Chapter Thirty-five - Convergence

Johnnie had rented a three-bedroom faux Key West-style cottage in a development that sat on the river a short distance from where it emptied into Dead Man's Bay. Michael had to struggle to get there. His hip where the gator had bit him was throbbing, although the morphine dulled the pain to a minor annoyance, it also dulled his thinking and made him lethargic to the point that he almost missed the boat landing. He corrected too late and ended up back paddling to reach it. By that time, Johnnie had seen him and wadded in to help him land the boat. "Damn bro, you look like a Filipina hooker in Subic Bay after the fleet left town. You okay?"

Michael nodded and offered a tired smile. He climbed out of the cockpit and grabbed the stern, while Johnnie lifted the bow. "Dude, I can get the boat. You look like shit. Just relax." Johnnie slid around the kayak until he cradled it under the cockpit and carried it up the boat ramp.

"Better get it out of sight—someone may be looking for it and me," said Michael.

"Oh shit, I know what that means," said Johnnie. He had accompanied Char, Michael, and a team of MARSOC operators on a raid launched against a missile base in the Venezuelan jungle two years ago. These guys were fire starters when it came to causing mayhem.

"I need to make a couple of calls and I'm gonna need a doctor," said Michael.

Johnnie started to speak and then caught himself. He was almost going to say he would get Sofia. "I'll see to it."

They drove to the cottage with the kayak in the back of a pickup Johnnie had rented. Char and Eddie were sitting at the kitchen table drinking coffee awaiting Michael's return. Michael lumbered into the kitchen, grabbed a cup from the cupboard, and poured himself some coffee. The two men sat waiting for Michael to say something. "Is there any food?" he said finally.

Char noticed the wound on Michael's thigh and gave him a concerned look. "We'll have Johnnie pick up something up after he finds a doctor. What the hell happened to you?"

"Long story. The short version is that they know we're here," replied Michael. "I'm going to take a shower—then we can talk." He exited to the back porch, pulled off his wetsuit, stepped under the outdoor shower, and rinsed off. Not caring that there might be other residents around, he contently stood naked under the spray.

***

"Early lunch?" asked Reynolds.

"Sure, as long as they have burgers," said Davis.

"It says they serve the best in Steinhatchee right there on the sign," replied Reynolds.

Davis turned to examine the changeable letter sign in front of the building—a Fifties-era block type with green aluminum awnings shading half frosted picture windows "Low bar to meet— there are probably less than six restaurants in this burg."

"Hopefully, we won't end up eating in all of them."

"No, I think we should see if Ray's Tasty Eats lives up to its reputation. What do you want to bet the waitress is named Flo?" said Reynolds.

"The lunch check," replied Davis.

They exited the Chevy Silverado pickup—Reynolds had bullshitted the dispatcher into believing they would be encountering some swampy terrain. In truth, he was thinking of buying one and thought that an extended test drive might be in order.

The restaurant's interior hadn't been changed since it was built. The owner had contracted with a lumber yard in Cedar Key to supply roughhewn cedar planks, which he finished and transformed into a long counter, booths and wall paneling.

Ray had long since died, but his son, Raymond Junior, shortened to simply J.R., had grown up worshipping at the feet of a father who had marched across parts of North Africa and most of Europe as part of Patton's Seventh Army. J.R. followed his old man's steps into the army, but his only brush with glory was a few years spent in Berlin guarding a turnstile at a checkpoint between east and west. He returned in 1990 to take over the diner from his then ailing father and J.R. hadn't left Steinhatchee since.

At ten after eleven in the morning, the breakfast crowd had already eaten and the lunch crowd hadn't yet arrived, so the two federal agents had the restaurant to themselves. They took a seat at a booth near the door and perused the acetate-covered menu. The owner, a white shirted man with a black bow tie and black pants, took their order. "What'll it be, gents?"

"Cheeseburger, medium fries, diet coke," said Davis.

"The same," said Reynolds. He read the man's name tag, "J.R. Are you the manager?"

"The owner, actually."

"Even better," said Reynolds, "got a minute to talk?"

"Sure, you're the only order, so it should take all of fifteen minutes to get you your food. Ten if you let me put it in now."

Reynolds took out his FBI credentials and flashed it. "The burgers can wait, have a seat."

J.R. did as instructed and slid into the booth next to Davis. He was visibly nervous. "What is this about?" he asked.

Reynolds smiled at the man in an attempt to calm him. "It doesn't involve you. Do you know a man by the name of Nicky Flynn?"

"Yeah, I know him. The guy is a scumbag. He owns a fish camp about three miles from here on the river. I'll write down the directions," said J.R.

"Seen him lately?" asked Davis.

"Yeah, he came in here to pick up a big order of food—enough to feed twelve to fifteen people. He used to do that after the kitchen at his camp closed down—but he hasn't had clients there in a long time."

Reynolds opened a portfolio binder and retrieved a photo showing a heavily tattooed man of about thirty to thirty five leaning up against a wall with anti-British graffiti painted across it.

"Seen an older version of this guy?"

"No," replied J.R.

Reynolds turned the clear document protector to a photograph of the *Good as Gold.* Before Reynolds could ask, Davis blurted out, "Seen this yacht?"

J.R. shook his head affirmatively. "Yeah, sure have."

"Tell me where and when," said Davis.

"I was out fishing with the kids yesterday. I saw her in Dead Man's Bay. An eighty foot Hatteras—kind of hard to forget. You normally don't see a boat like that around here. It looked like it was maneuvering further out to sea."

Davis smiled at Reynolds and addressed the owner. "That's all we need J.R. Now how about you get us those burgers?"

They followed the directions that J.R. had given them which led to a dirt road that disappeared into a near unbroken line of Florida Pine. On the edge of the main road, stood an old wood billboard that displayed the faded image of a man wearing waders reeling in a large striped bass. Reynolds continued down the main highway—deciding that they needed to talk through the details rather than showing up at the fish camp and with their dicks in hand

"So, what are we planning on doing? Just showing up without back up and arresting them all?" said Davis.

"We verify they are there and then call in HRT," said Reynolds, referring to the FBI's Hostage Rescue Team.

"How long will that take?" asked Davis.

Reynolds shrugged. "Hours, days, who knows? I'd have to notify the SAIC in Miami, give him a full report and hope he approves the raid."

"By that time they may be long gone," said Davis.

Didn't J.R. say the suspects are picking up food at the restaurant a couple of times a day?" asked Reynolds.

Davis smiled. "That's genius."

Reynolds pulled a U-turn in the center of the highway and ended up driving off the shoulder and into the soft Florida dirt. He floored the gas pedal and the beast responded in kind—the tires spun in the soft earth, shooting up twin rooster tails of dirt before the truck careened back on the road. "Hot damn son, that's what I'm talking about," shouted Reynolds. He pounded the roof with his palm a few times to add emphasis.

"Whatever," said Davis. The burger had not satisfied his ample appetite. His only interest at the moment was getting some chicken wings or something else to tide him over until dinner. They walked into the restaurant and were about to take the same booth when someone caught Davis' attention. It was slightly more crowded, with three more men that Davis took to be fishermen or truck drivers seated at the counter and a customer paying for takeout. J.R. had agreed to call them if someone from the fish camp came in to pick up an order, but this was something different. A thin blond-haired kid was paying for several meals packed in

Styrofoam that the cashier was busily placing into plastic bags.

Davis walked down to the end of the wall and slid into a booth facing the door. Reynolds slid in opposite him—immediately blocking Davis 'view of the young man.

"Move your head," said Davis.

"Why?" said Reynolds.

Davis didn't want to arouse suspicious so he clenched his teeth and spoke barely above a whisper, "Because the guy at the counter looks familiar."

Reynolds slid over to the window. Davis studied the face for a moment and the guy looked at him. Davis locked eyes with the man but he turned to the cashier to receive his change and quickly exited. Then it hit him. It was the young guy he had encountered with Char on the Coast Guard cutter in Key West.

The guy walked briskly to a Toyota Tundra parked in front of the restaurant. He jumped in the cab and slowly exited the gravel lot. Davis and Reynolds waited for the pickup to be out of sight and then exited. Reynolds, a graduate of the FBI's surveillance course, waited until the truck was almost out of sight before he pulled the Silverado onto the highway.

Johnnie checked his rear mirror looking for any telltale sign he was being followed. He saw a pickup pull onto the highway and figured it was one of the farmers he had seen seated at the counter. *The guy in the booth was the same agent that had hassled Char in Key West, but maybe I'm being paranoid. But, just because you're paranoid, doesn't mean they're not out to get you, thought Johnnie.*

That was a crazy thought to suddenly pop into his head and he decided to test that theory. Johnnie spied a logging road about fifty feet in front of him. He slowed the vehicle and turned onto the gravel road until he reached the tree line. He pulled a short distance down the road so he would not be visible to casual observation and exited the vehicle.

"I saw him turn off ahead," said Davis. They passed by the logging road and Davis turned to look. The road was as flat as an anorexic stripper, and he could just make out the truck about a hundred feet away.

"No sense playing a cat and mouse game. Let's see how our young friend feels about being charged with obstruction," said Reynolds. He opened the glove box, pulled out a police light and handed it to Davis, who slapped it on the roof of the cab. Reynolds pulled the truck off to the shoulder, executed a tire squealing U-turn and was soon propelling the truck back towards the logging road. "Man, I love this truck," said Reynolds. He turned down the logging road until he met the Tundra heading in the opposite direction.

***

"It's about time, you've been gone for about an hour and a half. We're starving," said Char. He was sitting in one of the arm chairs watching the news on a large flat screen television.

Johnnie walked in the door, followed by the two agents and he couldn't resist answering his boss. "Well, I hope you want bacon, because I brought at least four hundred pounds of it."

"On your feet, motherfucker," said Davis. He had his pistol drawn and pointed directly at Char. Reynolds followed closely behind him.

Eddie was startled by the entry of the two agents. He looked at the tall FBI agent and smiled. "Jason Reynolds, what the hell are you doing here?"

"I know you?" asked Reynolds.

"Yeah, Detective Lieutenant Eddie Doyle, formerly of the Pinellas County Sheriff's Department, but currently retired. We worked the Chavez kidnapping back in 2003."

"Jeez, that was a long time ago. Good memory," said Reynolds.

"Some might say eidetic," said Char. "By the way, Carl do either you or your buddy have a warrant?"

Michael walked in the room from the bathroom clad only in a towel. Davis pointed his service pistol at him as he entered. "Guys, do you mind keeping it down? The doctor is stitching me up and you're scaring the shit out of him." He gave Davis a conspiratorial grin, "I'd appreciate a steady hand—less of a scar that way."

Davis remembered Char's son being cocky, but not even acknowledging a weapon being pointed at him struck Davis as either crazy brave or just plain crazy.

"Let's everyone calm down," said Eddie. "Anyone want a cup of coffee?"

"Hey, Eddie," said Davis, "you ain't in charge of jack shit, you got it? I got a seizure order for an eighty foot yacht that this asshole has in his possession."

Eddie gave the man an incredulous look. "Oh, really, that's all you're worried about? From what I've been told, there are three suspects directly involved in multiple murders, including the death of that man's fiancée and a murder for hire, hunkered down right up the road. Add to that the fact that they have kidnapped his ex-wife," said Eddie, pointing towards Char "and I'm surprised that the entire HRT have not yet descended on the fish camp."

Eddie was pissed—this shit should not be happening just because certain federal agents wanted a little pay back for past misdeeds committed by Char Blackfox. "And all you're worried about is the administrative seizure of a boat. How much of a reward are you due?"

Davis didn't answer. Reynolds holstered his weapon and walked over to where Davis stood in a modified Weaver stance with his weapon pointed directly at Char. "Carl, put your sidearm away. These folks are victims—regardless of the seizure order. First things first, old man."

Reynolds turned towards Eddie, "Did you say you had coffee, old son?" Eddie nodded, "I'd love a cup, and I'm sure Carl could use one."

Eddie clasps his hands together, happy that he wasn't going to be an unarmed man at a shoot-out. "Great, how does everyone take it?"

Davis slowly lowered his weapon and returned it to its holster. He was convinced that any hope of getting a payoff for the seizure of the *Good As Good* was dissipating like a fart in the windsock. "Cream and two sugars."

Chapter Thirty-six - Settlement

"Their last best offer is eight and one quarter million," said Calvin Henshaw. "It's a pretty standard contract. I can have our attorney review it if you want, but there are no surprises. They'll just take over operations as is. If that's acceptable, we can do this all remotely."

Vicky looked at her diamond bejeweled Rolex President and smiled—it was 12:55—well before the deadline she had set. "No need for a review, just send it along. One question—how long will it take to get the funds wired?"

"Immediately upon settlement, which will be when all signatories sign the documents," replied Henshaw. "It should take a couple of hours to get everything in place. I'll call you back when we're ready to execute the sales contract and you can sign on-line."

"I've got three bank account numbers that I would like the

funds sent to. Let me know when you're ready to write them down," said Vicky. Flynn and Kelley watched and listened as Vicky conveyed the account numbers and amount as she had proven to equally as devious as they were. She ended the call and smiled at both men. "There, I've kept my part of the bargain. Once the paperwork is ready, I'll sign the papers and you'll both be paid."

"It will be over for me lassie when there is cash in me hand and I'm sipping a Guinness in me favorite pub in Kenmare. There were plenty of slips between the cup and the lip and ensuring that you're not one of them is my current priority," said Kelley.

He had a few more tasks to complete before setting sail for County Kerry. He intended to retire there—as someone other than Ken Q. Kelley—that name was wore out. The feds would be looking for the man responsible for so many dead—some that were currently still breathing, but why leave any loose ends?

"What do you want to do with Ann?" asked Flynn. He had locked her in one of his rooms, but aside from a sore shoulder, she was otherwise unharmed. Flynn had every intention of letting her go, but he was certain that Kelley had other ideas. "It looks like we're getting our money regardless of the insurance pay-out, so why not let her go?" he added.

"If you mean the hostage, forget it—she still has value," said Kelley. "Those two freaking maniacs are being careful because we have her. Without her they would be on us like a couple of bog-warriors on a shepherd's pie. Best we just keep her until we don't need her any longer. Then I'll see to her." Kelley was suddenly hornier than he had been in a while. *This calls for a drink and a piece of ass,* he thought.

Kelley gave Vicky a lascivious smile. "How about a drink to celebrate, eh Vicky?"

She unexpectedly returned his smile. "Sure, Kelley, why not? I got a bottle of Gentleman Jack in my room. Why don't you join me?"

Kelley laughed. "Oh, yes dear, I fully intend to join you."

Vicky stood up and smiled in return. "Just bring the ice—I can't drink hot whiskey." She walked out of the room like she was leaving the stage—insuring that she advertised her skills in the back. Buy one dance and you'll leave when you run out of money—that used to be her game.

Vicky ascended the stairs, got to her room and stripped naked. Kelley arrived a short time later with a bucket of ice. He entered, gazed upon her voluptuous nakedness and forgot about the drink. Vicky acted passionate this time—pretending to enjoy it. She badly needed to sell Kelley on something. He finished and poured himself four fingers of whiskey, shook a cigarette out of his pack, and reclined bare-assed in the old leather armchair—content for the moment, but he was still fighting more than just natural urges. He had thought he had weaned himself off of the mild opiate addiction he had fallen into—only to have the compulsion reappear as he neared the goal line.

Vicky reclined on the bed clad only in a sheet, smoking and thinking how best to broach the topic with the Irish hitman who had just soiled her loins. "Tell me Kelley, does two point five million garner you happiness?"

"I haven't really thought about it much," he regarded her with a sly smile, "Why? Do you want to give me more of your share?"

Vicky flicked an ash from the end of her cigarette. "I was

thinking that we might take Flynn's share—if he were no longer around," said Vicky. "I'll split it with you."

"If I do the dirty work?"

Vicky smiled demurely, "Of course, that would make it worth another million and a quarter."

Kelley smiled at her and shook his head. "You're a treacherous lass, you are. I'm glad you're not after my arse. What if I ask him what he's willing to pay me to off you?"

Vicky shook her finger at him, "There's no dance without me—my signature is needed to complete the sale and my money will be transferred to a numbered account a long way from here."

Kelley sipped his whiskey. "I'll give it some thought, but we need him and his men right now and once the transfers are made, there is no bleeding point—he'll have the money."

Vicky crushed out her cigarette and stood up on her knees. The sheet fell away from her body, revealing her pert breasts. "Timing is everything, Kelley. Something might interfere with the transfer into his account."

He approached her and wrapped his arms around her bare mid-drift. "A corpse doesn't usually complain," he said before lowering his mouth to suck one of her large nipples.

She placed her hand on the back of his head as she would a suckling child. "That's right Kelley—dead men tell no tales."

***

Flynn walked out of the conference room and into the lounge. He slid behind the ornate hand carved cedar bar, selected a half decent Scotch and poured himself a drink. *The Mick had taken his woman, but two and a half million could buy a lot of female companionship in Thailand or the Philippines. However, five million could buy even more.*

Before he met Vicky and was talked into being her accomplice, Flynn had busied himself with bringing back the resort's lost luster. He had worked at it slowly, like a sculptor painstakingly trying to coax an image from a block of granite. Funded by charter trips that never seemed to deliver enough profit, he thought making a deal with the devil would get him the funds he needed to complete the project. It now seemed like that would be impossible.

Flynn had given Vicky the best room in the house, a suite that he had diligently refurbished. He had been pouring what free money he had toward restoring the fish camp to its glory days and now it was all for naught. The rooms had never been redone and all the fixtures from the brass lamps to the glass door knobs were original and intact—it was just a matter of polishing a faded gem.

The old wood frame cedar bed was hand hewn by his father in the late forties. The room was paneled with the same rot resistant wood and time had imparted it with a certain rustic charm. The bathroom was original to the time period—with a claw-footed porcelain-lined cast iron tub, old style flush toilet and pedestal sink.

Flynn had made incremental changes, restoring the leather on original clubman arm chairs, changing out old mattresses and adding flat screen televisions and Wi-Fi to lure in technology-obsessed potential clients. He named the suite for his father, Joseph, and thought it would be the first of many changes at the lodge, but it appeared to be the first and last.

Josiah entered the swinging doors from the restaurant and

roused him from his reminiscence. "The men are wanting lunch, boss and I'm out of money."

Flynn sighed, reached into his wallet and withdrew five twenties. "Try to bring me some change this time."

"Sorry boss, but the boys eat like hungry gators when someone else is paying," said Josiah.

Chapter Thirty-seven - Reinforcements

The cottage was eerily quiet after the voices faded from the receiver's speaker. Eddie looked at Reynolds, as he seemed to be the agent more willing to listen. "If they consummate the deal electronically, they could be gone this evening or early tomorrow. We need to know when you can have reinforcements on the ground or we can decide to go without them."

Reynolds had made a few phone calls earlier and knew the disposition of reinforcements. "HRT is tied up with a terrorist incident and is unable to respond at this time. We can wait for the Miami office to organize a response team or we can coordinate with local authorities. Either way, this is going to take time."

"Time is a luxury we don't have," said Eddie. "These three have proven to be murderers, and they are holding Char's ex-wife as a hostage."

"We go in there with anything other than overwhelming force and we'll get our ass handed to us," said Reynolds.

"You have it," said Char. "Two federal agents, a retired detective lieutenant and three former elite war-fighters."

"We don't even know what we're up against," said Davis.

"Yes, we do," said Michael. He was sprawled face down on a king size bed with nothing more than a towel draped over his backside. His wounds had been stitched closed and the doctor had dosed him with a painkiller before he left. He felt pretty good. "Including Flynn and Kelley, I counted at least six men."

"J.R. says that they've been ordering a dozen separate meals each time," said Reynolds.

"Accounting for two non-combatants, that means they have about ten men hunkered down at the camp. Against six of us—one of which is a walking wounded," said Davis.

"Belay that bum scoop, shitbird," said Michael. "I'm just catching a few Zzzs. I'll be ready at O-Dark Thirty to go Oscar Mike."

Davis gave Eddie a puzzled look. "He says don't worry, he's resting, but he'll be ready when the time comes," said Eddie.

Char walked up to Reynolds and stood close enough to bump chests. "So, do we do this with or without the FBI?" he asked.

"We wait for HRT or the Miami office to get here. According to the SAIC, the latter can be here by some time tomorrow," said Reynolds.

"Tomorrow may be too late. You can't expect them to wait around after they have completed the sale," said Char.

"Then we stop it. Kill their internet access or delay the deal. I'll get on the phone to the dealership and ask them to slow everything down. We do it all the time," said Reynolds.

Michael jumped to his feet and confronted Reynolds. His speed startled the man. "They'll get suspicious and it's my mother's life that hangs in the balance. I've already lost a fiancée. No, we go with you or without—it's your decision."

Reynolds looked at Eddie for reassurance, but retired detective nodded his head in agreement. Michael locked eyes with Reynolds and then turned to Davis. "You guys can either participate or leave—just don't get in our way." Michael grabbed a stack of clothes Johnnie had gotten for him and started to get dressed.

"There is a legal way we can all do this together, said Eddie. "I'm surprised Davis didn't bring it up since forming a posse originated with the Marshal's Service—federal officers are empowered to deputize civilians under limited circumstances," said Eddie.

"Very limited circumstances," said Davis. "I am not sure any of these guys would qualify for deputization."

"I've read the directive—the U.S. Marshals Service Special Deputization program," said Eddie. "They are all certainly qualified with their personal weapons and two are still DOD personnel, but are off duty. We fill out and file the forms with the USMS via email. It at least gives us a modicum of cover—the worst that happens is you're out of a job."

"We're still outnumbered two to one. How do we conduct a raid with those odds?" asked Reynolds.

"No need to worry, we're bringing in reinforcements," said Michael.

Reynolds walked up to Char. "How sure are you that these three conspired to kill Harold Dennison?"

Char walked over to his rucksack and withdrew the dive computer he had taken from Dennison's gear while Char was aboard Flynn's boat. He handed it to the agent. "The dive computer is integrated with the air supply. The medical examiner and I verified that the air valve on Dennison's tank was turned off about twenty three minutes into the dive. Four minutes and fifty seven seconds later it was turned back on."

"Making it appear to the casual observer that the diver suffered some type of medical malady and drowned," said Eddie.

Char returned to his bag and withdrew Dennison's ice pick. "Michael took this from Kelley's boat. It's got Harold Dennison's initials on it and it fits a scabbard on his dive gear. We think Dennison managed to stab Kelley with it before he died."

"The chain of custody is going to be a problem," said Reynolds.

Char regarded Reynolds with a gravely serious expression. "Agent Reynolds, we came here to kill Kelley and Flynn—not take them into custody."

***

The Gulf Stream G550 touched down on the short airstrip at the Marine Corps Air Station in New River, near Jacksonville, North Carolina. It had a call sign temporarily assigned by the Colombian Air force that designated the aircraft as flying under a diplomatic flag for the government of Colombia.

Marco Ramos and Alberto Villegas sat side by side, in plush leather reclining chairs studying a map of the area surrounding the fish camp spread out on the table before them. They had two passengers to pick up here before flying on to the Cross City Airport, where Johnnie planned to meet them.

The pilots were directed to taxi the jet to a VIP boarding area normally reserved for General Officers, open the hatch and await their passengers.

About a minute after the steward popped the hatch open and lowered the boarding ladder, a tall black man climbed abroad and addressed the steward. "Marcus Dixon. Can I bring my equipment on board?"

Dixon was a critical skills operator who served with Michael in Venezuela. He still served on a team, but had just returned from a three month deployment to Afghanistan and was on leave.

"Yes, of course," said the steward. An unseen party began handing up various equipment bags and gun cases into the passenger compartment. The bags were stowed and the steward directed the two MARSOC operators to seats across from the Colombian Marines. Marco Ramos jumped to his feet and embraced him. Dixon quietly expressed sympathy for the loss of his cousin and Ramos in turn thanked Dixon for coming to his aid in a time of need.

Ramos had met Dixon only briefly after he had been shanghaied into acting as Liaison Officer between Dixon's unit and the Colombian Marine Corps (COLMAR) two years ago. Alberto Villegas, then commander of a COLMAR base near the Venezuelan border, had risked his life to evacuate wounded MARSOC operators after they had been ambushed.

The next man who climbed into the cabin had been the

communications chief of the same team. Juan Thomas, was now an instructor at the MARSOC Individual Training Course—teaching tactical communications during phase one of the rigorous seven month course. Both Marines had developed strong ties with Michael when he was forced to assume command after the regular Team Commander had been grievously wounded. Both of them felt they owed Michael for getting a badly compromised mission back on track.

The two new passengers took their seats and the jet was soon in route to northwest Florida. The flight was long and uneventful. The steward passed out box lunches and sodas to the new passengers. Dixon and Thomas ate heartily—they had been on enough missions to know to eat while they could as they couldn't be sure when they would get their next opportunity.

Approximately two and a half hours later, the jet touched down at a small airport in Taylor county about ten miles from Steinhatchee. A black GMC pickup and a Chevy Tahoe sat at the end of the tarmac awaiting the arrival of the jet. As soon as the plane was parked, the vehicles approached and the passengers began expeditiously offloading the bags and equipment.

Michael greeted each of the jet's passengers with a warm embrace. They had all served in combat together and so shared the bonds that are forged in the crucible of battle. "Once more unto the breach, dear friends," was all that he could think to say.

Chapter Thirty-eight - Line of Departure

They gathered in the twilight on the patio of the cottage—wearing an eclectic mix of combat uniforms and carrying an odd assortment of weapons; the Marines and Char wore old Vietnam-era jungle utilities that Dixon had scrounged and armed themselves with M4 carbines and M45 MEUSOC pistols. The agents wore similar black versions of the combat utility and carried nine millimeter SIG-Sauer P228 semi-automatic sidearm. Reynolds had also brought a 9mm Heckler and Koch MP5A5 submachine gun. Eddie opted for North Face khaki-colored cargo pants, a long sleeve plaid shirt and his venerable .38 caliber revolver.

"Bow your heads and join me in prayer," said Dixon. "Saint Michael, the Archangel, defend us in battle. Be our defense against the wickedness and snares of the devil. May God rebuke him, we humbly pray. And due thou, O Prince of the heavenly host, by the power of God, thrust into hell Satan, and all the evil spirits who prowl about the world seeking the ruin of souls. Amen."

"Amen," they said in unison.

"That's quite a prayer," said Reynolds.

"St. Michael is the patron saint of the Marines," said Michael.

"Because even God hates a pussy," said Thomas.

They all laughed—it broke the nervous tension that had engulfed them. Of the group, only Reynolds and Davis were untested in battle, but both had done high risk arrests. Johnnie would operate the Boston Whaler, provide medical support and evacuation—should it be needed.

Now that the team was assembled, Davis would swear them in as newly minted special deputies. Because of the nebulous legality of the situation, however, he doubted the legal authority he imparted would hold up in a court of law, but Eddie was right— Davis had lost a job before—at least this time he would be doing it for a good reason.

Reynolds and Davis would nominally lead the team of highly trained operators hell-bent on enacting vengeance on those well deserving it.

Michael walked in front of the group. "You all know your assignment. Make sure of your targets—no blue-on-blue incidents. We all come back from this one."

    ***

"They're coming in early tonight," said Josiah. The two men stood on the dock watching the boat slowly approach. Normally, the shuttle boat would arrive well after dark in order to avoid being seen unloading their felonious cargo.

"You sure it's them?" said the other man. He was an old marijuana peddler named Maynard Philbrick, who had recently gotten out of jail for selling OxyContin to teens. He used to say the trick was getting them hooked and then you could get whatever you wanted from them. He was charged with simple possession and unlawful sexual activity with certain minors. He managed to avoid the more serious charge of lewd offenses committed upon persons less than sixteen years of age, because the girl was out celebrating her sixteenth birthday. Still, the seven years he spent in Okeechobee was no picnic—he had to be held in protective custody the whole time to keep other prisoners from delivering a version of convict justice specifically reserved for child rapists.

Maynard looked at Josiah, thinking he hadn't heard the question and then Josiah fell backwards onto the hard wood of the dock. Perplexed, Maynard looked down at Josiah and then felt something smack into his chest—it felt like someone had punched him hard. He tried to cry out, but was out of breath. He tried to turn to run and something that felt like a ballpeen hammer hit the side of his head. He collapsed on the dock like a cheap folding chair exposed to a three hundred pound man.

The boat approached within a few feet of the dock. By turn, Michael, Thomas, and Dixon bounded off the boat. All of them carried silenced carbines. Once they were on the dock, Johnnie turned it hard, up throttled and cruised back downstream.

Michael had suspected they were using one of the old ramshackle cottages to store the grass until it could be broken down and redistributed. Knowing the lazy nature of swamp-rats, he checked the hut nearest the path from the dock and found it locked by a high security shrouded padlock. *Someone was safeguarding something of value. They probably should have spent a few more dollars on the hasp,* he thought. He detached a short breaker bar from his belt, inserted it between the door jam and hasp, applied some downward force, and wrenched the bracket from the doorframe. He could smell the pungent order of dry marijuana before the door was fully open. Small brick size bales of Mexican grass were stacked from floor to ceiling throughout the one bedroom cabin. Michael looked at his watch—it was 6:27. They had about three minutes to kill. He withdrew an M15 White Phosphorous grenade, pulled the retention ring, while holding the safety lever. The watch's second hand reached twelve, Michael tossed the grenade onto the stacks of grass and closed the door behind him.

The dry marijuana immediately caught fire from the powerful chemical accelerant emanating from the grenade. Seconds later, flames rose up from the stacks of pot towards the ceiling within the dilapidated wood structure. The conflagration generated dark billows of burning marijuana and wood. Dixon busied himself implanting a Claymore mine on the path leading from the lodge while the two other Raiders stood by watching the fire.

"Hoping for a contact high?" asked Thomas.

"No, all that shit ever did was make me horny and hungry," said Michael.

The three Marine Raiders took up a hasty position in the high foliage along the trail and awaited any responders. They heard excited shouts coming from the lodge and heard a series of thundering footfalls approaching the shack. Dixon held the firing device in his hand—once triggered, the mine would unleash a shit storm of 700 double ought buckshot propelled by 682 grams of composition C4 explosive with an effective killing range out to a hundred feet.

***

Eddie had been waiting for the driver, a red-haired, freckled-faced kid barely out of his teens, at Ray's Tasty Eats. J.R. had known Red since he was a youngster. He grew up as the illegitimate son of a local high school girl gone bad, who couldn't get away from Steinhatchee fast enough. Red was a good kid rubbing shoulders with the wrong people, but everyone had to make their own mistakes.

It went down easy. Eddie waited in the parking lot for the kid's order to arrive at the counter. Four large plastic bags were delivered. Eddie timed his arrival with the kid's departure and held the door open as he exited. "Let me help you with the other two bags, said Eddie. Before the kid could protest, Eddie grabbed the two sacks left on the counter and followed the kid to his truck. Red opened the cab, threw the bags in and anxiously turned to retrieve the sack Eddie carried. Red took the bags and was about to offer a word of thanks when he felt the two inch barrel of a revolver pressed into his ribs. Eddie looked at his watch—it was 7:15. He had fifteen minutes to make it to the gate.

The old Ford F100 puttered at the gate while Jarius pointed the barrel of his twelve gauge shotgun at the cab's extra occupant. "Who's this?" he asked.

"My cousin Eddie from Ocala—you said you wanted extra guys so I picked him up at my house. He had a fight with the wife, and he staying with me until it blows over."

"Well, Cousin Eddie, got a gun?" asked Jarius.

Eddie took the revolver from his holster and held it up for Jarius to see.

Jarius laughed heartily and then doubled over with a cough.

"Shit, you'd have better luck clubbing them with it."

The night erupted in light and noise. Darkness was suddenly and momentarily vanquished and replaced by a huge explosion by the river. The eruption was felt when the pressure wave it generated collided with Jarius—knocking him off his feet, sending the shotgun flying from his hands and momentarily stunning him.

Jarius looked in the direction of the noise to see smoke climbing up through the air in billowing black cascades. Eddie got out of the cab and pointed to a spot by the curb inside the gate. "Pull the truck up over there," said Eddie.

He ran to Jarius, who was struggling to get to his feet. The man reached for Eddie's hand, but Eddie parried the arm and brought the pistol grip of the .38 caliber revolver down in an arching blow that smashed into the man's balding head. "You were right, dickweed—I did have better luck clubbing you with it." Jarius moaned in pain and Eddie hit him again. Jarius fell back on the ground and didn't move.

Eddie ran towards the gate, pushed it fully open as a black SUV and a silver pickup truck powered into the compound. The vehicles emptied their occupants before they skidded to a stop in the muddy soil. Char, Ramos, and Villegas ran towards the main building as rounds zipped past them from someone firing near the building's entrance.

Char saw the muzzle flash from the enemy's weapon and directed return fire. "Fire, right front," he shouted. Ramos and Villagas engaged the enemy with automatic fire and the incoming rounds ceased. They approached the stairs and searched until they located the shooter. Char shined his Surefire gun light on the man hidden beneath the staircase. He was dead—having been hit numerous times in the face and neck. Char took the man's weapon, a Ruger Mini-14, and slung it over his back. *Better to have it and not need it*, he thought.

Ramos stealthily approached the stairs. He scanned up their length with his gun light and crept up a step at a time. Char followed, while Villegas provided rear security. Once Ramos reached midway, he dropped to the prone and crawled the rest of the way to the top. *El momento de la verdad*, thought Ramos—the moment of truth.

Michael, Dixon, and Thomas sprinted towards the lodge. "Pendejo!" Michael shouted. Villegas recognized the running password they had established and raised his weapon. He directed them into a stack facing the stairs as it was the only position that provided some cover. The three stacked up in a single file behind Villegas and waited for Ramos to call them forward. Ramos held his assault weapon over the landing and immediately received a large volume of fire. One round struck and penetrated the hand guard causing him to let go of the barrel. "Mierda!" said Ramos. *They were apparently lying in wait for the team just behind the entrance doors to the lodge.* The doors were propped open and furniture had been hastily stacked in the opening.

Ramos withdrew two frag grenades from his tactical vest and readied them. If any of the exploding devices hit a piece of the barricade, it could conceivably bounce back onto the entry team— that would be bad. He turned to look back at the stairs and noticed Michael was crawling to him carrying a familiar looking device— an AT-4CS. It was a disposable 84mm unguided, recoilless smoothbore weapon specifically designed to be employed against fortifications or armored vehicles in a confined space. It was yet another unexpended piece of ordnance that Michael had hoarded from their mission in Venezuela.

The weapon's exploding warhead would have a devastating

effect on the defender's barricade; however, getting a shot off before being killed would be tricky. Ramos looked at Michael. "I'll throw a grenade—once it explodes, fire off the AT-4." Michael nodded. Ramos pulled the pin of the grenade and lobbed it at the open space at the top of the barricade. Excited shouts came from inside the building as the defenders scattered to avoid the explosion. A loud detonation erupted from inside the lobby followed by assorted screams. Michael stood up aimed at the barricade and fired the rocket. A loud whoosh emitted from the bazooka as the rocket exited the tube. A second later, the warhead exploded against the barricade and destroyed it in a ball shaking eruption of fire, God-awful noise and splintered wood.

Ramos, Michael, Villegas, Thomas, and Eddie entered through the doorway in a tactical stack. Eddie hadn't done anything like that since a stint he had done on the Pinellas County SWAT during the first years of its existence.

The explosive devices had prevented the doorway from becoming a death funnel, as the team didn't need to slow down during its entry. Each member took up a predefined position to cover all areas of the room, but the lobby was undefended. Char casually followed the entry team with his weapon held loosely at his side.

Michael surveyed the damaged interior of the lobby and let out a low whistle. Three bodies lay haphazardly upon the lobby floor. Two were obviously dead—one was missing most of his forehead and another had a fist size hole in his back. The third man moaned in pain. Michael kicked the man's weapon away from him and gave him a cursory examination. He had small cuts about the face-probably caused by wood shrapnel from the breaching munitions and a wound to the stomach that was seeping blood. He turned towards Eddie. "Call in Davis and Reynolds. It's time to add a little legal respectability to this firefight."

"What are we going to do with him?" asked Thomas.

"Call Johnnie—have him medevac the guy," said Michael.

"It'll take at least two of us to move him. Better to let him bleed out," said Char.

Michael shook his head. "I'm not going to argue the point— we treat the wounded—regardless of what side they're on."

"Whatever, it can wait. We still have business to take care of," said Char.

Juan Thomas had been cross trained in combat lifesaving and had often been pressed into service when the Corpsman was too busy on numerous occasions. He began to treat the man's stomach wound, while the rest of the team conducted a search of the building.

The men began moving down the hallway towards the conference room in a staggered column. They stacked outside the door and entered. No one was there, but a recurring buzz emanated from the speakerphone. Michael looked at Ramos, who shrugged his shoulder. He touched the answer button and said hello.

"Is Mrs. Dennison there?"

"Who's speaking?" asked Michael.

"Calvin Henshaw, I'm the GM at her dealership—or rather I was. Is she still there?"

"She stepped out. What can I help you with?" said Michael.

"I just wanted to confirm with her that the sale has been consummated and the wire transfers have been made," said Henshaw.

"Great, thanks, I'll let her know." Michael reached over and ended the call. He looked at Char. "Apparently they sold the dealership. That means they're going to be running for the exit doors."

"Let's move. I think they're still in the building," said Char.

They approached the stairway and met Thomas at the bottom landing. "The guy we fucked up may die. We need to get him treatment," said Thomas. He began to say something else when numerous loud cracks erupted from midway up the right angled staircase. Someone had stuck a rifle around the banister at the quarter space landing and fired an unaimed burst towards the Marines.

Michael and the other men returned a barrage of gunfire at the rifle, but whoever had fired the rounds had retreated up the second flight of stairs. Heavy footfalls echoed overhead indicating the perpetrator was moving down the hallway on the second floor.

Thomas fell to the floor gravely wounded. He was conscious—having been struck in his stomach with a heavy caliber bullet. The exit wound had left a fist size hole in his back. Michael dropped to a knee, removed Thomas' IFAK and pulled out several QuikClot bandages. Char knelt down next to the wounded man. On Michael's signal they flipped him onto his stomach so they could treat the more severe wound. Thomas cried out in anguish. The other men, unsure of what to do, provided security at the foot of the stairs.

Michael grabbed his radio transceiver, "Johnnie, we need you in here to medevac Thomas. He's been shot."

"Roger, Skipper. I can be there in ten mikes," replied Johnnie.

They had set up their cabin as an aid station. The doctor that had treated Michael had been hired at an exorbitant rate to stand by there for just such an eventuality. Michael pushed a bandage into the wound cavity and Thomas again cried out in pain.

Eddie looked down at the wounded man and turned to Michael. He held up his pistol. "I'm not much good to you guys with this. I'll see to his wounds and get him to the boat—you guys go take care of business." Eddie didn't wait for an answer. He had spied an old gear trolley used for transporting equipment to and from the dock staged in the parking lot. It had four off-road bicycle tires and a flat wooden platform that would serve as a mobile stretcher.

Eddie tapped Dixon on the arm. "Give me a hand for a minute." They returned a few moments later with the trolley and gingerly loaded Thomas onto the platform.

"I'll help get him down the stairs. Then you're on your own," said Dixon. "I got a score to settle."

They pushed the trolley loaded with the wounded man onto the porch and the men cautiously carried it down the stairs. Michael grabbed Eddie's arm and drew him close, "Follow the path to the dock," he said as he pointed towards the blaze. "It's about fifty meters past the fire. Take care of yourself."

"You too," said Eddie. He began laboriously pushing the heavily laden cart down the muddy path. The light from the fire at the cabin had started to die down, but pungent black smoke continued to waft skyward. Eddie pushed the cart down the path towards the sputtering blaze, wondering whether he was doing something noble or cowardly.

Michael and the rest of the team filed back into the lobby. They formed a stack to ascend the stairs with Michael at point and Dixon immediately behind him. Michael pointed his weapon skyward, cognizant that the team would be exposed to plunging fire as they maneuvered up the stairs. One of the most hazardous conditions that a team is likely to encounter is a stairway with a turn between floors as the team would be blind to whatever was waiting for them on the upper floor.

***

Kelley opened the door to Vicky's room. Ann had been gagged and tied to an arm chair that stood in one corner of the room. Kelley opened the door to the spacious bathroom to find Vicky cowering in the bathtub. "Come on Vicky, cheer up—the time is at hand to begin final negotiations."

Flynn, lay in a prone position at the top of the stairs armed with a Heckler and Koch submachine gun that Kelley had supplied him. He pointed it at the spacial plane at the foot of the second flight of the staircase waiting for someone to step into his sight. He planned to fire up the point man and then retreat into a room halfway down the hall. Once the remnants of the team passed he would crack the door and kill as many of them as he could from a covered position while Kelley engaged from the front. If he and Kelley were lucky, they would kill them all in the crossfire. Then, he could get rid of Kelley.

Michael scoured the stairwell for any sign that an ambush awaited them. Step by step he moved up awaiting what he felt would be an inevitable fusillade of bullets aimed directly at him. Flynn felt sweat trickle down his brow, follow the curved line of his cheek, and descend into his collar. He saw a shadow begin to creep around the wall and he began a slow squeeze of the trigger.

Char opened the fire exit door at the end of the hall, identified the threat laying in ambush at the head of the stairs, brought his M4 carbine up to his shoulder and fired two, three round bursts.

The first three rounds went high and wide—striking the wooden bannister Flynn was using for shelter. Flynn turned to his right as to confront the threat as Char fired again. This time all three rounds struck Flynn in the chest and neck. Michael rounded the turn and fired at the wounded figure at the top of the staircase. The mortally wounded Flynn squeezed the trigger and held it as he died. The hammer fell, but did not fire. The last thought that went through his mind as he died was *that bastard Kelley fucked me over.*

Michael and the rest of the team clamored up the second flight of stairs. He looked down the hall at Char and smiled. Dixon, Davis, and Reynolds arrived at the top of the stairs still locked and ready to engage. Michael signaled with his hand to keep their muzzle down—lest they fire on his father, "Clear," said Michael. They repeated in unison and looked down the hall to see Char walking towards him.

Dixon shook his head. "Might have said something old man."

Reynolds picked up Flynn's weapon and examined it. "Why didn't he return fire?" he asked.

"Don't know, but I have a theory. No time for it now—let's clear the rest of the building," said Michael. "Dixon, go down to the front desk and look for a pass key, otherwise we'll be here all night."

Dixon returned in a few minutes with a key ring. "This was on a hook behind the desk." Michael took the ring—it had three keys on it. He approached one of the doors and tried each key until the key turned and unlocked the door. The team methodically worked their way down the hall. One of the rooms was marked with a brass plate announcing it to be a suite.

Michael unlocked the room, opened the door and the team

burst inside. In the center of the room sat Vicky tied to a chair. Whoever had bound her knew what he was doing. Her arms were tied behind the back of the chair with paracord, her ankles were similarly bound to the legs and she was gagged with a pillowcase. Her face was smeared with black lines where tears had washed mascara down her face. She pleaded with her eyes to be released.

Michael pulled off the gag. "Where's Kelley?"

"He left me. He took that old woman and left me. Please untie me."

"That old woman is my mother. Where did he take her?"

"I don't know. Please untie me," she repeated.

Michael walked behind her, withdrew his Ka-Bar and cut away the paracord first from her ankles and then from behind her back. Michael helped Vicky to her feet, but held onto her wrist as Agent Reynolds withdrew a set of handcuffs and expertly slapped them onto her wrists.

"What the hell are you doing?" she cried.

Reynolds spun her around to face him. He fixed her with a cold stare delivered from a lofty perch—all six foot four of him towering over her. "I'm arresting you for murder, conspiracy to murder, murder-for-hire, and a half dozen other charges. I'd arrest you for being a greedy bitch, but unfortunately that's still legal."

She let out a hysterical cry and fought against the handcuffs, but the petite woman was not match for the tall federal agent. He held her by the upper arm and stared down at her. "We can do this the easy way or the way that's going to make me enjoy cuffing and stuffing a cold-blooded killer. We have a few questions for you. Cooperate and things will go better for you," said Reynolds. He guided her to a straight back chair, aligned her so that she could sit sidesaddle and helped her sit down.

Michael looked down at Vicky, who sat sobbing softly. "Where's Kelley?" he asked.

Vicky shook her head, "He's gone. He took that old woman with him—I hope he rots in hell!"

"I'm going to send him there," said Michael. "Any idea which way he went?"

"He heard you calling for a boat to pick up the guy he shot. He was going to take it out to that yacht and trade the old lady for it."

"My mother," said Michael.

Vicky shook her head slowly and began softly sobbing again. "He'll kill her, he told me that himself."

T.S. O'Neil

Chapter Thirty-nine - Eidetic Eddie

Eddie pushed the cart carrying Juan Thomas past the smoldering remnants of the cabin. A tired and sweat-soaked Eddie audibly sighed in relief when he heard the launch approaching downriver. He felt newly energized by the sound and used what vigor he held in reserve to propel the cart down the muddy and root sown path towards the dock. The trail turned a corner to avoid a grove of running bamboo and then opened onto the dilapidated wooden pier. He pushed the cart onto the structure, released his grip on the handle and wiped his perspiring brow.

Eddie checked Thomas' bandage and found it saturated with blood. Thomas softly moaned as Eddie did so—but thankfully, he was otherwise unconscious.

Kelley ran down the path about twenty meters behind Eddie, dragging Ann by the wrist. She fell two times and each time she did, he would roughly drag her to her feet and pull her forward like a rag doll. The third time she fell, the palm of her hand found a fist-sized rock. She grabbed it and when he pulled her back up, she swung it at his head and heard an audible crack when it hit his skull.

"Fucking bitch," said Kelley.

"I told you I was going to get you," she said. She swung again, but he was able to block the blow. He expertly landed a short punch to her head causing her to drop the rock from her fist and fall onto the muddy path.

He touched his forehead and felt the viscous and sticky seeping flow of blood. "You feckin' gobshite. I'm going to need stitches," said Kelley.

Ann adopted a thick Irish accent, "you're going need a fecking grave-digger when I git done busting your cranium, you mick bastard."

Kelley was exhausted. He looked down at her and shook his head in frustration—causing it to throb. "Is it Saint Patrick's Day when the whole fecking world is Irish?"

Kelley reached down, grabbed her wrist, twisted it and dragged Ann to her feet. He pulled her face close to his and pointed his pistol at her head.

"Do that again, and I'll kill you."

She spat in his face. "Do it! Regardless of what you do to me, they're going to kill you." Kelley's face flushed a red hue with anger at the belittlement. He recalled spitting in the face of a limey soldier and felt ashamed for a moment. He wiped the spittle from his face and calmed himself.

"All right, listen, you behave and I'll let you go when this is over—I promise you. Now, git yur ass moving," said Kelley.

He pushed her this time. Ann staggered and looked at him—surprised that she was suddenly free. She broke into a run like a sprinter just a few meters shy of the finish line. Kelley pointed the pistol at her back, but she jumped off the path into the heavy undergrowth.

Kelley panicked—she was a lifeline—without a pistol barrel pushed against her forehead the kid or his old man would rip him apart. He ran down the path towards the dock, skirting the still smoldering building. The vegetation became sparser as he approached the river. He heard a motor launch in the distance and realized it would be the kid who worked as Char's mate—the same one who had pursued him in a Boston Whaler off the Dry Tortugas. *Shit, that felt like a year ago,* he thought.

Ann squatted down concealed by the underbrush and waited for a few moments in silence, hoping Kelley would lose interest in finding her. After what felt like an eternity, she plunged further into the dense foliage. She heard the sound of an approaching boat and briefly considered making a run to the river and then following it downstream towards the sound. She discounted the idea as the possibility of running back into the madman was too great.

Ann broke through the foliage and found herself back on the path, but now behind Kelley and closer to the still smoldering cabin. She cautiously approached the circle of abandoned cottages—thinking she could hunker down near or in one until help arrived and was surprised by the sight of two men frantically engaged in rescuing small packages from the burning ruins.

She froze rigid like a standing corpse—willing that they wouldn't see her in the darkness, but Maynard Philbrick had seen her in the periphery of his vision. She turned to run back down the path, but he was on her in a moment. Philbrick grabbed her wrist and twisted it outward—forcing her arms behind her back.

"Where do yew think yer goin?" He reached down between her legs with his free hand—immediately announcing a repellent intention. She raised her foot as high as she could and brought the wooden heel of her shoe down upon his boot. It hurt just enough to cause him to release his grip and she sprang free.

He lunged at her and she sidestepped him like a matador passing a bull. She bolted down the path towards the dock in a panic—forgetting the threat that waited for her there.

***

Kelley ran up behind Eddie and struck him on the back of the head with the butt of his pistol. The detective crumbled onto the dock. Kelley gazed down upon the body of the wounded man much like a child examining a bug. "You're in a bad way lad. I'm not sure yer long for this world," said Kelley.

Thomas' eyes fluttered open and he regards Kelley. "I'm not sure you are as well," said Thomas. Kelley laughed at the dying man's foolish bravado as he was seized by a jolting pain. He looked down to find a large knife sticking out of his hip. "Stabbed by a fucking dead man," said Kelley.

Thomas knew that he was probably going to die and decided to die as he lived—leaning into the wind. "Not dead yet," he said. Thomas struggled to get off the cart as Kelley brought the pistol up and blindly fired a half dozen rounds at the wounded man. A shot struck Thomas in the chest and he straightened his body so that he was almost standing straight. He forced himself to smile at his killer. "Better to die on your feet than to live on your knees," said Thomas. He fell forward onto the dock dead.

"Just fucking die already," said Kelley.

Ann turned the corner of the path in a sprint with Philbrick close behind. She ran onto the dock and almost tripped over Eddie's prostrate body. Kelley made a grab for her, but he tripped, hobbled by his wounded leg. She turned to escape and ran into the clutching arms of Maynard Philbrick.

"Bring her here," ordered Kelley. Philbrick enveloped Ann in a bear hug and carried to Kelley. "Good boy. Now go down river, in case the kid in the boat decides to turn around. If he does, shoot him."

Philbrick was annoyed by Kelley's insult, but even his boss, Flynn, treated the man with great deference, so Philbrick ignored the slight.

Eddie was momentarily knocked out. He slowly regained consciousness—feeling worse than the morning after he had downed a fifth of whiskey on a dare. He felt the apple size object pressing into his leg and he was momentarily puzzled as to its identity. It was hard and it hurt—wedged the way it was between the ground and his thigh. Then he remembered taking the grenade from Michael—more as a gesture and attempt at humor than a drastic course of action—should he need to employ one. *Well, now the chickens have come home to roost,* he thought. He hadn't thrown a grenade since MP Basic Training close to forty years ago. *It's just like riding a bike*, he thought and immediately discounted that oversimplification—*bikes don't blow up.*

Eddie felt his heart race and wondered whether he might be having a heart attack—decades of stress, booze and greasy food argued in this direction. Another feeling began to germinate in his scrotum and he stifled a chuckle. He remembered *the Grinch that Stole Christmas* from his childhood. It wasn't his heart that seemed to get larger, but his balls—Eddie immediately understood the phrase he had heard throughout his life—he suddenly grew a pair—and he felt that they might be brass.

Eddie rolled onto his side; thrust his hand into the cargo pocket of his pants and pulled out the baseball shaped object. Kelley stood less than six feet away, but his attention was directed towards the approaching boat. Eddie would have to roll the grenade towards Kelley's feet and then jump off the dock and into the water. *He would yell out to Ann and hope for the best*, he thought and then immediately discounted the idea. *Char and Michael would take turns skinning him alive if Eddie harmed her. This called for more of a grand gesture—the Hail Mary pass into the end zone. He tried to remember the length of time he would have and seemed to recall that it was between 4 to 5 seconds. Which one was it, 4 or 5? Shit, what difference did it make—one second was not a margin of error that need concern him. If he wasn't off the dock in a couple of seconds, it probably wouldn't matter.*

Eddie rolled onto his knees—the grenade held between his hands. He used his thumb to pop off the safety clip, grasped the pull ring with the ring finger of his left hand and wrenched it loose. He rolled the grenade towards where Kelley stood with his arm draped around Ann's neck, loosely holding an automatic pistol in his hand. At the same time he sprung from a crouch and launched himself at Ann's midsection. He closed his arms around her as he made contact and fell on the dock—still a few feet short of the edge. Ann grunted and began to protest, but Eddie rolled over her and used all his strength to launch her into the river. He followed a short second later.

Kelley didn't see the grenade until Eddie had entered the water. It rolled into his foot and bounced off, landing a few feet away. *Bloody hell*, thought Kelley, *the bastard just bollocked me.* Kelley dove off the dock just as the grenade detonated—he felt the heat of the blast on the back of his legs as he submerged and knew that he was probably hit. Kelley surfaced, his ears ringing from the explosion. He still clutched the pistol in his hand and that was good. He could feel his legs, but he winced in pain and remembered the Marine's knife was still sticking out of his thigh. Whatever damage the grenade had done, it had not been the coup de grâce it was intended to be.

Kelley looked over at where Ann and Eddie stood neck deep in the dark brown water and pointed the pistol at Eddie's face. "Come here you bastard and bring her with you." Eddie looked at him, puzzled to see that Kelley was still breathing. "I said come here. I have to tell you one more time and I'll shoot you in the face." Eddie swam over to the man and regarded him with a slight smile. "Cheeky monkey, ain't you, said Kelley.

"Beg pardon?" said Eddie.

"Never mind," said Kelley. He brought the pistol up as high as he could and then down in a powerful arc—striking Eddie's forehead with its barrel. The force of the blow opened a gash in Eddie's forehead. He immediately lost consciousness and his head slipped beneath the water. Ann screamed.

Kelley intended to let him drown, but after a moment's consideration, thought better of it. He needed someone to treat his wound and he knew that cops had at least a rudimentary level of training in first aid. Kelley reached down into the water, found the man's collar and dragged him to shore.

In the fog laden darkness of the false dawn, Johnnie couldn't quite make out what was happening on the dock, but he had heard an explosion a few minutes ago and was worried. He had an M4 carbine, but piloting the Boston Whaler to the dock required both hands. Johnnie throttled down the engine as he approached the dock, brought the carbine up to the ready position hoping he would be able to tell friend from foe. Johnnie walked the boat towards the dock and the scene slowly materialized in the gray of the morning fog. The Boston Whaler close to the pier. A woman stood on the dock with Kelley standing behind her holding a pistol to her forehead.

"Drop the weapon on the deck sonny-boy," said Kelley. "We're gonna need a lift out to that fancy boat of yours."

Chapter Forty - Blue Falcon

They were gathered in the main lobby trying to plan follow on actions in light of Kelley's escape. Reynolds and Davis had excused themselves to call in an after-action report to the field office in Miami. Apparently, there had been some second thoughts among the typical ass-covering careerists that exist in the upper ranks of all bureaucratic organizations, especially the FBI.

"So, tell me the bottom line," said Char.

"I called in to tell them we would be transferring a prisoner. My boss, the special agent in charge of the Miami field office, told me and Davis to stand down. We're going to transport the suspect to the Taylor County Jail until we can arrange transportation to Miami where she will await trial in federal court," said Reynolds.

"Oh yeah, and you guys are no longer deputized. That was my boss' addition to the conversation," said Davis.

"They think this thing has gotten way out of hand. They'll issue a warrant for Kelley's arrest and hope he turns up." said Reynolds.

"What about my mother?" asked Michael.

"I wish we could help, but if Davis and I do anything other than as instructed, we'll be lucky to get jobs as security guards at an old folk's home," said Reynolds.

Char's satellite phone buzzed. He pushed the answer button and walked outside to get a stronger signal.

"Hey mate, Ken Q. Kelley here. I'm just admiring the downright luxurious accouterments on this yacht of yours and thought that I'd give you a chance to say goodbye to your wife before I drop her in the briny deep."

"What do you want, Kelley?"

"This yacht, for one thing. Possession is nine-tenths of the law so I want the other tenth. Sign the title over to me and let's say two hundred thousand for gas money, and I'll give you back your old lady, and all the rest of them. Otherwise, I'll cut their throats and throw them overboard right now—except your wife—I've got some plans for her."

"All right, you can have it. Just don't hurt anyone," said Char.

"Look whose giving orders now. Listen to me now, boyo. I'll send the skinny kid in to get you at the dock. You leave that fecking Captain America on shore or it's no deal."

Char ended the call and walked back in the lobby. "Kelley's

got the yacht and your mother. He wants the title to the boat and two hundred thousand dollars," said Char.

"There's no title to that boat," said Michael.

"Apparently, Kelley doesn't know that. Otherwise, he'd already be gone," said Char.

"Don't worry, I'll have the Coast Guard seize your boat—that way I'll still get a reward for the seizure," said Davis.

Michael looked at the deputy marshal and then at Char. "They move in on that maniac and he'll kill my mother and the rest of them," said Michael.

"Optimistically, that probably won't happen. And if it does, I hope it doesn't ruin the carpeting," said Davis.

Michael fought the urge to slug the asshole in the face, but it served to reason the guy would fuck them over the first chance he got—all in the name of the forty or fifty thousand dollars he'd reap as a reward for the seizure. Luckily, they had anticipated that eventuality.

"Blue Falcon?" offered Char.

"Exactly my thoughts," said Michael.

"Gentlemen, if you'll excuse us, my son and I have some preparing to do. Dixon perhaps you can help us," said Char.

Char watched from the lodge's front porch as Reynolds and Davis escorted their prisoner to their truck. "Thanks for the help fellas. Don't worry about a thing—we'll take it from here. Goodbye Blue Falcon."

They both were puzzled by Char's last remark, but each man gave a short wave. Reynolds helped Vicky into the rear seat of the pickup and secured her seatbelt for the ride to jail.

Michael came out on the porch, stood next to Char, gazed down at the departing pickup truck. "Buddy fuckers."

"You know it. After all of this, that son of a bitch still wants to get his hands on our boat," said Char.

"We can't let that happen," said Michael.

"I'm not about to let that Irish terrorist have it either," said Char.

"Well then, our course of action seems clear," said Michael.

"As glass," said Char. "Tell me you can do what needs to be done."

"It'll break my heart to do it, but yeah—can do easy."

"You and me both. Who do you want to use?"

"This I do alone. The Colombians and Dixon have done enough."

"Knowing Kelley, he'll be watching."

"Let him watch. He ain't going to see anything."

***

They all sat in the main salon of the *Good as Gold*. Kelley reclined in an arm chair loosely holding his semi-automatic pistol while Eddie tended to his wounded leg. The Ka-Bar bayonet still protruded from his thigh. Eddie was afraid to remove the knife as he was sure it would cause major blood loss. *Shit, why do I care* thought Eddie, *If I can kill this guy it will all be over. But, if I do something that instills panic, the fucking crazy mick will shoot me and everyone else.*

"I can't remove the knife—it's probably better if I just dress the wound around and secure it in place," said Eddie.

Kelley nodded and took a deep slug from the bottle of Jameson he had retrieved from the bar. "Drinking alcohol will just increase the bleeding" cautioned Eddie.

"Who are you—my fecking Ma? Just dress the wound," said Kelley.

Eddie cut away Kelley's trouser leg with a pair of shears. The wound was in the center mass of the thigh, about four inches in length and a half inch wide—how it had missed a major artery was a mystery.

Eddie grabbed the Jameson's from Kelley's hand. Kelley started to resist "It's to clean the wound," said Eddie. Kelley released his grip on the bottle and Eddie liberally poured it over the wound until he felt satisfied it was disinfected. Kelley winced in pain. "Give it here, he said. Eddie handed him the bottle and Kelley took a long swig.

"The "Q" stands for Quinlan," said Eddie. He was bandaging the stab wound while Kelley worked diligently to finish the bottle. Kelley eyed him suspiciously. Eddie interpreted the look for license to speak further. "You killed a man in an apartment on Treasure Island on August 4th 1996. The same day you killed your wife, a beautiful young lady by the name of Kiley Reilly, along with her Australian boyfriend.

Kelley took another swig from the whiskey bottle, "What do you know about it, old man?"

"I was the detective on the case. Eddie Doyle, formerly of the Pinellas County Sheriff's Department, Robbery and Homicide."

"An Irish cop—go figure," said Kelley. "What is this old home week? Just finish your job and shut the fuck up."

"Just trying to make conversation. Your real name is Conor Brennan and you were a hit man for the Real IRA, correct?" asked Eddie.

Kelley brought the muzzle of his semi-automatic pistol about an inch from Eddie's right eyeball. "Jesus fecking Christ, do I have to shoot you to get you to shut yer yap?" He reached into his pocket and withdrew a small balloon and handed it to Eddie. "Know how to cook up a spoon of heroin?"

"I've seen it done before," said Eddie.

"That's an eighth of a gram. Put half of it in a spoon, cook it up and then inject it into my leg," said Kelley.

"You're the man with the gun," said Eddie. He immediately considered using the entire balloon which should put him out and might kill him.

Kelley as if reading his mind, pushed the pistol's muzzle in contact with Eddie's cheek. "Show me the dosage before you cook it. I want to be sure you don't try anything funny."

Ann got a spoon and matches from the kitchen. Eddie withdrew a syringe and prepared it for shooting. When ready, he handed it to Kelley, who unceremoniously plunged it into his leg next to the wound. After a few moments, Kelley felt a cool numbness replace the fiery pain. He brought the bottle to his lips for a short swallow, put his head back on the chair, and sighed in relief.

Johnnie had been gone for about a half hour. Kelley had given him twice that to get back or he would begin killing hostages, but as the euphoria washed over him, he relaxed and almost nodded off.

He regarded Eddie through half opened eyes. "So, you investigated the Paddle Board Killer?"

"Yeah, I did. Can I ask you a question about it?" asked Eddie.

Everyone wanted to know the same thing, so Kelley answered without being asked. "I wanted to see if I could do it. It turned out I could. I tried to recreate the act with the doctor, but I messed it up."

Eddie regarded him dispassionately, as he had seen a lot of unrepentant killers during his forty years of police work. "Yes, you only killed one of them."

"Shoddy work that," said Kelley. "My old boss, McKevitt, would have shot me in the kneecap for such a fuck-up."

Eddie was still reeling from the shot to the head the murderous thug had inflicted on him, but he wasn't about to let him slaughter them without a fight. "Yeah, you killed the woman who saved your life. I mean, who wouldn't?" said Eddie.

Kelley smiled and lazily pointed the gun in his direction. "The Paddle Board Killer may yet strike again. Do you want to be the last murder I commit?"

Eddie felt adrenaline course through his system and he visibly shivered. "Guess not," he said.

Maynard Philbrick descended from the pilot house into the main salon. He had been ordered to keep a gun to the pilot's head and watch for Char's arrival. He looked at Kelley and nodded. "The kid and the guy that looks like an Injun are heading this way."

Kelley sat up in his chair. "Anyone else with them?"

"Not that I can see," said Maynard.

"Help me up," said Kelley. Maynard walked behind the club chair, reached under Kelley's armpits and lifted him to his feet. Kelley tentatively tried to walk and found that the pain had been deadened sufficiently to allow him to do so unassisted. He walked over to Ann and gestured toward the stern with the pistol. "Show time, darling—your knight in shining armor has arrived."

She walked out on the stern and saw the launch approaching slowly. She saw Char standing in the bow and sighed in relief. He smiled at her. "Hi, Honey, are you okay?" *Maybe they would get out of this alive*, she thought. Kelley appeared behind her while Maynard ordered Eddie to the bridge.

***

Michael dressed in a wet suit and snorkel gear sat suspended by three deflated inner tubes that hung from the starboard side of the Boston Whaler. The tubes where tied to lines that suspended him about a foot from the water. He got wet but was totally concealed from view of anyone on the *Good as Gold*.

Johnnie threw Kelley the rope. It fell short and dropped back in the water. He tried again, but this time, the line sailed to the left—causing Kelley to turn around and retrieve the line. While he was distracted, Michael slipped out of the inner tubes and into the water. He sheltered at the stern— shielded by the hundred horsepower outboard motor and waited for Char to lure Kelley to the pilot house—on the pretext of using the computer console located there.

Kelley wrapped his left arm around Ann's neck and with his right hand kept the pistol aimed at her head. He slowly backed into the salon as Char came aboard. Johnnie waited on the launch—ready to depart in a hurry should anything go wrong.

Char followed Kelley into the main salon. He smiled slightly when he saw the knife protruding from Kelley's leg. "Jeez, Kelley what the fuck happened to your leg?"

"Never mind, asshole. Just know that I executed the fecking man after he stabbed me."

Char thought for a moment and realized it had to have been Thomas. "Too bad. Thomas was a good man. Better still when you consider that he stabbed you after being shot in the stomach."

"Yeah, he was a fecking peach, said Kelley. "Now can we stop the eulogy and get down to it."

"Sure, what do you want to do first?"

Kelley looked at him through drug-addled eyes. "Simple, you give me the title to the boat plus two hundred grand and then I sail away," said Kelley.

"That simple?" asked Char.

"I also give ya yer fecking bitch back," said Kelley. "And good luck with her."

Char smiled at Ann. "Have you been mean to Mister Kelley sweetheart?"

Ann smiled. "Maybe just a little."

"I should kill you both, but a deal is a deal and you fecking deserve each other," said Kelley.

Char took out an official looking title that Michael had downloaded from the internet and manipulated through a graphical editing tool. Luckily, Flynn had a decent quality color printer and the hotel seal looked like a notary stamp—if you didn't look too closely. "I'll sign this over to you. Let's go to the bridge and I can transfer the money to your account."

Kelley gestured with the pistol towards the bow. "Lead the way."

They walked up the short staircase to the bridge as Michael approached the swim platform on the yacht's stern. He pulled himself out of the water and stood up, watching as Kelley exited the main salon. Johnnie threw him a towel, and he quickly dried off—lest he leave a puddle of water in the boat's plush interior.

Michael slipped through the open sliders, quickly crossed the salon, and descended the staircase leading to the lower deck. Hopefully, Char would keep them occupied long enough to do what he needed to do.

"The satellite uplink needs to be reset," said Earl. "It happens all the time. It might take a few minutes to reboot and reacquire the signal."

"Just fecking hurry," said Kelley.

Char called Kelley over to the chart table and signed the document, annotating transfer of the vessel. Kelley signed the document with the name Maynard Philbrick—indicating that he would be jettisoning the persona of Ken Q. Kelley.

Char looked at the man and Kelley gave him a slight smile, "Mum's the word old son."

"None of my business," said Char.

A few minutes after fiddling with various computing hardware, Earl turned toward Char. "Internet is up," he announced.

"About fecking time," said Kelley. "Let's take care of the second part of the transaction."

Char nodded. "They say wives are expensive and ex-wives even more so." He logged on to his bank's website and initiated an electronic fund transfer to the account number Kelley provided. It would be difficult, but not impossible to cancel it if he could act soon.

Kelley patted him on the back. "Well, it looks like our business is done. I may be many things, but I'm a man of me word." He pointed the pistol at Char and motioned towards the stern. "Now get your crew and your whore off of my boat before I change my mind and execute all of you," said Kelley

Maynard swung his shotgun in a low arc towards the stern. "You heard the man. Git yer goat smelling ass off our boat."

"You're the boss," said Char. He addressed Ann, Earl, and Eddie. "Let's go while the getting's good." They filed off the bridge, descended the stairs into the main salon, and out the sliders onto the stern as Kelley followed after them.

One at a time, they stepped off the stern of the yacht onto the Boston Whaler. Char was the last one to step off the stern. He turned and gave the yacht one last look. "Gonna miss you *Good as Gold*. You were a fine boat."

"Don't worry yourself, I'll take good care of her," said Kelley. "Now cast off and get the feck out of here."

Johnnie quickly untied the lines, reversed the engine, turned the bow toward starboard and pushed the throttle lever forward. Kelley watched from the stern. He thought he caught a glimpse of something long and black hanging off the side, but perhaps it was just the boat's bumpers.

Kelley returned to the main salon, retrieved the bottle of Jameson and poured himself a drink in a cut glass tumbler he found behind the bar. He toasted the empty room. "Well done, Kelley old son, well done."

***

The resort where they had rented a cottage had a nice sandy beach near where the Steinhatchee River emptied into Dead Man's Bay. It was getting close to sundown, and the sun sat on the horizon bathing the beach in a warm golden hue. The resort had an open-sided structure sheltering two picnic tables. Johnnie and Earl had set one of the tables up as a rudimentary bar holding several bottles of liquor, some mixers, and a tub filled with ice and bottles of Corona beer. Char summoned everyone out onto the beach for a short ceremony to remember fallen comrades.

Dixon had called in the death to MARSOC's duty officer, and was told to leave the body where he had fallen as they would be dispatching an aircraft to retrieve the body and launch a line of duty investigation into his death. Dixon had covered Thomas' body with a tarpaulin, but couldn't leave it to be molested by the elements. After a short discussion with the lodge's manager, he and Michael moved Thomas into the near empty walk-in freezer and locked the door.

Aside from a few loose ends, it was over. Ann was free. Flynn was dead, but it had cost Char his yacht. Even if he kept it, the government through a greedy federal marshal would have moved in to seize it.

Reynolds and Davis returned from transporting Vicky to the Taylor County Jail. Davis approached Char on the beach and smiled at him. "I contacted the Coast Guard and gave them a full description of the yacht. Chances are good they'll seize it as Kelley sails out of the bay."

Char nodded in acknowledgement, but not necessarily in agreement. "We were just about to toast fallen comrades—you're a vodka martini man aren't you?"

"I'm on duty, so I probably shouldn't—but what the hell," said Davis. Michael could tell that the man was already counting the reward money from the seizure of the *Good as Gold*. Michael nodded at Earl, who quickly returned with a red solo cup filled with vodka.

Ramos and Villegas sat on a picnic table in the bohio drinking ice cold beers and conversing in rapid fire Spanish—no doubt about the firefight they had just been involved in.

The yacht was still in sight, slowly making its way out of the bay and into the open ocean. Char nodded at Michael. He retrieved his sat phone from his belt, punched in a number and waited.

"Lady and gentlemen, I propose a toast," said Char. The group turned their attention to him and patiently waited for him to continue.

"To fallen comrades. Our very dear friend Staff Sergeant Juan H. Thomas of the United States Marine Corps Special Operations Command."

The group repeated his toast and drank. Char locked eyes with Deputy Marshal Davis. "I'd like to propose one more toast. To the *Good as Gold*, may she rest in peace." Davis gave Char a puzzled look.

Michael pushed the send button on the sat phone that dialed a number of the cellular phone attached to a two pound block of C4 plastic explosive attached to one of the large diesel tanks. The electric charge generated by the ringer was enough to fire the blasting cap embedded in the explosive— causing it to explode and ignite the fuel tank on the yacht.

The yacht erupted in noise and flames. Even in the distance, the sound was deafening. The initial explosion was followed by the sympathetic detonation of another as the other fuel tank detonated. The surrounding water was showered with debris and a heavy plume of smoke billowed from what was left of the vessel. Char smiled. He hoped that the last thought that entered Kelley's mind before he was engulfed in flames was that all his evil acts had finally come back to take him straight to hell. "Yeah, karma's a bitch," he said.

Davis incredulously looked at the smoldering wreck in the distance, brought the red solo cup up to his lips and drank its entire contents. He dropped the cup onto the sand and then walked over to where Char stood looking at the burning ruin in the distance. "You bastard, you tricked me!" screamed Davis.

"I don't know what you're talking about. It could have been one of the exhaust fans in the engine room failed or an electrical short for all I know. Didn't anyone ever tell you the best-laid plans of mice and men often go awry?"

Davis stared at him—fuming with barely contained rage. Char knew the deputy had a short fuse and figured it was time to make an exit. "If there is anything else you want to charge me with, Marshal Davis, feel free to let me know. Otherwise, I'm going to have a drink with my ex-wife," said Char. He turned and walked away from the agent.

Reynolds found Davis and handed him another cup. "I figured you could use this. I called in the fire to the Coast Guard. They told me they would send a cutter, but if it's not a hazard to navigation, they will just let it burn itself out."

Davis nodded and took a long swig from the cup. He wiped his mouth with the back of his hand. "Fucking Char—he always manages to find some way to screw me over."

Reynolds nodded. "Yeah, he should come with a warning label—fuck with me at your own peril." Despite his anger, Davis laughed.

Reynolds slapped him on the back. "It's not so bad, bro. I'll share credit for Vicky's arrest with you. That should go a long way to getting you out of the doghouse."

Char entered the bohio to find Ann and Eddie Doyle seated next to each other at a picnic table. "What's all this then? My ex-wife having drinks and telling secrets with my employee."

"Yes, indeed we are," said Ann. "I didn't know that Eddie is married to your old girlfriend."

He shrugged. "Small world," said Char.

"Especially with you in it," said Eddie.

Michael had been sharing a beer with Dixon, having an informal wake to remember their friend Juan Thomas. He saw his mother and father talking to Eddie and excused himself, curious to hear what was being discussed. He was initially baffled as to what Eddie was saying—until he remembered where this all started—Fort Jefferson.

"You see, it was Mudd's luck that got him into trouble and then back out again. It's still unknown what Mudd's level of involvement was in the assassination of Abraham Lincoln. He just had the misfortune to be seen in the company of John Wilkes Booth on one occasion and to have treated him for a fractured leg in the aftermath."

"So, what good luck befell him?" asked Michael.

"He escaped the death penalty by a single vote of the military jury that sentenced him to life in prison," said Eddie. "And in 1867, there was an outbreak of yellow fever at the Fort."

"That doesn't sound lucky," said Ann.

"Ah, but for him it was. You see, the garrison's own doctor caught the fever and died. Mudd took over and was able to contain the outbreak. He so inspired the soldiers at the fort, they wrote a letter petitioning President Andrew Johnson to pardon him. He did so, and Mudd returned to his medical practice and rehabilitated the family farm in Maryland."

"What's that have to do with me?" asked Char.

It's pretty much the same for you and Michael. When I first heard of you both, you were on the run from the law. You started out as criminals and ended up heroes. You lost your boat just like Mudd lost his practice and his farm fell into disuse, but upon his release he was able to rehabilitate both. Thanks to you, the Paddle Board Killer—at least pieces of him, now lay at the bottom of the aptly named Dead Man's Bay," said Eddie.

"How about his marriage—was he able to repair that?" asked Char.

"Yes, he returned to married life with his wife, Frances. As far as I know, they remained together until his death," said Eddie.

Michael raised a beer to propose a toast. "Here's to Mudd's luck."

Char smiled slyly at Ann. "And to those that have it."

About the Author

T.S. O'Neil lives in Seminole Florida with his lovely wife, Suzanne. He is a veteran of the Unites States Marine Corps Reserve, the Unites States Army and is retired from the Army of the United States at the rank of Lieutenant Colonel. He is also the author of Tampa Star and Starfish Prime.

Other Books by T.S. O'Neil

Tampa Star

http://www.amazon.com/Tampa-Star-Blackfox-Chronicles-Book-ebook/dp/B00A6DSN5A

Starfish Prime

http://www.amazon.com/Starfish-Prime-Blackfox-Chronicles-Book-ebook/dp/B00IQXL2LO

www.ingramcontent.com/pod-product-compliance
Lightning Source LLC
Chambersburg PA
CBHW060516180626
46817CB00002B/377